I've travelled the world twice over,
Met the famous: saints and sinners,
Poets and artists, kings and queens,
Old stars and hopeful beginners,
I've been where no-one's been before,
Learned secrets from writers and cooks
All with one library ticket
To the wonderful world of books.

© JANICE JAMES.

OLD MRS. OMMANNEY IS DEAD

After the death of her husband, beautiful Camilla Ommanney found herself shadowed by John Marquis, a survivor of the accident that had left her a widow. Was he really the John Marquis Camilla had once loved, or was he, as she had terrifying reasons to believe, her husband come back from the dead to drive her insane . . . ? A cryptic message brings Inspector Finch to her aid to tear the mask off a murderer, and save the life and sanity of a tortured girl.

MARGARET ERSKINE

OLD MRS OMMANNEY IS DEAD.

Complete and Unabridged

ULVERSCROFT
Leicester

First published in the
United States of America in 1955

First Large Print Edition
published March 1991

British Library CIP Data

Erskine, Margaret
 Old Mrs. Ommanney is dead. — Large print ed. —
Ulverscroft large print series: mystery
Rn: Margaret Wetherby Williams I. Title
823.912 [F]

ISBN 0–7089–2389–5

Published by
F. A. Thorpe (Publishing) Ltd.
Anstey, Leicestershire
Set by Words & Graphics Ltd.
Anstey, Leicestershire
Printed and bound in Great Britain by
T. J. Press (Padstow) Ltd., Padstow, Cornwall

1

THE Ommanneys had always been prosperous. Rich themselves, they had, for the most part, married money. They had been soldiers and sportsmen and many of them had had a passion for trees. For these the great woods of Hammerford were a memorial. The trees stood now, tall and impassive, oak and beech and lime, dwarfing the village and making the squat church appear even more squat.

There was a long double row of cars parked outside the church. Cars were parked round the Green. A little group of chauffeurs stood silently together. A police sergeant and two constables stood in attitudes of frozen respect. Cottages had their front doors closed and their windows curtained.

Old Mrs. Ommanney was dead.

Inside the church was packed; from the Lord Lieutenant of the County to little Johnny Trimble, who brought the Sunday

1

newspapers to the Hall. And, in differing degrees, they were all aware of a queer, uneasy atmosphere.

Some put it down to the position of the church, over-shadowed as it was by great trees, so that, even at midday, it was full of shadows. Some to the harsh voice and wild eyes of the Rector.

To young Mrs. Ommanney the words of the burial service were no more than a background to her thought. Her unquiet mind was full of its own preoccupations.

She knew exactly where he was sitting. In her mind's eye she could see him. The tall, rather stiff figure. The handsome face with its regular and expressionless features. The vague, empty eyes. Only — were they vague still? That was the question that tormented her. Had done ever since Martin Templar had asked her if she had noticed any change in him.

When it had been decided that he should live in Hammerford she had wondered just what would happen if ever his memory should return. She had tried to put the idea out of her head. The doctors had said that such an eventuality was unlikely. Only a miracle, they said, could do it.

2

'And miracles,' she thought feverishly, 'don't happen any more.'

As the months had passed her fears had died away. John Marquis remained as he had been when he came out of hospital. Only sometimes, seeing him with Hugo, Camilla had experienced a feeling of panic. Suppose he should remember, suddenly, while they were together.

And then Martin had asked her if she had noticed any change. She had said no. It had been true at the time. But, after Martin had gone, she had remembered rather a curious thing. A feeling that had come to her lately. The feeling that she was being watched. That someone in the house was closely observant of her.

At first the idea had aroused nothing more than mild irritation. After Martin's question this had become tinged with another feeling — fear. She, in her turn, had watched. She had noticed how often John Marquis came to the Hall. She had seen him coming towards the house on the morning when her mother-in-law had died.

And someone had been in the powder room that morning.

3

She had been waiting for the night nurse to go downstairs. There had always been an interval of ten minutes between her departure and the appearance of the day nurse. Camilla knew because she had timed it.

Not that she had wanted more than a couple of minutes for what she had to do. She had slipped out of the powder room, closing the door behind her. She had hurried across the passage and into the great front bedroom without anyone's seeing her. That part of the house had been kept quiet because of the sick woman. She had come out again, reached the foot of the stairs when she had remembered.

The door of the powder room, which she had closed, had been open a few inches.

She stood there, sick with terror. Her veins had turned to ice. Her heart had thumped so that there had seemed no other sound but its pounding. She had forced herself to go back upstairs.

The door of the powder room had been closed.

The day nurse had appeared rustling and gleaming. "Good morning, Mrs. Hugo," she said.

"Good morning, Nurse," she had answered quite calmly. And she had walked away without glancing back.

Hugo touched her on the arm. She looked at him vacantly, lost, the pupils of her eyes dilated. She saw that, beyond him, the congregation were seating themselves for the lesson. Hurriedly she did the same. Forced herself to listen.

"For as in Adam all die . . . "

And then she felt it again. There, in the crowded church. That extraordinary sensation.

Someone was staring at her. Boring into her defenseless back. Someone who hated her. *Who had cause to hate her.*

She fought with an irresistible urge to look around.

She turned her head stealthily.

John Marquis had his eyes closed.

A great wave of relief swept over her. She was conscious of a feeling almost of affection for him. She had seen him so often like that. Leaning back, his face as quiet and composed as that of any of the effigies around him. His eyes closed —

But how long had they been closed? Had he, perhaps, shut them deliberately

5

as she had turned her head? And before that — ?

Young Mrs. Ommanney was not the only person preoccupied with her own thoughts. There was, for instance, Colonel Stonor, Chief Constable of the district.

He kept thinking of the letter he had sent his cousin, Sir Eustance Anson, Assistant Commissioner of New Scotland Yard. He could recall its contents, word for word.

'We've never had any trouble in Hammerford before,' he had written. 'It's an ordinary place enough. Just a couple of dozen cottages and a lot of trees. The Ommanneys have always liked trees.

'The whole business is so trivial, too. Lights are turned on where they were off before and off where they were on. Doors that were open are banged shut. Closed doors thrown open. Yet Wisbeach — he's the local P.C. — reports that the villagers are behaving as if each one of them had a dead body concealed under the parlor floor.'

Then he added, heaven knew why, 'Old Mrs. Ommanney is dead.'

In return he had expected a letter,

caustic perhaps or patently forbearing, on the best methods of catching a practical joker. Instead, what had happened?

Eustace had written to say that he was sending a full-blown Detective Inspector. 'He's as curious as a village postmistress, as wily as a fox, and has the physical endurance of a lifeboat coxswain.'

But Colonel Stonor had known more about him than that. He had known that the Inspector was one of the C.I.D.'s ace men. *A murder specialist.* Eustance hadn't described him as such but he, Colonel Stonor, knew the man by reputation.

And there wasn't any murder in Hammerford. There weren't any dead bodies under the parlor floor. And, certainly, there wasn't any chance that old Mrs. Ommanney had been murdered.

The only mystery about *her* was how she had managed to hold on to life so long. Just cussedness, he supposed, and the determination not to leave her daughter-in-law in possession.

Must have been pretty embarrassing all around, he reflected. The old lady propped up on her pillows, looking as old as God's mother and pretty well as immortal. Waiting, day after day, month after month, for Hugo to come and tell her that his wife was in the family way.

But the old lady had not been immortal. She died quite suddenly and peacefully at eleven o'clock one morning. He'd heard the news that same afternoon. And then, obeying some impulse too obscure to recall now, he had sat down and written that letter.

Colonel Stonor sighed heavily.

It was too late to recall it. Too late to stop the Inspector. He was probably on his way already. Might even then be waiting at the police station at Market Stalbridge.

Here the Colonel's mind fled back to that building. He saw it as it would probably appear to the C.I.D. man. Its grimy exterior. Its minarets above and its yellow tiles below. The figure of Justice, blindfolded, over the main entrance, subject of so many rude jokes.

He thought of his own desk, burned with innumerable cigarette ends and the initials R.S. (Robert Stonor), which he had carved one day during a particularly harassing session on the radio. England, playing against the Australians at the Oval, all out for 52. Ghastly business that had been.

He lost himself in a dream of green pitches and white flannels. Of magnificent innings and devastating bowling. And, at the back of the church, a very large, sleepy-looking man wondered what had come over the plump little army type, bobbing and nodding and looking most unsuitably happy in one of the front pews.

Septimus Finch was the seventh son of a well-known West Country solicitor. From his father he had inherited the tenacity that had taken him into the Metropolitan Police force as a uniformed constable. From his mother, a Cornish woman, he had inherited a sensitiveness to his surroundings that amounted almost to a sixth sense. With an aunt, the widow of an archdeacon, he shared a great curiosity concerning his fellow men. His other interests were poetry, parlor magic, and his old racing car, known as Wadsworth.

He did not look like anyone's idea of a detective. Not even the Assistant Commissioner's, who, while not wanting his men to look like detectives, did want them to look like some recognizable type.

A schoolmaster like A. Or a pushing, go ahead salesman like B. Or a successful professional man like C. Finch looked simply a large, lazy, good-tempered man in his middle thirties.

He had left London early that morning bound for Hammerford. He was wearing a dark suit, a somber tie, and a wide-brimmed black hat that would have graced the head of an assassin. Between tie and hat his bland face loomed as disarmingly as that of a baby.

He came through the town of Market Stalbridge. Beyond it he began to look out for the village of Hammerford. That village, ordinary enough; a couple of dozen cottages and a lot of trees. He stopped his car.

The view had opened out to one side where the ground fell sharply away. He found himself looking over a sea of leaves. Great woods, with here and there a field picked out like a pool of water and all overlaid with the soft haze of autumn.

'Now it wouldn't be down there,' he murmured aloud. 'Or would it?' The idea tickled his sense of humor. Colonel Stonor, he reflected, was perhaps a master of the art of understatement.

The road that ran down to the valley was narrow, winding and precipitous. There was a road sign that indicated not only that the hill was steep, but that there was a dangerous bend at its foot. There was, too, a single finger post half lost in trailing briars. Finch leaned from his car to decipher the timeworn lettering.

To Hammerford, it said. And, as if it had worked some ancient spell, he saw in the far distance above the trees, standing remote, tranquil, and with a pervasive melancholy, the somber red pile of a great house.

He backed the car. Swung it around into the opening of the lane. Quarter way down the hill a man stood at a gate leading into a field of sheep. He was tall and wonderfully handsome. He was wearing a green pork-pie hat, a pair of old flannel trousers, and a light-colored shooting coat patched with leather.

Perhaps it was because there had been something surprising, coming on him so unexpectedly with no other living person near nor any habitation in sight. Or perhaps the fact that Finch was nearing his destination had affected his judgment.

Whatever the reason, the picture of the man in the field, staring out across the wooded valley, had left behind a strange and rather horrifying impression.

At the foot of the hill there was a stone wall. When this ended the trees began. They stood on either side of the road, their branches meeting overhead. The slight breeze that had been perceptible on the high ground now failed completely. The day was still, silent and somehow ominous.

A bell began to toll in the tower of Hammerford church. Finch, who had not been hurrying, slackened speed still further. He did not want to reach the village until after the service had started. If, as seemed likely it were a big funeral, there would be reporters, local men but trained to recognize faces, and Finch's was not unknown. For the same reason he would not follow the cortege to the grave-side.

On the outskirts of the village he took a side turning. He parked his car in a clearing under some beech trees. At first there was only the sound of the tolling bell. Then a car went along the road behind him. Then another and another until they were passing in an almost continuous stream.

The sound ceased. The bell fell silent. There were left only the small sounds of the countryside. And suddenly Finch thought once more of the man he had seen on the hill. And he stirred, feeling again a sharp stab of uneasiness and repugnance.

Finch got into his car and drove into the village.

A police constable waved Wadsworth into a vacant space. He was a man of about thirty years of age. He had a thin intelligent face and steady brown eyes.

He opened the door of the car. "You'll have to hurry, sir," he said, "the service has begun." He stood back and saluted.

Finch slid his long legs to the ground. Ordinary civility, he wondered, or had the constable recognized him? He picked his way between the cars. You could not, he considered, see the village for the cars — cars and trees.

Inside the lych gate was a black notice board. On it, in gilt letters, was the name of the church, St. Peters, and that of the Rector, the Reverend Philip Ommanney. The churchyard was almost as tidy as a public park.

The door into the church was open. He walked in quietly and chose a chair by itself just inside the door. In spite of this every head in the back pews turned to look.

'Couldn't have made more of a sensation,' Finch thought, 'if I'd come in bowling a hoop.' He put his hat on another chair and sank on his knees.

When he arose the heads had turned away. He was conscious, though, of a sort of current running through the church. There was uneasiness there, and fear and a queer sort of vigilance. It was as if a large part of the congregation were thinking rhythmically of the same thing. He looked about him.

The Reverend Philip Ommanney was conducting the service. He was a tall, elegant-looking man with a thin, high-bred face, long, rather useless-looking hands, and restless movements. 'His age,' Finch thought, 'must be about sixty.' His voice was harsh. In the soft religious light before the altar his face had a tormented look.

In a front pew were four people. A spruce little man, plump and with a well-fed neck. At first sight he seemed to have nothing in common with either the thin elegant priest or the broad-shouldered young man who stood beside him and whom Finch took, rightly, to be Hugo Ommanney, the dead woman's son. The police, though look at ears. And the little man had Ommanney ears, small, delicately formed, and close to the head.

The woman beside him was taller than he. Taller and thinner and with fair faded hair dragged severely up under an expensive but uncompromising-looking hat. Finch felt that he could tell quite a lot about the wearer from that hat.

Hugo Ommanney gave the impression of being a big man. He was not particularly tall, but wide and square-shouldered. He had a round, bullet-shaped head covered with brown hair. It was close-cropped at the back, but broke obstinately into crisp-looking curls on top. He carried himself like a soldier.

The woman — or girl — who stood by him must be young Mrs. Ommanney. She was tiny, with a white, fragile-looking neck. Her hair . . . ? The color of stem ginger in syrup was the nearest that Finch could get to it.

There was something intriguing about

her appearance even from the back. But not so intriguing as her behavior. What was it that she was trying to see?

There! She was turning again. A colorless cheek, a lovely line from ear to jawbone, a chiselled nose, a flash of greenish eyes . . .

Subconsciously Finch had become aware of footsteps approaching the church. Now, suddenly, they were in the porch.

An elderly man came in through the open door. He was tall and distinguished-looking, He bore a distinct resemblance to the Reverend Philip. His clothes were expensive. His hands were smoothlooking and beautifully manicured. He carried a bowler hat and a walking stick with a silver knob. His head was slightly bowed. His air was one of grief and bereavement nobly borne.

Perhaps Finch moved. Or perhaps the newcomer was startled to find someone sitting so far back in the church. Whatever the reason he threw Finch a look that had nothing in it either of grief or nobility. It was at once quick, piercing and wary.

The glance and the well-kept hands were unmistakable. 'A wrong 'un,' thought Finch, much delighted. He wondered just

16

what place there was for a cardsharper in the family hierarchy.

A ripple of interest passed like a breeze over a cornfield. There were exclamations sensed rather than heard. Heads were turning on all sides. Among them was that of young Mrs. Ommanney.

Regardless of her surroundings, of interested eyes, she stared. Her whole face expressed an unbounded fury and astonishment.

The man walked right up the aisle. He paused purposefully at a pew directly behind the young Ommanneys. The mourners there moved up, reluctantly, Finch thought. The newcomer took his place in the vacant seat. Knelt devoutly for a moment. Then settled himself with a saintly and abstracted air.

The service went on.

"Therefore, my beloved brethren, be ye steadfast . . . "

The coffin was carried down the aisle. The Reverend Philip followed, his eyes cast down. He walked with an oddly uneven gait, so that Finch wondered whether he had an artificial leg.

The mourners came from their pews. Finch could get a good view now of the Ommanneys.

Hugo was a man of about thirty-two years of age. He had a high forehead, bold, rather insolent-looking green eyes, an obstinate chin and a small, full and yet determined mouth.

His wife was lovely. Like a miniature painted on ivory, pale, fragile, and exquisite. She had tiny hands and feet and walked delicately. She kept her eyes down. Her narrow pointed face now showed no expression.

The man whom Finch had designated 'a wrong 'un' walked just behind them. If he resembled the Rector of Hammerford he resembled Hugo Ommanney still more. They both had the same look of natural insolence and hauteur, washed over in his case with a thin veil of spurious benignity.

Behind this trio came the small neat man whom Finch had thought was also an Ommanney. His eyes were very blue. His face, though solemn enough now, was set in a genial mold. His wife, who walked by his side, was about fifty years of age. She looked excessively well bred, thin, faded, flat-chested and bloodless.

The other mourners came from their pews.

Ancient dowagers, middle-aged matrons, and their spouses. Sons and nephews bearing the imprint of the services. Fresh faced, healthy-looking girls not too well turned out. Representatives of public bodies, recognizable by their correct and glossy attire, so obviously kept for just such occasions.

And now the villagers, scuttling and hurrying with an odd effect of panic, of anxiety to be gone from the church. Their footsteps clatterd and echoed and died away.

Finch saw then that he was not alone. The man with the light tweed coat sat in one of the pews. Sat just about where Camilla Ommanney had been glancing so surreptitiously during the service.

As Finch watched from the shadows he bent forward, resting his head in his hands.

2

THE Ommanney Arms faced the church across the length of the Green. It was very old, with bulging whitewashed walls, crooked windows and a massive chimney stack. Over the door was painted: 'William Wyman, Licenced to sell Beer, Wine, Spirits and Tobacco.'

Finch pushed open the door and went in. He found himself in a passage-like hall. The walls were covered with shiny brown paper. A narrow staircase ran up to a dim landing. A stuffed pike looked sadly from a glass case on a side table. There was a visitors' book, its pages yellow with age and disuse. A smell of beer was superimposed on other scents, illusive as ghosts. Finch fancied that he could detect cheap linoleum, beeswax and pickled onions.

A murmur of voices came from behind a door which bore the inscription 'Public Bar.' Finch pushed it open.

Some half a dozen old men were there

drinking beer. The landlord, William Wyman, stood behind the bar. He was a strongly built man with a fresh-colored face that would have been open and pleasant had his eyes not been placed too close to his nose.

The conversation ceased abruptly. Faces turned, looking at Finch in silence. With no change of expression they appeared, if not actually hostile, then, at least, defensive.

The silence lasted but a moment. Wyman broke it.

"Good afternoon, sir," he said, smiling. He spoke in a slow country voice with a soft broadening of vowels. "What can I do for you?"

"I should be glad if you could put me up for few days," said Finch, and his own voice was soft and drawling.

Wyman's smile faded. "We don't cater for visitors."

"You'd best put up at the Bull in Market Stalbridge," said another man. He was a tall elderly fellow and looked like a gamekeeper.

"Aye. They're used to visitors there," said a little shrunken man. Finch was

21

to know him later as the owner of the village store.

So strangers were unwelcome. "If I can't have a room I shall camp out," Finch declared. "I noticed a little copse of larches as I came in. A nice site. Overlooks the village, too." He smiled blandly. And his black hat lay on the bar counter like a challenge.

His suggestion was a source of extreme discomfort to the old men and the publican. They looked at each other with glances of dismay and anxiety.

Wyman was the first to recover. He forced a smile. "I didn't say that we couldn't take a visitor," he said. "Only that we didn't cater for them. I can give you a room and welcome."

"I don't want to put you out," Finch murmured.

Wyman's manner grew almost ingratiating. "Say no more about it, sir." He glanced at the clock. "The wife shall make up your bed and get the room ready."

As he spoke he lifted the flap of the bar and came through. "This way, sir." He raised his voice. "Fred!"

An elderly man came from a room at the back.

22

"Look after the bar a minute," Wyman told him, "while I show this gentleman to his room."

The old man stared. "His *room*, Will?"

"Yes. He's staying here."

Wyman turned abruptly away. He led the way up the steep staircase. Finch followed him.

Behind them they left complete silence and Fred's face, hanging pale and blankly staring like the dial of a disused clock.

Several passages ran off from the landing. Dim passages furnished with odd corners and with allegorical pictures hanging on the shiny brown walls. Steps led up and steps led down. The wide boards were polished to the color of heather honey.

"Mind your head." Wyman threw open a crooked door.

The room beyond was clean. That was the most that could be said for it. It was sparsely furnished. The mattress, even from a distance, looked as if it were filled with potatoes.

The spring blind was down over the window. Finch, calculating swiftly, realized that it faced the Green. "This will do splendidly," he said.

Left alone, he walked over to the window. He lifted the blind a little, looking cautiously around the edge.

The scene had changed entirely in character. The committal service was over. On all sides cars were starting up, moving off. The police were active; waving them on, signalling with hands which held gloves immaculately white.

The young Ommanneys were getting into a dark car. The tall wolfish man and the tubby man with his lean wife were getting into another. The little army type spoke authoritatively to the sergeant. And Finch wondered with a feeling of surprise if he could be the local Chief Constable.

Three people walked across the Green. Two of them walked in front, the third followed behind. In spite of this the little group had the air of being, if not exactly a family group, then, at least, a friendly and intimate one.

The leading pair were women. One was tall with a strong grave face and an air of dignified repose. The other was a little mousey woman with a thin intellectual face. The third was a tall, well-grown young man. He had a round merry face, now set in sober lines, and an engaging air of youthful vitality.

They stood for a moment talking together. They separated. The mousey-looking woman went into a picturesque cottage. The other two entered a small square Georgian house that stood back behind a high hedge and in a fair-size garden.

Now the villagers were coming out. Hurrying still, popping into their homes. Closing the doors again. The sergeant and one of the constables stepped into a police car and drove away. The second constable, the one who had spoken to Finch, took a cycle out of the hedge and walked away, pushing it.

"So that *was* Wisbeach," Finch thought.

There was no sign of the man in the light tweed coat.

Finch dropped the blind into place. He went down to his meal.

Mrs. Wyman was waiting for him at the foot of the stairs. She was a plump, cheerful-looking woman some years younger than her husband.

"I laid for you in the saloon, sir," she said. "It's not likely there'll be many in there today."

It was next to the Public Bar. It had a communicating door. It was so comfortable-looking that Finch felt certain that the Wymans had had nothing to do with its furnishing.

It had a small semi-circle bar of heavy mahogany and tall stools with brown leather tops. A long mirror hung on the wall, giving an illusion of space. A couple of small tables, one of which was laid for lunch, half a dozen comfortable chairs and an oak settle with a thick red cushion made up the rest of the furnishings. Glasses of all shapes and sizes twinkled from shelves behind the bar. There was a heartening display of bottles. The whole suggested a custom that was at once small, prosperous and constant.

"Mr. Wyman isn't one for coffee," said his wife, "but if you'd like some afterwards I'll send the girl out for it." She added in what Finch took to be a reassuring tone of voice, "I was in service up at the Hall before I married — in the kitchen."

Said Finch solemnly, "That's wonderful news," as indeed it was.

He was fond of good food. And somehow the sight of the lumpy mattress in his bedroom had suggested damp potatoes, disintergrating suet dumplings and yellowing cabbage. Instead he had an excellent stew, rich with field mushrooms, and half of an immense apple tart, obviously his share of the Wymans' own meal.

When he congratulated his hostess on this last she laughed. "The master — old Mr. Ommanney that was — used to send out to the kitchen. 'Tell Mrs. Marsh,' he'd say, 'that Milly's to make the pastry.' Cook didn't use to like it but Mr. Andrew wasn't one you could go against. Mr. Hugo's the same. They both liked their own way but Mr. Andrew was master until the day of his death."

Finch, feeling that it would further antagonize her husband, had decided against questioning Mrs. Wyman. This was the only piece of information he had from her. Later, sitting on a stool and with Wyman joining him in drink, he began in earnest.

"A fine funeral this morning," he remarked. "Surprising for such a rural area."

"Plenty of people around here," Wyman responded. "Big people,too." He added inquisitively, "You didn't know the family then?"

Finch shook his head. "I was sent as a representative. No one else available." He added, "Had the old lady been ill long?"

"Two years. She never got over the death of Mister Arthur, her elder son." Wyman added with lugubrious relish. "Took to her bed when she heard of it and never rose again."

"Bad luck," Finch murmured. And then, "How did the son die?"

"Broke his neck in a motoring accident."

Finch shook a commiserating head. "Leave a widow and children?"

"No children but there was a widow." Wyman swept a cloth over the shiny surface of the bar, watching his own reflection and frowning to himself. "Educated abroad, she was. Traveled all over the place when she was no more than a toddler. Went as far as Turkey, so I've been told. When war broke out she was put in a convent in Switzerland and there she stayed until she was nineteen." He looked at Finch with an expression of great seriousness. "Stands to reason a life like that would make her different to most people."

28

"It was certainly unusual," Finch agreed. Wyman nodded his head. "Unusual! You've said it, sir."

The outer door opened. A carelessly dressed man came in. He wore an old shirt, open and showing a muscular neck, a pair of shabby grey flannel trousers, and a torn, paint-stained coat. He had a sanguine complexion. His iron-grey hair was short and bristly. He had a long, thin-lipped mouth and eyes that were at once malicious and knowledgeable. He looked angry, though that might have been only with things in general. Finch fancied that he had been drinking already.

"'Afternoon, Wyman," he said. "Double gin, please."

"'Afternoon, Mr. Templar." Wyman put his drink on the counter.

Templar perched himself on a stool. Sat eating salted nuts with a hand so hairy that it might almost have been fur-backed. Indeed Finch remarked that he was an extraordinarily hairy man. Hair grew on his chest. It grew in his ears and on his wrists. It sprouted in his nostrils and curled in separate wiry hairs on his cheekbones.

"You down for the funeral?" Templar asked Finch without looking up.

"Yes, I thought I'd stay on for a couple of days. This looks a nice quiet spot and I could do with a rest."

Templar grinned to himself. "Not so quiet as you'd think. Someone in the village has been acting the fool. Getting into other people's houses without their knowing it. Banging doors and turning on lights. Kid's stuff but the village seems scared to death." He laughed, emptied his glass and ordered another double gin.

Finch caught the oddest expression flitting across Wyman's face. Doubt and anger and something that had looked like fear. It had gone before Finch could pin it down.

"You shouldn't laugh, Mr. Templar," said Wyman. "No, it isn't right to laugh." And his small eyes went past the two men in an uneasy survey of the farthest corners of the room.

Templar's laugh was louder this time. "You see? What did I tell you?" He caught Finch's eye and winked. "And you wouldn't have said that our friend here was a nervous type, now would you?"

Before either Finch or the landlord could answer the outer door opened. The man in the light-colored tweed coat stood there looking in.

Finch saw now the reason for his earlier unfavourable impression, his instinctive revulsion.

Nothing about the newcomer's face was as God had made it. Instead it was a miracle of plastic surgery. But the doctor's skill, which had restored the face, had not been able to restore the brain. The eyes were empty of everything but a curious innocence, an innocence so unnatural in a man of his age as to be rather shocking.

"Hello there, Bill Bowman!" he cried. His voice was thin and lacking in resonance. "Same as usual."

"'Afternoon, Mr. Marquis." As the landlord reached up for a whiskey bottle on a shelf behind him Finch was surprised to see that his hand was shaking.

"Hello, Johnny! Come and sit down." Templar pushed a stool towards him with one foot.

John Marquis seated himself. He looked with anxious enquiry at Finch. "Do I know you?" he asked.

Finch shook his head. "I've never been down here before."

Marquis's eyes cleared. "That's all right then." He turned to Wyman. "It's quiet here this afternoon, isn't it?"

"That's because of old Mrs. Ommanney's funeral," said Wyman.

"Did I know her?"

"The old lady was already bedridden when you came here to live."

"So I didn't know her. I must try to remember that." Marquis repeated the words like a child learning a lesson. "I didn't know old Mrs. Ommanney. She was already bedridden when I came here to live."

"That's right, sir," said Wyman. And Finch saw that a line of sweat had broken out on his forehead.

Finch was conscious that there had been a curious undercurrent in this exchange. It was, he reflected, like teaching oneself a foreign language from a book and then hearing it spoken by natives of that country. Unintelligible but vaguely familiar.

Templar picked up his glass. "Suppose we oughtn't to be here" he said with sudden alcoholic gloom. "But it's not the right thing to drink alone so what's the answer?" He held his glass up to the light for a moment with a sour, unhappy smile. Then he tilted his head and poured the contents down his throat.

The talk grew desultory. Touched on the funeral and other local matters.

John Marquis pushed his glass across the counter. "The same again, Bill Bowman."

Wyman put both hands flat on the bar. "For God's sake don't call me that, sir," he begged hoarsely. "The name's Wyman — William Wyman."

John Marquis looked bewildered, lost. "Wyman? Then what makes me call you — that other?"

"I couldn't say sir." The landlord's voice was surly. He poured out a second whiskey and soda. He put it down with a bang and his look was both obscure and defensive.

"I saw a big Elizabethan house from the top of the hill," Finch murmured when he was certain that the previous line of conversation had petered out.

"That would have been Hammerford Hall." The note of constraint was still in Wyman's voice.

"Who owns it now?"

"Mr. Hugo, old Mrs. Ommanney's second son."

"He had a lady with him in church," said Finch. And saw Templar turn and give him an amused stare.

"His wife," said Wyman shortly. He clattered the glasses together as if to terminate the conversation.

"And where is Arthur Ommanney's widow?"

"She married again." Wyman gave Finch an ugly look. He pushed open the door into the Public Bar and went through. His voice came back to the saloon. He was calling 'Time' in an angry tone though the clock said ten minutes to three.

"Dear me!" said Finch plaintively. "What have I said wrong? Who *is* Arthur's widow?"

"Her name's Camilla."

"Nice name. And Hugo's wife?"

"Still Camilla." Templar drew a large and invisible C on the bar with a blunt forefinger. Then stared at the spot with a look both sardonic and ugly. "Old Wyman," he said at last, "doesn't think the second marriage decent, though he'd die rather than say so — and that goes for the village, too."

He stopped speaking and the words seemed to hang in the air as if they were important. When they had quite gone Finch broke the silence.

"Were the brothers alike?"

"No. Arthur, so I'm told, had oodles of charm. A real golden boy."

"And what has Hugo?"

Templar gave a sudden hiccuping chuckle. "The Hall, my boy, and all that goes with it. Ah well! *Laurel is green for a season, and love is sweet for a day.*" He slipped off his stool and his face was angry again.

Finch looked gloomy with him for a moment. "Something in that," he murmured. And the next two lines of Swinburne's poem chased themselves through his mind.

"But love grows bitter with treason,
And laurel outlives not May."

It had been, he reflected, an odd sort of conversation. But then Templar had been more than a little drunk.

The man with the plastic face had said nothing all this time. Just sat gazing at his handsome reflection in the long mirror. As if, Finch thought, hoping to surprise the man he had once been.

The two men gone, Wyman came back to the saloon.

"What'll you take, sir — seeing that you're staying in the house? No, nothing more for me, thank you all the same." Wyman picked up a cloth and swept it over the counter. "Fact is," he said apologetically, "Mr. Marquis gets me down. Asking the same thing over and over. Never remembering what you tell him. And looking at you with eyes that empty they fairly make your flesh creep."

"What was it? The war?"

"No, sir. More recent than that. He was a passenger in the car when Mr. Arthur was killed. Burned terrible, he was. Two years in hospital and came out remembering nothing."

"What a shocking thing. Was he married?"

"No, sir. Had no relations nearer than an uncle."

"Lucky thing, that. Who was the other man who came in here?"

"That was Mr. Templar — Mr. Martin Templar," he amplified as if Finch might

36

recognize the name. "He's a painter of sorts."

"One of the modern school, you mean?"

"I couldn't say about that, sir. I've seen some of his pictures. They looked well enough to my mind. The sea mostly." Which, Finch reflected, made Hammerford a queer place of residence.

"Has he lived here long?"

"Came last May. Took old Major Cockerell's house furnished."

And that, Finch decided, made it queerer still.

Finch fetched his suitcase from his car. He unpacked it, putting its contents into the rather rickety chest of drawers. As he did so, he found himself listening. Not for anything in particular, but for the sound of some form of human activity.

He straightened his back. Stood listening intently. There was nothing: no sound of voices. No footsteps on the road outside.

He walked over to the window and let up the spring blind. The village he saw, had come into its own again, though in rather a forbidding way. Because of the trees sunlight went early from Hammerford. The cottages stood now for the most part in a kind of twilight gloom.

Windows were uncovered and vacant with a dim hint of furniture beyond. Front doors were still closed. No one walked in the gardens, or stood about on the Green. Over to the left he could see the great carpet of flowers which hid the disturbed earth of the churchyard.

And no one walked there, either.

3

MARKET STALBRIDGE was a busy, ugly place. It was market day. Though most of the trading was over the streets were still congested. A long line of dusty and battered-looking cars, some stationary, some on the move, seemed to give the lie to the contention that farmers are a prosperous body. Finch was not deceived. A country man himself, he knew their canny preference for money in the bank to any outward show.

He drove his car, Wadsworth, into the courtyard of the police station. He got out and looked with mild surprise at the architecture. He gave his card to a rosy-faced constable.

A tall burly man with dark eyes came into the charge room. He looked like a farmer and was a farmer's son. He wrung Finch's hand with vigor.

"I'm Superintendent Laker," he said, introducing himself. "The Chief Constable, I'm sorry to say, isn't here. But if you'll come along to my room I'll be pleased to do what I can for you."

The passage had the usual rather depressing smell of disinfectant and strong soap. Laker's room, though, was a cheerful place. He appeared pleased and yet slightly surprised to see the C.I.D. man.

"It was good of you to come," he said. He broke off to order tea to be sent in from the canteen and to offer Finch a cigarette. "But, to be frank, I can't understand why you did."

"Sir Eustance told me that someone had been terrorizing the village of Hammerford." Finch's small, softly drawling voice surprised the Superintendent as much as did the assassin's hat. "He's never tried to terrorize a village himself but he feels it must be difficult and not to be embarked upon lightheartedly."

"Something in that," Laker conceded. "But why send you?"

Finch shrugged. "Blood is thicker than water."

"Blood?" Laker seemed startled. "Ah! I see what you mean. Colonel Stonor and Sir Eustance. I thought for a moment . . . " His voice trailed away.

"And then," said Finch gently, "Colonel Stonor put at the end of his letter, 'Old Mrs. Ommanney is dead.' "

It took a few seconds for this to sink in. Laker stared, then turned crimson. He opened his mouth. Closed it again on all the rude words he had been going to say. "Mr. Finch," he said at last and with admirable restraint, "the Colonel must have put that in as a bit of gossip between cousins, as it were. For if there's one thing that's certain in this world it is that old Mrs. Ommanney died a natural death."

Finch looked at him in pained surprise. "That," he said sadly, "makes things very, very difficult."

"I can't think how Sir Eustace came to make the mistake," said Laker loyally.

Finch only sighed. He was wondering just how much of a mistake it would prove to have been. That he himself would not have been sent had Colonel Stonor not written those words was certain. But he *had* written them. And they must have meant something at the time. Just which of the family did he suspect? And for what reason?

"What will you do now?" Laker asked. He

41

found the silence embarrassing, particularly as he had just realized that the cause of the Chief Constable's absence from the police station sat before him.

"I shall go back to Hammerford and wait for fresh instructions."

"Back?" Laker seized on the word.

"I went to the funeral," said Finch gently. He added meditatively, "I was brought up in the country, where people enjoy a funeral even more than a wedding. It holds more elements of drama. But in Hammerford they weren't enjoying this one. They were as nervous as sparrows with a hawk overhead. It was a big funeral, too. Wonderful wreaths — only no one came to admire 'em. If a vampire had been buried there the village couldn't have given the grave a wider berth."

"Old Mrs. Ommanney," said Laker stiffly, "was very much respected. She'd lived at Hammerford Hall for nearly forty years. She was attached to the village. She chose the spot where she was buried herself. Said she'd like to be within sound of the village life."

"And now the village is frightened — too frightened to go near her."

Laker frowned. "You've been talking to Wisbeach."

"Not talking — but I think I saw him. Thin-faced man. Brown eyes. About thirty. Looks intelligent."

"That's him," said Laker heavily, "though I don't know about the intelligence."

"Tell me about the practical joker? When did he start?"

"It began late one evening on Saturday, August 22. Mrs. Markham was the first victim. She's a widow. Lives in a square white house which overlooks the Green — "

Finch nodded. "I've seen it — and her."

"Mrs. Markham was sitting downstairs reading when she saw by the glow thrown on the lawn that someone had switched on the lights in the bedrooms upstairs. She knew that the house should have been empty but for herself. And, not being a nervous lady, she went upstairs to investigate. It's a four-bedroomed house. They were all empty but in each one the light had been switched on from just inside the door."

"Mrs. Markham lives alone?"

"No, a young lad called Lionel Glover lives with her. His grandmother was sister to the last generation of Ommanneys and aunt to Arthur and Hugo Ommanney. She made a poor match and her daughter, Lionel's mother, made a worse one. Both his parents were killed in one of the air raids on London. As he was related to the Ommanneys they made themselves responsible for him. The Markhams — her husband was alive then — had no children of their own and they were glad to take him in. Besides Mr. Markham had been an invalid for some time and they must have been thankful for the extra money. The boy's training now to be a solicitor. He's in the office of Skindle and Drew here in Market Stalbridge."

"And he was not home when the Joker called?"

"No. He was over at the Rectory working for his exam. He'd failed once, so I'm told. Next, there was the case of old Delves. He was digging in his front garden one evening when suddenly the front door slammed so violently that everything in the cottage rattled and a couple of photographs on the sitting room wall fell down. A moment later the back door slammed. And so it went on. The whole village was talking about it.

Then, suddenly, eight days later, silence clamped down on it. No one, bar the gentry, had anything further to say. Anyone who brought up the subject — and that went for Wisbeach, too — was met with blank faces and averted eyes."

"But the Joker was still functioning."

"Wisbeach says yes. Only yesterday he was riding along Tuffits Lane when he saw the lights come on, one after the other, in the two upstairs rooms of a nearby cottage. He saw the owner, Sam Trotter, who was working in his front garden, look up at the windows and then, deliberately, go on digging. When Wisbeach spoke to him about it Trotter declared that he'd been upstairs himself and forgotten to turn the lights off. Wisbeach knew that he lied. And Sam Trotter knew that he knew. But that was Sam's story and he stuck to it."

"What was his manner?"

"Truculent — so Wisbeach says."

"Wisbeach thinks they know who's responsible?"

The Superintendent nodded. "They know all right — but they're not saying."

As he spoke he had a sudden mental picture of Hammerford with its blank windows and closed doors. Its houses standing dark and secretive in the thin autumn air. And the figure of Wisbeach outside it all — an alien.

"It does happen," he told Finch rather stiffly. "Even in England it happens."

Finch nodded. "There was a case in a Dorset village where the manager of some dog kennels was killed. And there was an old man stabbed with a hayfork under the Meon Hill. Yes, it happens all right."

"But you're thinking of murder," Laker protested.

Finch looked at him mildly. "The Yard don't really like me thinking of anything else."

Tea was bought in on a tray. Laker poured it out — passed Finch a plate of rather stale buns.

"I had a map of the village made and I've been marking the houses where the Joker is known to have operated," Laker remarked. He felt in a drawer. "There's a key at the side. Names of the people living in the cottages, date and so on. You may be able to spot what plan he's working on. I'm damned if I've been able to."

"Thanks. It'll be must useful." Finch

was glad of an opportunity to abandon his bun.

He took a quick comprehensive look at the map before folding it up and putting it away. "It's good," he said.

Laker, who had drawn it himself, merely nodded.

"Are there any known practical jokers in Hammerford?"

"As young men, the Ommanneys were great hands at it. Queer things they did, too. Some of them got into the newspapers. Reading them, you couldn't help but know who was responsible. They were young gentlemen of quite fantastic spirits. Still it's not likely that Mr. Hugo has started again at his age and with first his brother and then his mother dead."

"But it is interesting that there is a tradition of practical joking in the village. Tell me about the Ommanneys."

"How much do you know?"

Said Finch, "Old Mrs. Ommanney is dead. Arthur Ommanney is dead. Hugo is still alive and villagers don't like Camilla because she married both brothers."

"There's more to it than that," said Laker. "Arthur Ommanney married Camilla in spite of his mother's disapproval. His father had died about nine months before. Arthur had always spent a great deal of time at Hammerford, which was only right, seeing that he was the elder son. No sooner had he married though than she took him off to London and all we got was an occasional flying visit. They'd come down for a couple of nights. He'd be driving some great showy car. She'd be all scent and furs and the latest fashion."

"She didn't look like that at the funeral. She was quite plainly dressed — not even new clothes, by the look of them."

"Because Mr. Hugo won't have it. He's not easily led like his brother. He knows what he wants and he sees that he gets it," which was, in a way, an echo of what Mrs. Wyman had said. "He keeps her down here where she belongs."

Laker went on, "Hugo Ommanney was serving abroad when his brother married. He'd never met his sister-in-law until he came back with his regiment. There was a family reunion at the Hall and that started it. Mr. Hugo — he dropped his military rank when he came in for the property — fell for his brother's wife at first sight. From then on the two brothers were at each other's throats like a couple of mad dogs. And she not seeming to care how unseemly a spectacle it made. Going out sometimes with one, sometimes with the other. And within a month of Mr. Hugo coming home his brother smashed himself up in his car."

Finch raised an eyebrow. "It wasn't an accident?"

"The jury brought it in as one. But the motorist whom Arthur Ommanney overtook a couple of minutes before the accident said that he was driving like a maniac."

"Rather hard on his passenger, wasn't it?"

"Mr. Arthur must have been out of his mind," said Laker, and there was regret and anger in his voice.

"What happened exactly?"

"The accident took place just outside Ringwood. Mr. Arthur had brought a new car, a Super Martin, and was driving it from London to Bournemouth. It was a frosty morning. The car skidded. Turned completely around twice. Shot through a hedge. Struck a tree, turned over, and burst into flames. Arthur was killed instantaneously. The other poor fellow, John Marquis, was trapped. When he was got out he was a human torch. Horrible! And then, within six months of all that, Arthur's widow must needs marry her brother-in-law."

"Where was she at the time of the accident?"

"Staying with some cousins near Guildford."

"I see. Are the Ommanneys well off?"

"Yes. Mr. Hugo's father, Andrew Ommanney, had money, and then, just after the First World War, he married a rich childless widow, the lady who was buried today. Mr. Hugo couldn't have afforded to keep up the Hall if it hadn't been for her money. She was in her late thirties when she married for the second time but she had the two boys — which is more than young Mrs. Ommanney has managed."

"Give her time," said Finch, recalling the childlike face and figure.

Laker looked sceptical. "She was married

over three years to Mr. Arthur. He was killed in May of 1952. She's been married two years to Mr. Hugo." He smiled, tight-lipped. "But there, I may be prejudiced. I don't like the lady myself. I don't even like her looks, though I remember she made something of a sensation in London society. Had her picture in everything. The rare and lovely Mrs. Ommanney, one picture called her."

Laker seemed to linger over this tribute. He might not approve of Camilla Ommanney's behavior or even of her looks. But Hugo's pale-faced wife did stir his imagination. And that, Finch fancied, was no mean achievement.

"I believe I saw some other members of the family at the funeral," Finch murmured.

"Yes, old Mrs. Ommanney had three brothers-in-law still living. Sir Kenneth was there with his wife. He married Lady Sybil Voase, daughter of an Irish peer. They're a devoted couple. Never separated — perhaps because they have no children. They've been staying at the Hall for some time, waiting to get into their own house. Then the Rector is Sir Kenneth's brother. He's unmarried."

"And the third? There was a tall, rather wolfish-looking man?"

Laker was surprised. "The Major? Major Guy Ommanney?"

Finch's face sharpened. So that was why — "I've heard that name . . ." He caught Laker's look of wry amusement. "Wasn't he mixed up in some card scandal just before the last war? Caught cheating at cards?"

"That's the man. A second Tranby Croft affair, the newspapers called it. There was even a Royalty mixed up in it, if only a minor one. A young Indian prince over here with his tutor."

Finch nodded. "There was a libel case that the Major lost. It made a lot of talk. Some people took his part, I remember."

"More fools they," said Laker robustly. "Around here we knew the Major."

"Was he married?"

"Yes. But she'd left him long ago."

"By herself?"

Laker stared. "For what it's worth — no. She's been dead some years now. But she was a no-good little thing."

Little? Did Camilla resemble her — and in more ways than one? Finch tucked the question away in his mind. When he had more time he'd take it out again — but not in front of Superintendent Laker.

"But his relations down here stood by the Major, did they?"

Laker nodded. "They're great people for family. Besides, they probably thought that he was less likely to strike the headlines again if they kept in touch with him. Yes, we saw quite a lot of him until about four months ago. Then he disappeared and it was rumored that he'd been kicked out of the house. However, no sooner was the old lady dead than he was down here once more, staying at the Hall. Yesterday, though, he left again of his own accord. That was why I was surprised when you said that he was in church today."

"D'you know why he was thrown out?"

"Haven't a clue."

"Caught cheating again perhaps."

Laker guffawed. "No one about here would have been such a — fool as to play cards with him. I tell you we knew the Major."

"How does he live?"

"Honestly, I hope. The family may help

him. I know for a fact that they paid for the girl's schooling."

"There was a girl then?"

Laker stared. "Of course there was. Camilla Ommanney is the Major's daughter."

4

IT was getting dark when Finch drove into Hammerford. The village seemed to have retired for the night though there was a slip of light showing around the blinds of its one shop.

As Finch's car turned in by the Green its lamps raked the churchyard. They lit up an old stone vault and a marble angel pointing upwards. The humpbacked gravestones became old people, shawled and moving towards the church. Daisies sprang up like stars upon the grass.

Finch had driven some way when a thought struck him.

There had been no daisies growing in the churchyard. And anyway the flowers that he had seen were too large for daisies. Too large and too bright.

He stopped his car. He got out. There was a faint queasy feeling in the pit of his stomach. He stood for a moment looking over the church wall, getting his eyes accustomed to the dark.

Gradually the churchyard took shape. The stone vault came into view. The marble angel. The humpbacked congregation. The daisies . . .

He pushed open the heavy wooden gate. It scraped on the gravel and a breath of wind stirred the trees overhead. Except for this there was no sound. He walked across the grass.

He stooped and picked up one of the white scraps. It was a petal from a Madonna lily. It lay in his hand as light as a wisp of chiffon and the faint scent it gave off had a sad, evocative flavour.

He looked about him. Torn flowers were strewn everywhere. He picked up a few. Let them trickle from his fingers, Freesias, carnations, lilies . . .

The empty darkness tore at his nerves. Odd thoughts echoed disquietingly in his mind. Mental images crowded in on him. Blind-eyed cottages, Wyman's frightened face, the uneasy congregation, legends of vampires and open graves.

Where Mrs. Ommanney had been buried had seemed, in the light of day, a peaceful and pleasant spot. Now not a particle of light penetrated to it through the tall trees. It was as dark as the inside of a grave, as dark and almost as silent. Finch struck a match. The tiny flame dipped and curled, throwing a wavering, uncertain light. A granite cross rose in his path.

'Scared to the memory of Arthur Bliss Ommanney.'

The match flared and went out. The cross vanished. Darkness returned, pressing in on him. He struck another match.

He was standing beside the grave of old Mrs. Ommanney. The scent of flowers was strong and cloying. All about him the arrangement of wreaths lay unaltered. Only the grave itself had been shorn of flowers. The earth showed bare and unsightly, but at least it was undisturbed.

A small bit of white pasteboard caught his eye. A corner torn from a mourner's card.

Hugo and Ca —

Hugo and Camilla! The dead woman's son and daughter-in-law.

The place seemed full of ghosts. Old Mrs. Ommanney and her darling son. Hugo of the cool eyes and small determined mouth. Camilla, who had been married to both brothers. And had, Finch suspected, loved neither.

Just inside the lych gate his foot struck something hard. He stooped and picked it up. It was the stout wire frame on which a wreath had been built, but so bent, so twisted, and crushed as to be scarcely recognizable.

He stood quite still, looking at it. A madman or a giant did this. And, with the thought, the figure of the Joker seemed to materialize from the darkness. To become known, if not by name, then at least by character, for fury lay in the mangled wires and malice stared up from the torn flowers.

The door of the village store opened. The light flowed out. Templar followed it, calling "Good night" over his shoulder to someone in the shop. He paused in surprise. He thought that Finch looked impressive, even formidable, standing there in the gateway. A moment later he saw that he had been mistaken. The tall, lazy-looking figure had dropped whatever he had been holding. He was coming through the gateway.

'Must have been a trick of the light,'

Templar thought. He said aloud, "Hello! Anything wrong?"

"Someone's been destroying the wreaths on old Mrs. Ommanney's grave."

Templar gave a soundless whistle. "Never thought he'd do a think like that."

"Who d'you mean?"

"Why, the Reverend, of course."

"You think he's the Joker you were telling me about?"

"Who else? He has a thing about lights and doors. Can't leave 'em alone. There's a special name for it."

"Compulsion neurosis?"

"That's it. Sometimes the poor chap has to turn the lights off in his room as may as thirty-six times. Always in multiples of four. The same with doors. Takes him at least fifteen minutes to leave his house, so he told me."

"*He* told you."

"Yes. We're by the way of being buddies. He likes my company for the same reason that Johnny Marquis likes that of Hugo. Gives him a sense of reality." Templar added with coarse good humor, "Makes him feel he's all there when he isn't."

"Makes me feel I want a drink," said

Finch. "Come back to the pub and have one on me. First, though, I suppose I ought to tell someone about this business."

"Drinks first," Templar declared. "I'll ring the local P.C. when I get back to my place."

He climbed into the car. "Ever seen the Rector walking through the village?" he continued. "Hop-skip-jump. Touch this bit of railing. Avoid that crack in the path."

"So that was it! I noticed it in church. He ought to see a psychiatrist."

Templar made a wide gesture with his arm. "Aw, why should he? It adds to the gayety of village life to have a screwball parson. At one time, so I'm told he used to read the last verse of each lesson in church not less than four times. People used to come from all over the country to hear him."

"What happened?" Finch turned the car into the yard at the back of the inn. "Someone else read the lessons?"

"Hugo Ommanney tried that. But either the old man knew his Bible by heart or else he mugged it up beforehand." Templar got out of the now stationary car with a clumsy rolling motion. "No, what happened was this: when Hugo was all set to say, 'Here endeth,' the Rector'd pipe up and say his party piece."

Templar's rich chuckle rolled around the silent yard. He took Finch's arm. "Come on. Let's go in and frighten our friend Wyman."

The landlord heard them come in. He appeared through the door which led from the Public Bar.

Templar waited until they had been served, then he said, "Have you heard that our friend the Joker has been at it again? Sacrilege this time, no less. He's been destroying the wreaths on old Mrs. Ommanney's grave."

Wyman's face turned a dirty grey. "Whose wreaths?" he asked hoarsely.

Templar nodded. "That's quite a point." His tone was mockingly judicial. He turned to Finch. "Whose wreaths?" he repeated.

"Seems to have been those sent by the family," Finch answered.

Wyman gave a groan. "Oh, my God!" he muttered. He looked on the point of collapse.

Templar stared. "Here, hold up! What's the matter, man?"

Wyman shook his head slowly. He was making a great effort to appear as usual. "Why, nothing, sir. Nothing at all. You took me by surprise. That was all." He smiled in a ghastly way. "Sacrilege? Just think of that, now."

Moving stiffly, like a man in the grip of a nightmare, he turned and walked out of the saloon. A moment later there came the sound of the sitting-room door closing. The key turned in the lock.

"Well, I'll be damned," said Templar. "What d'you make of that?"

Mrs. Wyman waited on Finch at supper. She seemed more bewildered than frightened, he thought. Her thoughts were plainly elsewhere. She fumbled and dropped things, then smiled placatingly.

Wyman himself was back in the Public Bar, a sour, unsmiling man. It was very quiet there and a sort of gloom hung over the house.

Finch went up to his bedroom. He locked the door, drew down the blinds, and then spread Laker's map out on the bed.

Like the Superintendent before him, he could not see that the Joker had worked to any particular plan. He did notice, however, that not one of the houses visited by the Joker had had children or young people living in them. And that no less than five of the nine householders had the adjective 'old' before their names. Old Tom Delves. Old Mr. and Mrs. Lowe.

One answer to this was that young people will talk and that old people are slower to hear and see an intruder. Another was that the Joker took no great pains to remain unseen, because, having picked his house, he knew that he could count on the loyalty of the older inhabitants of Hammerford.

The only exception had been the Georgian house. There the householder had been only middle-aged and there was someone young living in the house. Against this was the fact that Mrs. Markham could have been seen by any passer-by sitting downstairs reading; while Lionel's whereabouts were probably known to everyone in the village.

Finch was by training bound to be a bit suspicious of this reasoning. Because the Georgian house had been the first to suffer. Because it *had* been the exception. Because, like poison-pen writers, the first to complain is often the author of the very action of which she complains, Mrs.

Markham was suspect.

One thing, though, was certain, the Joker was someone who hated (a) old Mrs. Ommanney, (b) the Ommanneys, (c) the remaining Ommanneys, being one himself (herself).

Finch had just slipped the map into his pocket when he heard a car slowing up in front of the inn. He switched off the light and looked from the window.

A smart Sunbeam-Talbot stood on the opposite side of the road. There was a bus stop a little farther on.

'Come to meet someone,' Finch thought. He stayed watching.

The bus came in, lighting up the darkened village with an almost carnival air.

The door of the car farthest from the driver opened. Major Guy Ommanney stepped out. He wore an overcoat and carried a suitcase. He slammed the car door, walked over to the bus, and climbed aboard. He passed down the bus and sat directly behind the driver. He took a book from his pocket and became, to all appearances, immersed in it.

He went on reading as the bus left. He was the only passenger.

The two-seater started up. It circled the Green and sped away. It turned into the drive of the Hall, roaring beneath the trees, making a lacelike pattern of leaves overhead.

'So the Major's been thrown out again,' Finch thought. 'Must be getting monotonous.' He looked at his watch. The time was ten minutes past ten.

He pulled the bedroom blind down again. For some time he was busy writing his report. He finished this, went quietly down the stairs and out of the pub.

The village was lost now, sunk deep in the immemorial silence of the tall trees. The lanes were twisting and narrow, haunted fitfully by moonlight. Scattered cottages were linked to the village by wooded paths. Sheep moved in the near darkness. An owl floated from a high tree. All about him was the uncaring solitude of night.

He passed a cottage that housed the local police force. He came to the gates of the Hall. There were no lodges; for this, though nearest to the village, was not the main entrance of the estate. The gates were open. They hung from massive brick-built piers. Surmounting each pier, Finch could discern a strange beast, unknown outside heraldry, supporters to the Ommanney coat of arms.

Beyond the gates was no glimmer of light to suggest a house. Trees hid it and made of the drive a dark tunnel.

Finch stiffened suddenly, listening.

At first there seemed nothing. Then, as he stood there, there came to him in the silence the faraway sound of footsteps.

They drew nearer. A branch cracked in the far side of the hedge. There was a rustling and a snapping. A dark figure emerged on to the road.

The Major had returned.

His overcoat was over his arm. He carried his suitcase. He passed so close to where Finch stood in the shadows that the detective could see his eyeballs gleaming in the moonlight. Could see, too, that he was smiling to himself. And that, Finch decided, under the circumstances, boded no good to anyone.

The Major stepped into the shadows and immediately was lost to view. A moment later he had switched on a flashlight. Finch watched the light jogging along, the Major's shining toecaps coming and going in its radius like twin pistons.

The drive must have curved, for the light vanished suddenly. For a time the trees threw back the echo of his passage. This faded and finally was gone.

There were left only the silence, the darkness, and the two strange beasts peering down from their high perch.

5

THE churchyard had been tidied up. Old Mrs. Ommanney's grave gleamed under a massed covering of white and pink chrysanthemums.

Finch watched the village wake up to life. A few farm workers leaving their cottages. Small children walking to the village school and, later, bigger ones catching the bus to Market Stalbridge. Women came out and cleaned their door steps.

The proprietor of the village shop let up his blinds. The little mousey woman came out of her cottage. She mounted a bicycle and pedaled energetically away.

The milkman made his rounds, and then the postman. They did not linger to gossip. It seemed that the news of the Major's return was not yet known.

Finch went downstairs.

Wyman and Fred were standing at the open front door. They turned when they heard his footsteps and wished him good morning. "Just waiting for the brewer's man," Wyman explained. He looked surly. His eyes were heavy, as if he had not slept.

"Splendid," said Finch. He tapped the pike's glass case. "Who caught this fellow?"

Wyman's face brightened. "I did, sir. In the Otway — the other side of the county."

"That's a salmon river, isn't it?"

"That's right, sir. My old uncle was water bailiff to Sir John Penberry."

"Any fishing around here?"

"Not what you could call fishing. I tried to interest both Mr. Arthur and Mr. Hugo but it was no good. Too slow, they said."

This was very much Finch's opinion of the sport. He had, however, done quite a bit on the Torridge while staying, as a boy, with a clerical uncle. The landlord and he talked fishing until Fred called out that the brewer's truck was in sight. They parted on cordial terms.

Finch went in to his breakfast.

A few minutes later the door opened. The Reverend Philip Ommanney strode in. His tall thin body was buttoned into his cassock. His face was heavily lined. His deep-set eyes glowed. It was a tormented, melancholy face.

"Good morning," he said, unsmiling and in his harsh voice. "I must apologize for interrupting you so early but I understand that you were the first to find the destruction in the churchyard."

He waved aside Finch's offer of coffee. He drew up a second chair to the table and seated himself opposite. He listened while Finch spoke, drumming with his long fingers on the table, fidgeting in his seat. The whole conversation took place to the sound of rolling barrels and Wyman's voice shouting directions. "And you saw no one?" he asked.

"I had a fleeting impression that someone was there," Finch answered. "But if that were correct they were just outside the radius of the car's lamps and had gone by the time I entered the churchyard. And certainly the damage hadn't been done long."

"It had not been done at seven-thirty for I myself passed through the churchyard at that time." The Rector was worrying one of the buttons at his neck.

Finch's eyes narrowed. "And I arrived at seven fifty-two."

The Rector looked up sharply. "Wisbeach

did not telephone to me until half past eight."

"That was because there's no telephone here. Mr. Templar offered to ring up Wisbeach from his house."

Philip Ommanney nodded. "That ribald and earthy man," he murmured. It seemed to Finch a pretty fair description of the painter.

"You did not know my late sister-in-law, I think?" And something in his tone of voice told the C.I.D. man that they were approaching the real reason for the Rector's visit.

"It was never my fortune to do so," Finch answered formally.

"You represented some company, I believe?"

Finch smiled slightly. "I might be said to represent the village."

The Reverend Philip Ommanney appeared to turn this over in his mind. He moved a pepper pot, setting it down with meticulous care, so that it covered an old coffee stain. "By that you mean that you are a newspaper reporter?"

Was that what had been in the Rector's mind all along? Finch shook his head. "I'm a policeman," he said simply.

"A policeman!" The Rector seemed as much relieved as surprised. He looked curiously at Finch. "Forgive me! I find that difficult to believe."

Finch passed him his I.D. card. "Colonel Stonor was worried," he explained, "not so much by what was happening as by the inhabitants' reaction to it. Someone turns on lights and bangs doors — and the villagers are frightened. It didn't seem to make sense." He added drily, "After last night, though, I'm not so sure."

The Rector nodded to himself. He said in a low voice, "I too. After last night I am not so sure. That tangle of wire — "

"There was only one?"

"There were four. Only one of them, however, was crushed out of recognition. Perhaps the miscreant was disturbed. Or perhaps" — Philip Ommanney's harsh voice dropped still further — "perhaps only that one wreath aroused his hatred."

"Whose wreath was it?"

Philip Ommanney hesitated. Not, Finch felt, from any desire for concealment, but rather from a primitive feeling that to say the name aloud might bring disaster to its owner. "It was my nephew's wreath," he said at last. "It was from Hugo — and his wife."

"Has he any known enemy?"

The Rector started. "No. no! Not to my knowledge. No, certainly not."

"Yet I think you have someone in mind."

The Rector's eyes avoided Finch's. "I had thought — " he stumbled. "John Marquis!" He rapped out the name. He went on with growing confidence, "Once the daily woman has gone there is no one to say whether he is in or out. He takes no notice of time. Some days he is up at cockcrow. Others he will sleep all day and go out at nightfall. And who can say what thoughts torment his shadowy mind?"

"I understand that he remembers nothing — not even what is said to him day by day."

Philip Ommanney's long fingers groped for the pepper pot. "But suppose," he muttered to it, "suppose his memory has come back? Might he not blame the Ommanneys because one of them made him what he is today?"

"But why Hugo?"

Said the Rector, "He loved him — that would make his sense of betrayal the more bitter, would it not?"

"I thought that it was Arthur Ommanney who was his friend?"

"I am speaking of after the accident. It was then that he turned to Hugo. Even in the hospital he would remember him and be pleased to see him when his own uncle had become a stranger. And down here he has followed him about like a child. When he has had one of his wandering fits and has gone off for several days, the first place he makes for on his return is the Hall. Indeed one might even suppose that it is a sudden urge for Hugo's company that brings him back, since I have known him to get there at three o'clock in the morning and search around until he finds a way in. No burglar could be more persistent or successful."

"And your nephew?"

"He has been wonderful with him. Never impatient, never unkind. My nephew, Inspector, has immense self-control, an entire absence of nerves, and, perhaps, little imagination."

"I see. And please don't call me Inspector. My usefulness would be gone if anyone heard you." Finch added, "Have you noticed anything that suggests that Mr. Marquis is recovering his memory?"

The Rector hesitated. "Nothing definite. And yet, and yet — I feel that there is a difference in the man himself."

Finch thought of Camilla Ommanney's behavior in church.

"D'you know if anyone else has had the same thought?"

"I believe that it is entirely my own idea."

"And young Mrs. Ommanney? What does she feel about it?"

"Camilla? We none of us know what Camilla feels."

"She remains neutral perhaps."

Philip Ommanney gave an abrupt high laugh that startled Finch. "Neutral!" he echoed. "Perhaps that is the answer. Camilla remains neutral."

Finch had the feeling that the Rector was alluding to something more than young Mrs. Ommanney's reaction to John Marquis.

Breakfast over, Finch went out to the telephone box on the Green. He put through a call to Scotland Yard. He asked for Inspector Drew. He was the Yard's social expert. His job was to know and remember not only those who were in society but those who hung dubiously on its fringe.

Drew's brisk voice proclaimed its identity from the London end. In return Finch gave his own name.

"Hello, my boy! I heard you had gone into the country. What's cooking down your way?"

"I've found some refugees from the bright lights. Notably one, Major Guy Ommanney."

"That chap! You have all the luck. What's he up to now?"

"It's a little difficult to say. He seems to have been thrown out of the ancestral home and come back. Been thrown out and again returned. Though what it's all about I don't know. Tell me, how does he live?"

"Very well, thank you. And will do as long as there are any snobs in the world."

"How's that?"

"He's what one might call a professional guest. It's quite an angle. He takes his distinguished presence to some expensive and moderately fashionable place. Puts up in a cheap room and then looks for a likely subject. Some rich old couple — or may be just a rich old girl — anyway someone who's feeling a bit out of things. He brushes up an acquaintanceship. Brings into the conversation a few titled relations. Regrets that owing to the illness of Lord So-and-So he's not on his yacht or grouse moor or whatever is correct for the time of year. They're flattered and excited. And in no time the Major's being entertained by them, motored about, invited to stay at their homes."

"Does it stop there?"

"We suspect not. But we've never managed to get anyone to lodge a definite complaint."

"Too bad," Finch murmured sympathetically. "There's a daughter — ?"

"Yes. I remember her at the time of the trial. You're sure to have heard of that? Yes, well, she was in court. A pale-faced little thing with a lot of odd-colored hair. Amazing self-control. James, of the London *Guardian*, called her the Dead-Pan Fairy. Her presence was supposed to have a good effect on the jury but it counted against the Major. Mr. Justice Kale was the judge. He liked children. And you would see him wondering what sort of a father would put his girl in such a position."

"She seems to have done well for herself. Married a cousin who has a nice place down here. Fellow called Arthur Ommanney. They were around and about in London until he killed himself in a motoring accident."

"Yes, I remember them. Very bright and gay and busy getting nowhere at great speed. No harm in them though. What happened to her after his death?"

"Within six months she married her brother-in-law."

Inspector Drew's laugh came down to Finch. "Just her mother's girl over again! I never could keep track of the number of men she married."

"I haven't heard much of her. What was she like?"

"A tiny thing. Known as the Pocket Venus. She was a tramp though. She was killed in a train smash in South America in company with a dance band leader with whom she was said to be living."

As Finch came from the telephone box

Wisbeach passed wheeling his bicycle. "Good morning, sir," he said, saluting.

"Have we met before?" Finch asked.

"No, sir. I recognized you from your photographs."

Finch looked at him quizzically. "The use of that last word in the plural marks you out as a fitting subject for promotion."

Wisbeach grinned back cheerfully. "I wish it did, sir. I thought it'd help when I got Mr. Marquis out of a burning barn but nothing came of it. Perhaps because I didn't manage to save the barn."

"What is the story?"

"It was about a month ago, sir. I was passing Hurst Farm when I saw smoke and flames coming from a barn. The farm's a small place and Mr. Inglis, I knew, was away for the day. I got nearer and heard someone screaming inside — just like a pig having its throat cut. I thought at first that it was a pig. The door had jammed but I got hold of a bit of heavy wood and broke in. Mr. Marquis came stumbling out in a terrible state. Not burned but crying and shaking. I didn't half have a time quieting him down. I couldn't do anything to save the barn. It was too far gone and there wasn't any water. Luckily it stood some way off in a field by itself."

"And I suppose it was Mr. Marquis who caught the barn on fire?"

"Must have been, sir. He often goes into a farm building to sleep. The farmers hereabouts are quite used to him suddenly turning up."

"They'll be a bit wary of him if he's going to do that sort of thing," said Finch. Then he asked, "Seen anything of the Major?"

"There was some sort of trouble up at the Hall last night. The Major is supposed to have hit young Mrs. Ommanney and Mr. Hugo put him on the last bus with his luggage and saw him off."

"He didn't see him off far enough. The Major came back. I saw him myself, going up the Hall drive."

Wisbeach shook his head. "If he's at the Hall no one knows it."

The mousey-looking woman passed, still bicycling energetically. She divided a bright smile between the two men. "Such a lovely morning," she called, swerving erratically towards them.

"Look out, miss!" Wisbeach shouted, springing out of the way.

"I'm all right," she called back. She waved her hand and rode on, dismounting in front of her cottage.

"That's Miss Buss, sir," Wisbeach explained. "A very nice lady but somehow she can't manage a bicycle. Maybe she took to it too late in life. She's a retired schoolteacher. Very highly qualified, so I've been told."

Finch nodded. "Anywhere in the park where the Major could lie up?"

"There's two or three concrete pillboxes left over from the war, but I doubt if the Major'd find them. They're so overgrown now. Then there's what they call the Italian House, sir. It's empty but it's got some furniture in it. Sir Kenneth had it done up. He would have moved in this week if it hadn't been for old Mrs. Ommanney dying."

"I'll go there and have a look for the Major."

Wisbeach looked startled. "Excuse me asking, sir, but is he wanted for anything?"

"Not in the way you mean. But I'm anxious about him." Finch looked at his wrist watch. "It's now twenty minutes to eleven. That means that nearly twelve hours have passed since the Major's return — and still no one has heard from him. And that, for a person of the Major's character, strikes me as highly unnatural."

Wisbeach nodded. "Anything I can do, sir?" he asked soberly.

"You can have a few discreet words with the bus conductor when he gets in. Meanwhile, how do I find the Italian House and shall I be trespassing?"

"Only in a technical sense, sir," said Wisbeach, answering the last question first. "We all use the park. The family don't mind as long as we keep out of sight of the Hall and don't disturb the pheasants. The Italian House is easy enough to find. If you walk up the drive for some way you'll see a track running off to the left. It'll bring you to the house. You can't miss it."

There was no one about at the gates to the park. The two strange beasts looked down from their brick-built piers. Beyond them the tree-lined drive curved gently. Finch walked on and on. Every moment he expected to encounter someone from the Hall. No one came. He seemed to have the place to himself. It was very peaceful and pleasant. Everywhere was the neatness that speaks of wealth.

The day was again still and warm, though it seemed to Finch that the hint of approaching autumn had become accentuated. Leaves came spinning down with scarcely a breath of wind to speed them. He came to the track. It seemed to have been made by the successive passage of trucks. The ground was heavily rutted and some of the young trees had been torn up bodily.

It was not long before the character of the woods changed. They became neglected and overcrowded. The trees were moss-grown. Fungus sprang up at their feet or hung in pale, bracket-shaped wedges from the trunks themselves. Young saplings pressed in on him and the undergrowth was thick and untrammelled. But for a slight sighing of the wind the silence was absolute.

He came on a melancholy grove of yew trees, blue black, old and twisted and sprawling in grotesque shapes. Here an axe had been used to clear the track. Torn branches lay withering on the ground.

A house was set in a clearing. The Italian House, small and beautiful and built of pale stone. There seemed no other entrance but the hacked and truck-made path by which he had come.

The house had the look of a place long abandoned; the windows, uncurtained, confronted him with a lidless stare. An attempt had been made to clear the garden. The sour earth had been roughly turned. The bleached and yellowing grass cut with a scythe.

Finch stood there in the silence and listened for a sound. None came. He walked slowly up the moss-grown path.

He broke the stagnant silence by a vigorous knocking on the front door. A knocking that seemed to wake a place long sealed by silence. The echoes died. There was nothing more to hear; neither sound nor stir.

He peered in at the windows. There was some furniture in this house. It had an alien, even a startled air. It seemed in no sense part of the scene. It stood away from the walls as if expecting every moment to be called for and taken away.

At the back a tall narrow iron gate broke the ring of yew trees. A window in the house stood open. For some reason he did not connect it with the Major. As he looked at it a queer little feeling of uneasiness came to him. He fancied for a moment that something darker than the shadow of a tree stood beside him in the thin sunlight.

He climbed into the room beyond. It was a kitchen. A lot of money had been spent on it. It was all gleaming tiles and electric gadgets. The color scheme was primrose yellow and white. It was bright, cheerful, yet after a moment Finch felt a chill come over him.

Something lay over the house like a desolating cloud.

He called, "Anyone here?" And his voice ran echoing before him into all the silent rooms.

He walked along the passage. He pushed open a baize door and became aware that somewhere near water was running splashing. He was now in the main part of the house. Four ornamental doors painted a soft green scumbled with gold, were set at intervals in walls treated to represent green marble.

He opened the first door on right. A window faced him across the width of a narrow room. Beyond it was a small enclosed courtyard. An old, half-dead fig tree grew against one wall. A fountain threw up a jet of water that fell again into a marble bowl.

He opened the door wider and looked in.

The Major was there.

He lay on an antique bed in a great pool of blood. His throat had been cut almost from ear to ear.

6

THERE was a telephone in the hall. Finch picked up the receiver. Almost at once a voice said, "Number please."

He was soon through to Superintendent Laker. "Someone has murdered the Major," he told him.

"Who says so?" Laker sounded as if, with the slightest encouragement, he would dispute the statement.

"I do. I just found him. You know the Italian House — ?"

"I know of it," Laker answered, as if the distinction were important.

"So did the Major. He's there — with his throat cut."

"No chance of its being suicide?"

"None. For one thing there's no weapon."

There was a pause. "Right! I'll be out. Take me a good half hour, though."

"I'll be waiting for you." Finch replaced the receiver.

The Superintendent, at his end, did the

same. He stood for a moment thinking in a confused sort of way. The room seemed full of the echo of his own voice. 'Blood,' he had said to the C.I.D. man only the day before as if he had a premonition. And now here it was — buckets of it, most likely.

He roused himself. Half an hour? It'd be nearer an hour if he didn't get moving. He went along to Colonel Stonor's room. He thought suddenly that if anyone had had a premonition, it had been the Chief Constable. The idea amused him. He knocked and went in.

Colonel Stonor was signing some papers in a rather school-boyish hand. "If you've come for these — " he began. "Oh, it's you, Laker."

"Mr. Finch has just rung up, sir, from Hammerford — "

The Colonel started as if his tongue had touched on an exposed nerve. "If he wants permission to dig up the old lady he can't have it."

"It wasn't about old Mrs. Ommanney, sir. It's the Major. He's had his throat cut." Laker repeated what he had been told over the telephone.

The Colonel's jaw dropped. "But this

is ghastly." he said. "Ghastly! Don't you see, Laker? The murderer's bound to be someone in the family. They all hated him. Why," he added, warming to his theme, "if we hadn't buried her yesterday, we might even have had to arrest old Mrs. Ommanney."

"It might be one of the villagers surely, sir. From what Wisbeach says they've been in a queer sort of mood lately."

Colonel Stonor rejected this. "The village wouldn't have gone near the Italian House. The place has a bad name."

"Of course," said Laker. "I've heard rumors of what the house was used *for* — "

"Yes, well something dashed queer happened there — and I'm talking of over a century ago. Since then the villagers have avoided the place. And though the Ommanneys kept the house in repair no one ever lived there again."

"Until Sir Kenneth came along."

"And look what's come of that," said the Colonel as if he had scored a point.

Laker nodded. "You'll be handing over the case to the Inspector, I suppose?"

"Yes, of — " the Colonel broke off, pondering. "Now, don't let's be too hasty.

You go up there, Laker, and have a look around. Make certain there's no chance of its having been suicide. This inspector fella isn't likely to have moved the Major. The weapon may be out of sight. Under the body, for all we know."

Laker agreed dutifully. He had little faith, though, in the Chief Constable's idea.

In the Italian House, Finch made a rapid survey of the rooms. He went from one to the next and all the time the sound of water followed him. The gay splashing and eddying of the little fountain in the enclosed courtyard. It seemed to fill the house like voices whispering together.

He looked from the windows. From every one the view was the same. The neglected garden, the wall of dark and dusty-looking yews. And beyond the leafy tops of the tall crowding trees.

The rooms themselves were all light and airy and delicately decorated with plaster work panels. The floors were parquet downstairs and richly carpeted upstairs. The curtains were of brocade. There were some beautiful pieces of furniture. Yet, when he had been through all the house, he marvelled that anyone should choose to live here. Redecorated, it remained neither more nor less desolate and remote in time.

He went back to the room where the murdered man lay. He stood at the door making a mental inventory of what he saw.

The only furniture in the room was a day bed, upholstered in crimson velvet, a mahogany chair with an upholstered back and seat covered in rose damask, and a mirror in an elaborate mahogany frame. The chair was one of a set of six. The other five were in the hall. The mirror hung very low on the wall as if formerly it had been in a much higher room. As if it had been hung in its present position only to be out of the way.

Major Guy Ommanney lay on his back. His head rested on the round, bolster-shaped pillow of crimson velvet which belonged to the day bed. His body was wrapped in a handsome brocade curtain so large that it must, Finch decided, have been meant for a portiere. His stockinged feet and legs were uncovered, as if he had

OMOID7

swung them into the air in a sudden abortive effort to rise. He wore a silk dressing gown over his shirt and underwear.

His coat and trousers, collar and tie were arranged over the back of the chair. His shoes, neatly treed, stood under it. All were as carefully arranged as the tools of a good workman, which Finch reflected, in a sense they had been.

A suitcase stood open on the chair seat. A small pile of personal possessions, the contents of his pockets, lay on the mantelpiece along with a novel in a bright dust-jacket, a flashlight and a pair of doeskin gloves smoothed flat and with the fingers pulled out neatly.

There was cigarette ash flicked lavishly over the parquet floor to one side of the day bed. Three cigarette stubs lay in the fireplace.

Finch opened the french window on to the paved courtyard. He walked out, looking about him curiously.

Three of the walls were pierced with windows. The fourth, on the kitchen side, was blank. It was here that the old fig tree grew. Its leaves were yellowing and it had some pitted-looking fruit. The soil under it was damp and soft. In it, close to the paved edge, was the imprint of the rounded toe of a shoe.

He went back into the room. He glanced at his wrist watch. Forty-three minutes since he had telephoned. And still the local police had not come.

He returned to the hall, and stood looking out on the scene, shoulders hunched, hands thrust deep into his pockets.

Beyond him the melancholy room rustled with ghosts and echoed the little sound of murmuring water that seemed the very voice and core of secrecy.

A police car came into sight, bouncing up the rough track. It stopped and Superintendent Laker and three plainclothes men stepped from it. They paused a moment, staring at the house before coming up the path.

Finch went to the front door. "Your case, I think."

Laker smiled sourly. "For the moment, yes." He stepped over the threshold. Stood looking about him inquisitively. "Very nice," he said. "Very nice indeed. When I heard that Sir Kenneth planned to live here," he told Finch, "I thought he must be off his rocker. But it's certainly a lovely little place."

Finch looked at him sadly. "I still think he must be off his rocker."

Laker shook his head. "It's nice," he said again. "Very tasteful." He added, "The police surgeon is going to be late but we may as well get on. Where is the Major?"

"This way." Finch preceded the local men. He stood aside at the open door. "I'm afraid he's not looking his best," he murmured in his small voice.

Superintendent Laker had never seen anything like it, but his was a phlegmatic temperament. He stood stolidly in the doorway looking first at the body of the dead man, then around the room.

He looked out of the window. His eyes came to rest on the little fountain. Its gay inconsequence seemed to shake him. "For Chris' sake!" he muttered. He crossed to the body. "But what on earth was he doing sleeping here?"

"There was some trouble up at the Hall. The Major got thrown out, so Wisbeach was telling me. But we were both in full view of the village at the time so I didn't like to press him for details."

Laker sent one of the plainclothes men out to the car. The uniformed driver was to take it and bring back the local man.

"You're certain that it wasn't suicide?"

Finch shook his head. "There's not even any attempt to make it look like suicide. Apart from the fact that the weapon is missing, the victim's arms are still under the bed clothes. Then the wound is all wrong. In suicide it should be slightly inclined downward and should tend to become shallower as it reaches its destination. Here, though, it is uniformly severe and situated low down in the neck. Finally one can even see where the victim awoke and attempted to sit up." Finch pointed. "There! Where the knife has slipped."

"He was asleep then?" Laker added indignantly, as if the Major had been engaged in some sort of sporting activity, "It didn't give him a chance."

Finch nodded his agreement. "And the curtain he had wrapped himself in held him down effectually as if he'd been sewn up in a sack."

"Any evidence as to the identity of the murderer?"

"None at the moment. He — or she — appears to have entered by a back window."

Laker gave him a shrewd look. "Whoever it was must have known that the Major was sleeping here."

"I fancy that's going to be quite an important point. Incidentally the major was wearing a light overcoat. I don't see it anywhere about."

"It's probably hanging up somewhere."

Said Finch mildly, "I wondered if the murderer might have slipped it on to cut its owner's throat."

Laker stared. Then sent two of his men to search for the coat.

While Laker and Finch had been talking, the local sergeant had been setting up his photographic apparatus. He was an enthusiast. He had photographed the scene of motor accidents, of housebreaking and chicken stealing. He had photographed scenes of imaginary disasters manufactured by himself.

His passion for photography had become a joke to his fellow police officers. "Don't touch it until McClansland White has seen it," had become a catch phrase. It applied to everything from an overturned bottle of ink to a pretty girl seen passing in the street.

His face now was white with suppressed excitement. He photographed the dead body — and the blood on the parquet floor. He photographed the cigarette ash and the stubs. He photographed the chair, the mirror and the mantlepiece. A police constable spotted the footprint under the fig tree and he photographed that. While Finch told Laker what he knew of the affair the sergeant's camera clicked and clicked, like a dressmaker's scissors.

Laker went through the dead man's suitcase. It was skilfully packed. Its contents were all expensive. Ebony-backed hair brushes. Fine linen handkerchiefs with the monogram 'G.O.' embroidered on them. Handmade shoes . . .

"He did himself well," Laker muttered. He picked up a morocco card case. Inside were half a dozen of the Major's visiting cards. "Five Desmond Place, Park Lane. Park Lane!" he repeated on a rising note.

Finch smiled faintly. "It's not such a grand address as it sounds. I know that part. Desmond Place is one of those odd little cuttings that abound in the West End. There's a warehouse belonging to a house-furnishing company on one side. A few shops on the other. No.5, I fancy is a greengrocer. The Major probably had a flat over the shop. Or even a flat over the flat belonging to the greengrocer."

Laker grunted. He replaced the card case. "A safety razor," he muttered. "A hundred Players in a box — "

"He seems to have been a heavy smoker. There're three stubs in the fireplace."

"All Players? That's not much help. Two out of three people smoke them."

"But not with a holder."

Laker's eyes followed Finch's to where the little pile of objects lay on the mantelpiece. Among them was a short amber cigarette holder with a narrow gold band.

"That's nice," said Laker. It was a favorite word of his. "Nothing flashy about any of the Major's possessions."

"No, he couldn't afford to look flashy," said Finch drily.

Laker glanced at him sharply. Then turned away to paw the objects over. "A flashlight, a pair of doeskin gloves — " He turned suddenly. "What did you say?"

"I didn't speak."

Laker grunted. "Must be that damned

fountain." He picked up a ring with some half dozen keys on it. He sent the remaining plainclothes man to see if any of the keys fitted locks in the Italian House.

He picked up the dead man's wallet. "Plenty of money here," he said. "A pile of bills under the elastic band on one side. And a roll of crumpled bills on the other."

Finch had been standing by the window. Now he ambled forward. "That's interesting." He took the wallet from the Superintendent. Stood looking down at it, brows furrowed.

"What's interesting in it?"

"The untidy roll of bills. They are what one is always looking for, a deviation from the normal. The Major," he added in his murmuring voice, "was such a tidy man."

"Tidy!" said Laker. "Look at the cigarette ash everywhere."

"That," said Finch, "seems to be another deviation from the normal. I can only suppose that Sir Kenneth was responsible in part for the Major's expulsion from the Hall. And all this is the measure of the Major's contempt. He was making use of his brother's house. He flicked ash over his floor, turned on his fountain, ate his figs — you'll find the skin of one in the grate. If he'd lived to walk out of the house he'd probably have gone off leaving the lights burning and the water running in the bathroom."

"You can't know that," said Laker, shocked. "You can't say that he'd have done this or that. The dead don't speak."

"Don't they?" Finch tossed the wallet on to the mantelpiece. He moved to stand by the day bed, facing the Superintendent across the motionless and ghastly figure of the dead man. "Murder," he said, "is a matter of character. The victim did this — or that — because it was in character. The murderer the same. That's how, in the end, we shall catch him."

He moved, turning his back on the day bed. "For instance, we can see, from the position of the cigarette ash, that the Major sat on the edge of the day bed facing the chair. He sat there while he smoked three cigarettes. Even if he were a chain smoker that means that he sat there for at least twenty minutes. He didn't sit on the chair, though he'd taken the trouble to bring it in from the hall.

Why? Because his coat and trousers were on it? Certainly not. The Major, from his age and from what we can deduce from his belongings, was a fastidious, luxury-loving man. The last person to sit about in an empty and unheated house in his underwear."

Laker's face lightened with sudden excitement. "You mean — someone else sat in the chair?"

Finch nodded. "The someone who gave him the roll of bills perhaps. The someone who stepped inadvertently on to the soft earth under the fig tree . . . " His voice trailed away.

In his mind's eye there rose a picture of the Major in his Savile Row suit, with his handmade shoes and his amber cigarette holder. He talked and gesticulated and flicked his ash nonchalantly about him. After his visitor had gone? Had he strolled in the enclosed courtyard, oblivious of danger? Turned on the little fountain? The little fountain whose gay splashing was presently to drown the stealthy approach of the murderer.

The man with the key ring returned. The Yale key fitted the front door lock.

None of the other keys was of use in the Italian House.

Another man hurried in. He carried a light overcoat. "I found it pushed into a bush outside the front door, sir," he said. "The Major's name is on the lining. There's blood on the sleeves and down the front."

Laker gave an exclamation. "The murderer did wear it then."

"Looks like it, sir."

Laker took it. Stared at it a moment. "The police surgeon had better have it and make certain that the blood is from the same group as the Major's," he muttered.

"It'd be a good idea to send his clothes and shoes to the Yard laboratory," said Finch. "There's about three quarters of an hour unaccounted for in the Major's life last night. He left in a bus for Market Stalbridge at ten minutes past ten. He didn't turn up at the entrance gates to the Hall until close on eleven o'clock. An analysis of the dust on his shoes and clothes may give us a hint where he went during that time."

"I'll see to that." Laker added fretfully, "Dr. Piper's being a long time."

Finch nodded. "Lucky the Major's not dying — instead of just being dead," he murmured in his soft drawl.

Wisbeach arrived. The driver of the police car followed him in.

"I was out on my beat, sir," Wisbeach explained. "Then we saw the bus come into the village. And I waited to have a word with the conductor, following instructions from Inspector Finch, sir. I hope that was right."

"Quite right," said Laker. "What did the conductor say?"

"Need we stay here to hear it?" Finch asked. Wisbeach, he had noticed, was turning green.

"No need at all," said Laker promptly. Only the thought that he might appear a sissy in the eyes of the C.I.D. man had deterred him from suggesting a move some time ago. "We can go back to the hall."

Finch asked Wisbeach if he had seen much of the Major in the village during his stay at the Hall.

"Yes, sir. He was about quite a lot."

"Hear any gossip about him?"

Wisbeach smiled faintly. "I'm not exactly popular these days. But Dora Penny, who's in service up at the Hall, told my wife that he seemed very interested in the practical joker. And I did hear that he was standing drinks all round in the Public Bar on the Monday evening. And that wasn't like him. The Major never paid for anything if he could help it."

"It wasn't very seemly, either," Laker sniffed, "seeing he'd come down for a funeral."

"I should imagine that self-interest was the Major's only consideration," said Finch. "He probably thought that a knowledge of the Joker's identity might be useful and didn't bother about anything else."

"Well, let's hear what the bus conductor said."

They had reached the hall. Laker seated himself on a chair similar to the one which the Major had taken to the other room. Finch, tall and sleepy-looking, lounged against the chimney piece. Wisbeach remained standing in the center of the room. He looked very alert and smart, his back very straight and his cap held under his arm.

"The conductor said sir, that Major Ommanney was the only passenger on the bus. He said that no sooner were they out of sight of the last cottage than he began to slap his pockets. Then he called out, 'Stop the bus, man. I've forgotten something. I must go back.' The conductor reminded him that it was the only bus to Market Stalbridge that night and the Major said that he couldn't help it and that he'd have to take a car. The last the conductor saw of him he was walking back very fast towards the village."

"Were those more or less the conductor's own words, 'no sooner were they out of sight of the last cottage'?" Finch asked.

"Yes, sir. He knew the Major and wondered what he was up to. He was laughing about it and said to me that the people at the Hall must have had a nasty surprise when he turned up again."

"Had you told him the Major was dead?" Laker asked.

"No sir. Mr. Finch told me to be careful. I stopped the police car out of sight and entered into casual conversation with him, as you might say."

Laker nodded. "Good! Did you see anyone about late last night?"

"Only Mr. Marquis, sir. He passed my

house about a quarter to twelve, walking away from the village. I was just going out. That's how I came to see him. I didn't see him again though — nor anyone else."

"He was going away from the village? That would mean that he could have been going into the park," said Laker. "Which way did you go?"

"In the opposite direction, sir. Up past Fowler's Farm. They've been losing chickens from there, so I thought I'd have a look around. It was all quiet enough, though, last night."

"Well — that seems to cover that." Laker glanced interrogatively at Finch. "Then let's get on to the trouble at the Hall. How did you come to hear of it?"

Wisbeach shifted his weight from one foot to the other. "It was owing to Dora Penny being my wife's cousin sir. She came down late last night to tell us about it."

Laker nodded. "Go on."

"It began, sir, after the last visitor had left. Dora was looking out of her bedroom window at the top of the house when she saw young Mrs. Ommanney and the Major walking towards the ornamental water. They didn't say anything to each other until they got there. Then they walked up and down talking hard. Sometimes Mrs. Ommanney would stand still and talk and the Major would listen and nod his head as if to show that he was taking it all in. At other times he'd speak and then she'd listen. Of course Dora couldn't hear what they were saying, but being so high up, she could keep them in sight as they walked nearly all the time."

"Doesn't sound as if they were quarrelling," Laker interjected.

"They must have been, sir," Wisbeach differed in the most respectful tone, "because the Major suddenly lifted up his hand and boxed her ears — "

"Boxed young Mrs. Ommanney's ears?" Laker was shocked.

"Yes, sir. A fair clump, Dora says. Mrs. Ommanney didn't do anything. Didn't even speak. Just stood there like she does, quite still and sort of blank. But Mr. Hugo must have seen what happened because he came tearing out of the house. Said something to the Major. And the Major bowed and walked back to the house."

"And Hugo Ommanney?" Finch asked. "What did he do?"

"Well, Dora says, sir" — Wisbeach accentuated the girl's name as if to dissociate himself from what was to come — "Dora says Mr. Hugo carried on proper daft. Kissing his wife on her mouth and then on her hands and stroking her hair — though Dora couldn't see that she was upset at all."

Laker, too, was embarrassed at such unmanly behavior. He said hurriedly, "And then Mr. Hugo took the Major to catch the bus?"

"Yes, sir."

"At ten-ten," said Finch in his soft drawl. "Rather a long hiatus in time between the blow and the Major's departure, wasn't there?"

Wisbeach looked at him. "There was more trouble at dinner, sir. Though none of the girls could find out what it was about. Mary King usually helps Mr. Carter — he's the butler — to wait at table. Last night there was melon from the hothouses to begin with, so Mary wasn't wanted. When she went along the passage for the second course she met Mr. Carter coming to meet her. Awful he looked, she said. His face sort of mottled and his eyes starting out

108

of his head." Wisbeach was warming to his story. "'I shan't want you in the dining room tonight,' he told her, very stiff and discouraging. 'You can put the dishes on the side table outside and I'll take them in.'"

"And did Mary manage to hear anything of what was said in the dining room?" Finch asked.

"No, sir, though I gather it wasn't for want of trying. But the doors at the Hall are thick and the girls a bit frightened of Mr. Carter, so Mary didn't dare go too near in case he came out and caught her."

"And still we haven't come to ten-ten and all that," said Finch murmuring.

"No, sir. But Dora saw what led up to it. It was getting on for ten o'clock and she'd gone up to do the bedrooms. She was crossing the landing at the head of the main staircase when Sir Kenneth came bursting out of the drawing room. 'Either that fellow leaves the house,' he bawls, 'or I do.' And he followed it up with a lot of bad words. And Mr. Hugo following him, says, quite quiet and cool like he always is, 'The Major shall go. I'm getting a bit tired of him myself. I'll take him down and see him off on the last bus,'And then he looks at his watch. 'Eight minutes, Major,' he says in the pleasantest tone in the world. 'When that's up I'll put you out.'"

"Was there any mention of money?" Laker asked.

Wisbeach looked at him quickly, as if wondering what had prompted the question. "Yes, sir. Dora heard the Major say, 'I fear that I shall not get further than the bus stop,' and Mr. Hugo takes up. 'No money, I suppose? That's soon remedied.' And he takes out his wallet and counts out some bills. Ten, Dora thought it was. And then Mr. Hugo looks again at his watch. He rings for Carter and orders the car around. And Dora had to move, and move fast, because the Major was coming up the stairs. So she crossed the landing and slipped into Lady Sybil's bedroom."

Laker, meanwhile, had been counting the notes under the elastic band. 'Ten,' he signalled to Finch, mouthing the word soundlessly.

"How did the Major look?" Finch asked. He nodded an acknowledgment to Laker.

"He was smiling, Dora says, sir, but sort of savage-like."

"Where was she while all this was going on?" Finch asked.

"Crouching down behind the bannisters, sir. They're all carved. And she'd pulled off her white apron so it wouldn't be seen."

"Evidently a young woman of resource."

"It's the films does it, sir." Wisbeach smiled tolerantly. "Dora spends all her spare time in the picture house at Market Stalbridge."

"But what happened after Dora hid in Lady Sybil's room?" Laker asked.

"I couldn't say, sir. Dora saw our clock just then. She gave a scream and said she'd catch it from Mr. Carter if she weren't in by half past ten. And off she rushed on her bicycle."

"The Ommanneys have the reputation of being a devoted couple?" Finch asked.

Wisbeach looked undecided. "Well, sir, he fair worships her."

Finch raised an eyebrow. "The devotion is one-sided, you think?"

"I don't rightly know, sir. But that's what they say in the village. Both Mr. Hugo and Mr. Arthur doted on her but — well, sir, it's difficult to tell how she feels. She's always so sort of — detached. Pleasant-like but — you don't feel she's really interested."

The ambulance and the police surgeon arrived almost together. Laker sent Wisbeach out to tell the ambulance attendants that they would have to wait.

Piper was a brisk little man. He was prematurely bald. His eyes behind large horn-rimmed glasses, were shrewd and humorous. He wore a bowler hat on the back of his head, as if he had forgotten it.

He hurried up the path, raking the windows with curious glances. "Sorry I'm late," he said. And his eyes flickered around the hall, taking it all in.

The mysterious reputation of the house, Finch reflected, seemed well established.

"So the Major's come to grief at last," the police surgeon remarked as he followed the Superintendent down the passage, with Finch bringing up the rear.

He paused in the doorway. "Well, I'll be — " He crossed to the body. He examined the wound. "Messy! Decidedly messy. Still, the murderer was doing all right until the Major woke up to what was happening."

He gave a cackle of amusement at his own wit. He looked at Finch and then sidelong at the Superintendent. "Trouble with you, Laker, is that you've no sense of humor. Not like the gentleman over by the fireplace."

"The gentleman by the fireplace," Laker retorted acidly — for no particular reason he and the doctor were antipathetic — "is used to murder. He happens to be a C.I.D. Inspector from Scotland Yard."

"Is that so?" Dr. Piper favored Finch with a frankly interested stare before returning to his work.

"No need to describe the Major. We all knew him, naughty old man. He's been dead not less than ten hours, not more than thirteen. And if you can let me know when he dined and on what, the stomach content should fix the time a great deal more accurately."

"He may have eaten a fig some time after eleven o'clock," Finch murmured.

Piper nodded. "I'll look for it. The weapon used to kill the Major was a knife. Razor-sharp but not a razor, since it had a cutting edge both sides. The murderer was right-handed — which isn't much help to you. He stood at the head of the bed to do his stuff so as to avoid the blood. For all that he probably got some on his sleeves. The blood must have spouted like water from a fire hose."

"He appeared to have worn the Major's overcoat to do the job." said Laker. "There's a fair amount of blood on it. I'd be obliged if you'd make certain that it's all from the same blood group as the Major's."

The police surgeon nodded. "Can do!" he said. He continued, "It's a severe wound. The carotid artery has been severed. But that doesn't mean that the murderer is necessarily a man. Given a knife as sharp as this one must have been and the victim asleep, a child could have done it."

"Even in these days of juvenile crime, I think we can rule out that supposition," said Laker waspishly.

"It doesn't sound likely," Piper acknowledged. He put his bag on the dead Major's stomach and began to repack it.

Laker looked at it, snorted indignantly. "If you've quite finished I'll tell the ambulance men to come in."

Dr. Piper gave him permission with

an airy wave of his hand. "In the bad old days," he said, "I'd have sewn up the Major's neck, dressed him decently and entered the cause of death as heart failure."

"Was that what happened before?" Finch asked.

The doctor nodded. "The story goes back to the 1840s, when Ralf Ommanney married a woman who was reputed to be the ugliest in the county — if not in England. Married her for her money. The Ommanneys always had an eye for the shekels. Having done so, he built this house. Here he entertained a succession of lady friends. The stories that got about would make your hair stand on end. And here on the 12th November, 1852, one of them took a dislike to him and cut his throat while he was sleeping."

"No wonder you were startled when you saw the Major. How did you come to know about it."

"My father told me. He had it from his father, who was the doctor called in by the Ommanneys. I remember the date because the 12th November happens to be my birthday."

"The Ommanneys seem to go in for women in a big way."

"You're thinking of the two brothers? Yes, there's a strong streak of sensuality in the Ommanneys. Ralf with his women, willing and unwilling. Guy, running wild as a young man and, as an older one, turning his knowledge and charm to good account. Philip, sublimating sex to a love of God and wrecking his nervous system in the process. And Arthur and Hugo, obsessed by their little cousin Camilla."

"What made you say that about the Major?"

"Oh, he had his admirers, even in Market Stalbridge. One or two of my patients, for instance; the wealthy female ones. They doted on him. Sent him expensive presents at Christmas and on his birthday." Dr. Piper added in mocking falsetto, " 'The dear Major! So distinguished-looking! Such charming manners!' "

"Was he a patient of yours?"

"No, no! The Ommanneys changed their doctor just after Ralf Ommanney died." The two ambulance men appeared and carried away the corpse. "Ah, there goes the Major! I must be off. Good day to you, Inspector. If I can help you in any way just look me up."

Dr. Piper nodded, clapped his bowler on to the back of his head and followed the stretcher from the room.

7

HAMMERFORD HALL had been built in the thirteenth century as a country house for a rich London merchant. Three centuries later it had passed into the possession of the Ommanney family through the marriage of one John Ommanney with its heiress.

It was he who built the great Elizabethan red brick house with its long mullioned windows, its massive chimney and square towers at each corner. Except for some slight modernization it had remained through the centuries structurally as he had left it.

The grounds surrounding the house, as might have been expected, consisted principally of immense sweeping lawns designed to show off the great trees in which the Ommanneys delighted.

Standing in groups or in splendid isolation were gigantic plane trees, magnificent spreading cedars, ilex, oaks and limes. An artificial lake had been made with the sole purpose of reflecting the dark hanging woods beyond.

Four people were sitting on the lawn in front of the house. The same four who had occupied the front pew of old Mrs. Ommanney's funeral. They sat now in cane chairs with newspapers and drinks and an air of comfort and ease.

It was Sir Kenneth who first saw the police car. He leaned forward and said something to his nephew. Hugo turned his head to look. He put down his glass, and as Finch and Laker stepped from the car, came walking leisurely towards them.

"Good morning, Superintendent," he said in a pleasant, impersonal voice. "I was going to write and thank you for the excellent management of traffic yesterday. Now you're here I can do it in person instead."

Laker said, "Thank you, sir," in a voice so gloomy that no one could have thought him anything but the bearer of bad news.

Hugo looked at him consideringly. "What was it you came to see me about?"

"It's the Major, sir," said Laker stiffly. "He's dead — with his throat cut."

For a moment Hugo Ommanney appeared startled out of his usual calm. "Good God!"

And then, "Where was this? In London?"

"No, sir. Here — in the Italian House."

"Here? But I — " Hugo broke off. "I see. He came back again." He added abruptly, "We must tell this to the others."

Always interview witnesses one at a time. Laker hesitated, and was lost. Hugo Ommanney had turned on his heel and was walking back across the lawn. There was nothing for Laker and Finch to do but follow him.

A young police constable scrambled out of the police car and hurried after them. He carried a large notebook and looked as unhappy as Laker felt. This was in no part due to any feeling for the Ommanneys. The constable, Hunt by name, had the gravest doubts as to his capabilities as a shorthand reporter.

Sir Kenneth, a small, pink, and well-scrubbed gentleman, was smiling as he watched their approach. He was very carefully and correctly dressed in a grey flannel suit faultlessly pressed.

The two women were doing needlework. Lady Sybil wore a thin black woollen frock and a black cardigan. Camilla had on an old navy blue linen blouse and faded navy blue slacks with drainpipe legs. There was a pair of expensive sandals on her tiny feet. Her odd-colored hair was drawn smoothly back and tied with a narrow black ribbon bow. Finch looked at it with interest. If it were a sign of mourning it was a very small one. And what, he wondered, had happened to the scent and furs and latest fashions, of which the Superintendent had spoken?

"Laker's brought us some bad news," said Hugo. "The Major came back some time last night. And now," he added baldly, as if it would upset the dead man's daughter no more than anyone else, "he's been found with his throat cut."

"Oh!" said Lady Sybil in distress. "Oh!"

Camilla said nothing. She bent her head. A curious stillness came over her, a blankness of face. Finch found himself staring, fascinated by its oddly slanting planes. Speculating on what might be going on behind those brilliant narrow eyes and the smooth ivory brow.

"Damn the fellow!" said Sir Kenneth explosively. "What made him do a thing like that?"

Said Laker, "It wasn't suicide, Sir Kenneth."

The little man stared. Then shook his head impatiently. "No, no! Stupid of me. Guy knew his nuisance value too well to do a thing like that."

"Murder?" said Hugo, lifting his brows. "That seems incredible."

"That's the way it is, Mr. Hugo," said Laker unhappily.

"Where was he found?" asked Sir Kenneth.

Laker made a vaguely propitiatory gesture with his hands. "In the Italian House. He was sleeping there."

Sir Kenneth's gaze became fixed, the fresh color on his cheeks deepened. "That was too bad of him! Too bad altogether."

"It's a bad show whichever way you look at it," said Hugo. And he frowned, jingling some coins in his pocket.

The Superintendent introduced the C.I.D. man. "The Inspector came down on another matter. But as he is likely to take charge of the case I brought him along."

The Ommanneys acknowledged the introduction. They looked at Finch, coolly and pleasantly and, it would appear, not a bit perturbed.

"I think I saw you in church," said

Sir Kenneth. He was smiling again. "Or perhaps it was your hat I saw."

Laker cleared his throat loudly. It had an ominous sound. It was, in fact, merely nervous. He was simply hating this. "The Inspector will want to ask you some questions. Hunt here will take down what you say and later you will be able to read and sign your statements."

"Of course," said Hugo quietly. He looked at the hovering and unhappy Hunt. "Hadn't the constable better have a seat — and a table to write on? Here! He can have this."

Hugo whipped up the table, drinks and all and set it down before the startled policeman. "There! Use that. Pour yourself a drink, too, if you feel like it."

"Hunt will not have a drink," said Laker, scandalized. He went on, "The Inspector understands that there were a succession of disagreements between the Major and different members of the household. For instance" — he looked delicately at his boots as he said it — "down by the lake."

Camilla raised her head. She looked at the Superintendent with an air of great candor. "Oh yes," she said, "that was after tea. I took the Major there. I wanted to talk to him." She had a light, clear voice. "I thought that I'd offer him half my dress allowance to stay away from here."

"My dear Camilla!" Sir Kenneth protested.

"Half your — !" Laker was shocked. "Did Mr. Hugo know?"

"Hadn't a clue." Hugo Ommanney looked faintly amused. "Though I'd had something of the same idea myself."

Finch found this answer illuminating. At any other time Laker's remark, involuntary as it had been, would have been taken as an impertinence by the owner of Hammerford Hall. Now he smiled and passed it over. His annoyance had not been allowed to cloud his brain.

Camilla looked across at her husband. "I wish I'd known," she said brightly. "I would much rather you paid him than I did."

"And now," said Finch, "no one need pay him," and watched that curious blankness spread again over the pale secretive face.

"So it would seem," said Hugo drily.

"How did your talk with Major Ommanney work out?" Finch asked Camilla.

"Not very well. You see, I couldn't

124

think of any way of making sure that he would keep his word and that made us quarrel."

"He'd broken it once already, hadn't he?"

"Oh, did you know that?" Camilla's tone was one of surprised admiration. "Yes, I gave him fourteen pounds on condition that he stayed away until after the funeral."

"Why?"

"I thought that it would be nicer without him."

"But if you gave him fourteen pounds on Wednesday morning, why by the next day, did he appear to have none?"

"He made a point of having none when he came down here. He knew that someone would have to give him money. He was awfully careful like that. He wouldn't even take a return ticket. Hugo, or Aunt May, when she was alive, had to pay his fare back."

"First class, too," said Hugo ruefully.

Superintendent Laker shifted unhappily. How did people of this class usually behave when one of the number had been murdered? He hadn't expected them to cry and moan over the Major — no, not even his daughter. It was well known she had had no cause to like him. But this — this tea-party atmosphere. Mr. Hugo so pleasant and Sir Kenneth smiling away.

"What reason did the Major give for coming down here on Monday?" Finch asked.

"He said that he'd seen the announcement of Aunt May's death in *The Times* and thought that she might have left him something in her will."

"And had she?"

"No. I don't think he really expected it."

"How did he seem on the Monday?"

"Very pleasant and polite. He said how much he'd always admired Aunt May and that he'd like to attend the funeral service."

"And you agreed and then changed your mind?"

"Oh no! It was the Major who changed. He said that, with so many friends and relations coming, he thought that after all he'd rather not be here."

"And when you saw him in church you were angry?"

Camilla opened her greenish eyes. "Wouldn't you have been? He'd taken my money and then broken his word. It was because he couldn't see any way of making himself look trustworthy that he lost his temper." She added with a bright look, "That's when he hit me."

"He shouldn't have done that," said Sir Kenneth, though without any great conviction.

Lady Sybil looked down her long thin nose. Laker was shocked all over again. Hugo said nothing. Just sat there with an air of quiet attention, one leg crossed over the other, clasping an ankle in well-shaped muscular hands.

It was difficult to tell what he was thinking. Difficult to see him as the Superintendent had described him with his brother, 'like two mad dogs at each other's throats.' Or as Dora had seen him, 'carrying on proper daft.' Indeed in the face of his cool composure it was difficult to imagine him as anything that he, Finch, had been told. There was something almost uncanny in the thought of so much self-control.

As for Camilla, Finch fancied that she

had introduced the subject of the blow deliberately so as to distract his mind from some aspect of the affair.

"I saw him from the hall window," said Hugo. "I came out and told him he'd better leave by the first train next morning. I didn't want to make more talk than there had been already but the Major wouldn't have it like that. He spent the rest of the afternoon being as offensive as possible. And, since we all knew each other well, that was very offensive indeed. Finally I rang up Martin Templar, the painter, and asked him to come to dinner, thinking the presence of a stranger might curb the Major. I ought to have known better."

"Jove, yes!" said Sir Kenneth feelingly. "The last straw as far as I was concerned was when Guy began to make up items for the nine o'clock news." He smiled at Finch. His blue eyes sparkled with a sort of icy glitter that had nothing in it of amusement. "And I thought I'd got over all feeling on *that* point long ago."

"What was the point?" Finch asked.

Sir Kenneth looked surprised. "There you are, you see! I take it for granted that everyone knows. Shows really that I'm not injured." He explained, "Some years ago, there was trouble in my territory in South-West Africa. I took what steps I thought fit to put down the troublemakers. Later I was charged with having been unduly harsh. There was an enquiry at which I was exonerated. And recent events, I consider, have more than vindicated my action."

After that first involuntary exclamation of distress Lady Sybil had not spoken. Had just sat there, head a little bent, whipping lace on to a handkerchief in a graceful, unhurried manner as if there were nothing of more importance taking place. Occasionally she had raised her lids a little and looked bleakly at some speaker. These quick chilling glances had been shared out rather impartially, Finch thought. Now she said, raising neither her voice nor her lids, "Kenneth, remember your blood pressure."

"By that time," said Hugo, "I felt that we'd all had enough of the Major. I told him I'd give him eight minutes to pack."

"Where were you all this time?"

"We had been listening to the radio in the drawing room. Sir Kenneth lost his temper and rushed into the hall. Martin Templar and myself followed him, the ladies remained where they were."

"Were you together all the time after dinner? Or had the Major the opportunity to go upstairs?"

It was Sir Kenneth who answered. "We were together. The Major stuck like the proverbial leech — and was just about as unpleasant."

"And while the Major was packing?"

"I stayed in the hall waiting for him," said Hugo. "The other two went into the small library to have a drink."

"And was the Major only eight minutes?"

"Seven and a half to be exact."

"You motored him straight down to the bus and came straight back?"

"Yes."

"And then?"

"We all foregathered in the small library and drank ourselves into a better frame of mind. Lady Sybil and my wife went up to bed early — about half past ten. Templar left soon after. Sir Kenneth kept me company until nearly twelve."

"Did Major Ommanney make any attack on Mr. Templar at the dinner table?"

"Yes — in a mild sort of way. But there was nothing to suggest that they had known each other if that's what you're getting at."

Lionel Glover came racing around the corner of the house. His round face was flushed. His blue eyes were sparkling with excitement. He was very colorfully dressed in an old tweed coat of a rather loud dog's-tooth pattern of red and green, a bright canary yellow pull-over and green corduroy trousers.

"I say!" he called. "It's all over the village that the Major — " He saw Finch and Laker. He broke off, looking embarrassed. "Hello, Superintendent!" he said awkwardly.

"Ah, the juvenile delinquent," said Sir Kenneth, the utmost bon-homie in his voice.

Hugo tipped his head a little. His green eyes looked greener than ever. His small mouth grinned. "They're saying that the Major's been found with his throat cut? It's quite true. No need to be so pleased about it."

Lionel looked abashed. "I wasn't pleased, only excited. It's such an extraordinary thing to have happened. I've read dozens

of detective books but I never expected
to have a murder right on our doorstep.
Actually," he added with dignity, "I've
always felt I'd make a pretty good detective
myself."

8

"**I** UNDERSTAND that Major Omman-ney had been forbidden the Hall some months ago?" Finch was continuing his interrogation.

Hugo nodded. "I found that he was getting money from John Marquis. Mr. Marquis, as you may have heard, has lost his memory. He is also — suggestible. The Major had been calling on him and telling him that he owed him money. Mr. Marquis's bank manager became alarmed at the number of cheques he was cashing and rang me up about it. I happened to have noticed that the Major, for once, seemed to have plenty of money on him and I put two and two together."

"So it was you who forbade him the house?"

"Certainly."

"Yet when he turned up here last Monday you were quite willing for him to stay?"

"Like my wife I realized that I should

have to come to some financial arrangement with him."

"Did you tell him so?"

"No, I wanted to know how I stood financially first."

"You thought that Mrs. Ommanney might have left her money away from you?"

Hugo looked mildly surprised. "No, I knew that she had left it to me."

"An understood thing," murmured Sir Kenneth.

At this point it occurred to Finch that there was very little expression in the retired Colonial Governor's eyes. He, Finch, might as well be looking at two brightly colored beer-bottle caps. Nor, for that matter, was there very much mirth in his perpetual smile.

"I was waiting to talk the matter over with Mr. Drew, the family lawyer," said Hugo. "He would have given me some idea as to what the estate could comfortably afford after the death duties had been paid."

"I see. Thank you." Finch turned to Sir Kenneth. "How many keys are there to the Italian House?"

Sir Kenneth looked startled. "Six. I had a new lock put on the front door and six keys cut. The back door, as you may have noticed, had an old-fashioned lock and is kept bolted."

"Do you keep all the keys in your possession?"

"Certainly. In a drawer in my dressing table upstairs. All but one. That I carry about with me." Sir Kenneth slipped two fingers into a waistpocket and brought out a key.

"When did you see them last?"

"Yesterday evening — just before dinner. I happened to open the drawer while looking for something else."

"When were you last in the Italian House?"

"On the Monday," answered Sir Kenneth, "after my sister-in-law's death. I slipped down to the Italian House and told the men who were laying the carpets that the work would have to stop. I took back the key I had given them and, when they had left, I closed up the house."

"And no one has been there since?"

"No one." It was Sir Kenneth who answered. There was no disagreement.

Said Sir Kenneth, "Am I to understand that my brother Guy had one of the keys?"

"Yes, he had it on his key ring."

"And my money in his wallet," said Hugo in a rueful tone of voice.

"But, my dear boy, it's not the same thing at all," protested Sir Kenneth in an excited tone. His face had grown scarlet again. "You *gave* him the money. He must have slipped into my room and helped himself to the key."

"Had Major Ommanney any keys to the Hall?"

"Quite possibly." It was Hugo who answered. "If you care to show me his key ring I can soon tell you."

Laker fished in his pocket and drew out the keys.

Hugo Ommanney ran them through his fingers. "None of those belongs to the Hall," he said positively.

Finch became aware that Camilla was no longer paying any attention to the conversation. All her interest — and it was wholehearted if surreptitious — was fixed on some point beyond Sir Kenneth's left shoulder. Finch's gaze followed in the same direction.

John Marquis was standing down by the lake. Standing quite still, his tall figure and faultless profile outlined against some dark bushes.

Seeing him, Finch felt again that queer stirring of uneasiness for which he could give no reason.

Everyone was looking now.

"Hello, Johnny!" Hugo called.

"Come and sit down, my boy," said Sir Kenneth.

Lady Sybil moved her workbasket from the chair beside her and Lionel gave it a friendly push in the direction of the newcomer.

Only Camilla said nothing. She had, Finch noted, made several clumsy stitches in the embroidery on which she was working. 'She doesn't like him,' he thought. And then, 'It's more than that. She's afraid of him.' The Rector had been wrong. John Marquis, it seemed, was one subject on which Camilla was not neutral.

Marquis approached in an oddly tentative manner. His eyes, with their curious innocence, passed doubtfully over the smiling, welcoming faces. He was like

137

a child unsure of itself in the company of grownups.

He glanced at Laker without recognition. He looked at Finch and his forehead creased painfully.

"Good morning, Mr. Marquis," said Finch. "We met yesterday in the Ommanney Arms."

John Marquis's face cleared. "Good morning," he said. And he smiled a pleased smile that grew as he met Hugo's glance of friendly recognition.

He sat down in the chair next to Lady Sybil. Became absorbed into the little group. Only, to Finch's mind, there seemed to have come some change. He found himself sharing in Camilla's disquietude. To him — as to her — the day seemed colder and less bright. It was as though the newcomer had spread a peculiar kind of blight, almost of desolation, about him.

"Was the Major known to have had any enemies?" Finch asked. "Or, failing that, did he give the impression of being afraid of anyone?"

"The answer," said Hugo slowly, "is, I think, no — in both cases."

"Though we know nothing of his life in

London," Sir Kenneth pointed out.

"Thank you. You have all been very patient." Finch rose to his feet. "I think that's all the questions that can usefully be asked at this stage?" He glanced interrogatively at the Superintendent.

"Yes, yes," said Laker hurriedly, though he sounded dissatisfied. And Hunt gave up taking notes as if his life depended on it.

"One other point. I'm afraid we must ask you all to have your fingerprints taken. Also to give us the names of any firms who have had men working in the Italian House. There's so many fingerprints there that at present we have no idea which to discount."

"Exactly!" said Laker in a tone of deep relief. He had foreseen the necessity but not the explanation that would make it acceptable, if not palatable.

The Ommanneys made no objection. Lionel, indeed, seemed delighted at the prospect. He held up his hands and studied his finger tips as if seeing them for the first time as a matter of whorls and ridges.

The Superintendent turned to Sir Kenneth. "I should be glad if you would come down to the Italian House at your earliest convenience," he said. "It is important for us to know whether anything has been added or taken away from the room in which the Major was found."

The two police officers had agreed to divide forces on leaving the Hall. Finch was anxious to see Martin Templar. Laker wanted to get back to his men still working at the scene of the murder.

Sir Kenneth glanced at his watch. "Ten minutes to one. And lunch is at half past. Be all right if I come down after? Say two-fifteen?"

"That will do nicely, Sir Kenneth," Laker answered.

"If we could have a look at the Major's bedroom," said Finch smoothly. "And then speak to the staff."

"Of course!" Hugo answered. "Lionel, show the Inspector upstairs. And then tell Carter to collect the servants."

"Oh, whizzo!" said the young man, springing to his feet. He led the way across the grass.

"It's a wonderful place," Finch remarked, running his eyes along its vast facade. "Is it ever open to the public?"

"Never. Sometimes, though, antiquarians

or learned bodies of some sort or another write to know if they can look it over." Lionel added with a nonchalant air that deceived neither of his hearers, "If I'm not too busy I usually show 'em around myself."

"Must be quite a job," murmured Finch.

"They do tend to ask a hell of a lot," said Lionel grandly.

The hall was huge, dim and silent. It had a magnificent hammer-beam roof, high and remote. An elaborately carved staircase wound its way upwards. Dark tapestries depicting the heroes of Greek mythology hung on the walls.

It had been warm enough outside. Here, though, the temperature varied little. A great fire burned on the hearth to combat the uniform chilliness. In front of it were deep armchairs and a couple of settees. Leather screens kept off the drafts.

Lionel led the way upstairs, bounding ahead. Occasionally he paused and threw some statement back over his shoulder. "Of course the Major was a pain in the neck to the rest of the family, but I liked him . . . If you want to know anything about the village you ask me." And then, with an affronted air, "I don't know why I wasn't asked up to dinner last night. I'd have done better than that chap Templar." He added darkly, "I bet he just egged the Major on. He's a chap with a most peculiar sense of humor."

On the first floor the architect had contrived an amazing number of staircases, little landings and oddly angled corridors. The dark furniture merged into the darker paneling and the tree outside threw a deceptive pattern of leaves across the floor.

Lionel pointed across the landing. "That's Lady Sybil's room. The others all chose rooms on the south side, except the Major. He liked to have the room he had when he lived here as a boy."

He led the way down a wide dim corridor. He threw open a door; stood flattening himself against it for Finch and Laker to pass. "I'll just nip down and tell Carter you want to speak to the servants. Then I'll wait for you in the hall. That all right?" He divided a warm and brilliant smile between the two men before he vanished.

Finch stood at the doorway listening

to his soft quick footsteps fading in the distance. When they had quite gone he went into the room and closed the door.

"Thought we were going to have trouble getting rid of that young man," Laker growled.

Finch shook his head. "Not this time," he murmured. "He had something else he wanted to do."

Laker stared. "What was that?"

Finch shrugged. "I don't know — but it will come out in time." He was making a rapid yet efficient search of the room. Lionel Glover had said that the Major had always had this room. He might at one time or another have contrived some hiding place in it. It was a big room with paneled walls and an elaborate plaster ceiling. The furniture, though, was of a later date. It was mostly walnut of the early eighteenth century and the bed was a half tester with green hanging. The windows looked north, across more timbered lawn and into a continuation of the same dark woods.

Laker watched Finch sourly. "I don't understand any of it," he burst out. "All that double talk. The family so open and

143

above board. And young Mrs. Ommanney. So bright and cheerful. Hasn't she any decent feelings?"

Finch paused in his search. "Don't make any mistake," he said. "Their conversation was by understatement out of fear."

"Well I didn't like it."

"I liked Sir Kenneth's constant grin much less. It was like the Cheshire cat's. I shouldn't be at all surprised to meet the grin at any time without its owner."

Laker ignored this. "You didn't ask about the roll of bills," he complained.

"What was the use? It could only have been Lady Sybil or Camilla Ommanney who gave them to the Major. And they'd both have had to deny it in front of their husbands."

"Not likely to have been Lady Sybil. It might have been one of the maids though. The Major had a way with women."

"In that case the money would have been given willingly. Not rolled and crumpled." Finch gave a last glance around the room. He had satisfied himself that there was no hiding place there. Or, at least, none susceptible to this type of search. "Let's have a look at Lady Sybil's room. I have an idea that Dora could have seen this doorway from there."

He led the way down the quiet passage, so quiet that the house might have been empty. He knocked, then opened the door into Lady Sybil's room.

It was a large paneled room which at one time had been painted white. The hangings were of pale blue silk. The carpet had a snuff-colored background and a pattern of formal flower sprays in pink and blue.

Lady Sybil's own possessions were plain, expensive and in excellent, if uninspired, taste.

Finch walked quickly across to a shoe cupboard and opened the door. "No good. They're too narrow," he said.

He joined Laker by the door, nearly closed it and looked through the crack. "I can see the door of the Major's room," he murmured. "That's a bit of luck. Dora's not the sort of girl to let anything get past her."

He crossed the landing searching for Sir Kenneth's bedroom. After several false moves he came on a room that was obviously in use by the retired Colonial Governor. It held a panama hat of such sedate lines that it could have belonged to no one else.

It was a big room and full of stately pieces of English lacquer. Half a dozen people might have slept in the bed without overcrowding. The dressing table was six feet long. The immense mirror was of red lacquer surmounted by a magnificent gold clock. It rested on a stand that had six shallow-fronted drawers.

For the first time Laker smiled. "Sir Kenneth must look a queer little fellow among all this," he said, with the tolerant condescension of the big man for a small one.

Finch said nothing. If this room were Sir Kenneth's choice, it threw an odd, rather disquieting light on his character. It suggested that his lack of inches was the dominant factor in his life. Against it his pride forced him to retaliate. He must be able to see himself as dominating his surroundings at whatever cost to them or to himself. Of such are the tyrants and dictators of life.

Finch pulled open the dressing-table drawers one after the other until he came to one that had the latch keys in it. There were four. "With the key Sir Kenneth has in his pocket and the one on the key ring that makes the six," Finch murmured. "All present and correct."

They found Hugo's room. A large, rather bare room, furnished with heavy oak pieces. What aids to comfort there were were strictly for use. Heavy ash trays which could not be tipped over. Goose-neck reading lamps. A telephone near the bed and some books on estate management and scientific farming bore out the impression given by the rest of the room.

Finch opened the next door along the passage. He stared in some surprise. It was a charming room of rosy chintz, pale water color on the white paneled walls and old-fashioned silver on the dressing table.

Of the two doors opening on the far side one led into a luxurious bathroom and the other into a dressing room where the wall space was taken up on three sides by built-in cupboards. Opening them, Finch saw rows and rows of frocks and suits, furs, hats and gloves. Camilla, it seemed, had plenty of fine clothes even if she did not wear them.

He picked the shoes up one after the

other looking at the soles. One belonging to a pair of black patent shoes he put in his pocket to give to Laker. The sole was damp and it might well fit the print in the soft earth under the fig tree.

"That's the lot," he said, rejoining Laker. The Superintendent had stayed at the head of the passage with some idea of raising the alarm if he saw anyone coming.

There was no sign of Lionel Glover in the great hall.

Said Finch, "D'you know the plan of this floor?" He rang the bell.

Laker shook his head. "The small library is somewhere on the south side," he said. "I remember seeing Mr. Andrew several times in there. The drawing room, I believe, looks over the front. And they've a whole lot of other reception rooms, including a long gallery on the first floor."

Carter entered the room. He was a tall thin man with a long sallow face and rather cold eyes. Finch could well imagine that the younger maidservants were afraid of him.

"I understand that you wish to speak to the staff," he said. "I have assembled them in the housekeeper's room."

And so he had. They stood drawn up like soldiers in a row. Finch ran his eye along the line. Faces blank or curious. Eyes avid or frightened. Thin housekeeper, fat cook. A smart-looking chauffeur in uniform. Carter appeared to be the only male indoor servant.

After a few minutes the cook excused herself, taking her two satellites with her. Then the housekeeper and the chauffeur left. But there was no dislodging Carter.

"I'm sorry we've come at such an awkward time," said Finch. "Perhaps we could have a chat with you later."

Carter waved a thin angular hand. "No, no. The luncheon table is laid."

"And the girl, Mary King, isn't here anyway," Laker growled.

"I thought she could be better spared than myself," said Carter implacably.

"I see that Major Ommaney's bedroom has been cleaned since he left," said Finch.

"That was Dora," Carter answered before anyone else could speak.

"And perhaps it was Dora who did the bedrooms last night?"

"Dora," said Carter repressively, "always

does the bedrooms at night."

"Which is Dora?" For that at least, Finch thought, would be a step forward.

A small brunette with a tip-tilted nose and very round eyes made an instinctive movement, then seemed to be trying to shrink to a point of invisibility.

"Dora," said Carter, "is the third from where I am standing." From the tone of voice he might just as well have added, "And where I can very well see her."

Finch turned to her. Neither his voice nor his expression at the moment could have startled anyone. "So you are Dora?"

"Yes, sir," the girl whispered. Then glanced at the butler as if even this admission might get her into trouble.

"I understand that you saw the Major come upstairs last night."

"Yes, sir."

"What did he do?"

"Went into his room."

"Did you see him come out again?"

"Yes, sir." Dora gave him a guarded look. Her eyes filled with tears.

It seemed hopeless. And to have interviewed her alone would only have precipitated an attack of hysterics. The mistake, Finch saw, had been in not interviewing the servants before going upstairs. He remembered, though, something that Wisbeach had said about the girl.

Had he been in court he would have been challenged for leading his witness. But here there was no opposing counsel and no judge. Only the butler, whose wits did not match his anxiety, and a rather empty-headed girl reared on the tradition of the cinema.

In a couple of minutes Dora had forgotten the butler. Was seeing herself as the heroine of a true-life drama. As a fragile, driven creature, caught up in the crude story of more earthy mortals. From all of which there emerged certain facts.

Shorn of their trimmings, they were these:

The Major had not come from his bedroom until he had appeared with his suitcase. Carrying this, he had walked down the stairs. Hugo Ommanney, in the hall, had made some conventional remark to which the Major had not replied. The pair of them had left the house, stepped into the car and driven away.

Dora's own behavior, shorn of the

flattering veil illusion lent it by Finch, was as follows:

As soon as she had seen that Major Ommanney was coming upstairs she had fled across the landing into Lady Sybil's darkened room. From there she had kept watch on the Major's door. There had been no one else on that floor at the time. Nor had anyone come up. And except for Hugo ordering the car around, no words had been spoken in her hearing.

As soon as the car had left the house she had gone along to the Major's room. There had been nothing there. Nothing forgotten. No farewell message. And — here a prosaic note was introduced — no money. But then, said Dora with a toss of her head and a return to reality, it was well known that the Major never tipped — no matter how long he stayed.

The staff dismissed, the two police officers had a talk with the butler. He declared that all the staff had been in bed by half past ten. At which time he himself had made the rounds, assuring himself that the doors and windows were securely fastened. Then he too had gone to bed.

Carter gave an account of what had been said at the dinner table. "I've seen the Major like that before," he told them. "Very aggravating and — well, petulant, you might say. He was a very trying gentleman in some of his moods — "

"A nice manly speech," Finch murmured pensively, as he walked down the long stone-flagged passage towards the hall.

"Carter's a good type." Laker agreed appreciatively.

"Only," Finch pointed out, "you'll notice there was nothing there to mottle the most modest of cheeks."

"Damn it," said Laker incensed, "no more there was!"

In the hall Lionel was waiting for them. He was sitting in a great oak armchair. He bounded blithely to his feet. "There you are!" he cried, as if he had been waiting for them all the time.

"As you say," Finch murmured agreeably. But Laker's glance was dark and suspicious.

9

THE weatherboard cottage, rented from Major Cockerell, was long and low. Its lines uncluttered by shrub or climbing plant. The paved path ran with military precision to the front door. The neat garden was mostly lawn and enclosed by a high hedge.

In a hammock, slung between two apple trees, lay Martin Templar. He lay on his back, his head cradled in the crook of his arm. His eyes closed. Thin sunlight dappled his face and picked out in bright color the heavy crop of fruit above him.

He opened one eye and looked at Finch. "Hello! You see in me one of the few rebels against the monstrous assumption that there is something intrinsically noble in work."

"Is that why the village calls you a painter of sorts?" Finch unlatched the gate and strolled across the grass.

"Very likely, though I'm no abstractionist," said Templar equably. "Have a drink?

154

Non-alcoholic if you like." He reared up suddenly. "Tell you what! I'll get some beer." He padded away.

It was very peaceful in the garden. The sunlight was pleasantly warm. There was the mingled scent of stocks and wallflowers and cut grass. The droning of bees in the Michaelmas daisies filled the air.

Martin Templar came back. He carried several pint bottles and a deck chair. His pockets bulged with a glass in each.

He nipped the cap off two bottles with practiced dexterity. "Don't know what you think," he remarked, pouring out two glasses, "but I like a head on it." He passed a glass and the half-full bottle to Finch. Sank into the hammock with his own drink. "Cheers!" he murmured. He emptied his glass, put it down on the grass and settled in his previous position, staring up into the trees.

"So Hugo Ommanney rang up," Finch remarked pleasantly.

The head turned. "What makes you think that?"

"Your offer of a non-alcoholic drink."

"Of course. Silly of me." Templar laughed

but his vanity had been hurt. "Not that it matters."

"No, but it's interesting. What did he tell you?"

"That the Major had sneaked back last night and that someone had cut his throat. Said that the police were sure to be around and apologized for any inconvenience caused by same."

"And very civil spoken of him, too," Finch murmured. "Had you met the Major before last night?"

"Saw him twice. Once in the pub, where he was making himself very agreeable to everyone. Once on Tuesday morning when he called in to pass the time of day."

"Did he mention the Joker?"

"Yes. Wanted to know if he'd visited me. I said no and pointed out that the terrain was hardly suitable for a quiet getaway."

"Did he give the impression that he had discovered the Joker's identity?"

Templar shook his head. "No — and if the Joker and the murderer are one and the same, I don't know it either."

"You don't think that the Rector might have decided that it was his duty to rid the world of the Major?"

"He might — but he wouldn't kill him without giving him a chance to repent. The Reverend is very hot on repentance, expiation and atonement."

"He doesn't believe 'Between the stirrup and the ground I mercy ask'd, I mercy found'?"

"No, poor devil! There's no easy way for anything the Reverend undertakes." Templar laughed suddenly, opening one eye to look at Finch. "Amusing to know that in dozens of homes tomorrow people will be saying, 'Just think, that nice Major Ommanney has been found with his throat cut.'"

"What happened at dinner last night?" Finch asked. He drained his glass and put it down between his feet.

"Dinner?" Templar opened both eyes. His thin cat's mouth stretched in a grin of pure malice. "Never heard anything like it. Hugo Ommanney was white with passion. The others were comparatively easy meat, but in my opinion, it takes something to rouse Hugo."

"What did the Major say?"

"He recalled the days when, it seems, Hugo was madly jealous of his brother

Arthur. He insinuated that Arthur had set out with the deliberate intention of killing himself in his car. Then he call Sir Kenneth Simon Legree and that started a slanging match across the table." Templar chuckled in retrospective amusement. "After the ladies had left the table, the Major speculated with a singular lack of delicacy on the possible causes of the lack of virility in the younger generation."

"And Mrs. Ommanney?"

Martin Templar's face changed in some subtle way. "She never has much to say." He added irrelevantly, "She was wearing a yellow chiffon frock, all pleats . . . " His voice trailed away as if he were seeing the scene over again. As if he were held fascinated by what he saw. Or was it, Finch wondered, the thought of Camilla that held him?

Templar laughed harshly, as though dispelling a dream. "That dinner was amusing!" he cried, as if forcing himself to see it so. "Hugo as white as Sir Kenneth was red and the Major smirking and showing a great mouth full of teeth like a horse."

"And Lady Sybil?"

"She epitomized the triumph of good breeding over embarrassment. Her conduct was impeccable. Obviously in the past Sir Kenneth could have shot a hundred natives dead at her feet and she wouldn't have turned a hair."

"Is that what he did? Shoot some natives?"

"Yes — so I've heard. Did it all himself — like shooting clay pigeons." Templar paused. Then added, "And smiling, I suppose. You noticed that smile?"

"I have. What's the matter with him?"

"Undoubtedly he's gone mad. Like a rogue elephant. A pigmy rogue elephant."

"An interesting analogy." said Finch drily.

There was a pause, infinitesimal but definite, before Templar spoke. "I imagine that a thing like that must tend to cut you off from your fellows," he said, in what was for him a rather stiff tone of voice.

Finch changed the subject. "What did you do after you left the Hall last night?"

"I cut across the park and home. Saw no one on the way. Had a last drink and went to bed."

"You have no servants sleeping in?"

"No. And, as you no doubt have noticed, no neighbours."

"And perhaps no reason for wanting to murder the Major?"

"I wasn't spared, if that's what you wanted to know. The Major seemed to get quite a lot of fun out of the fact that I had painted a portrait of Camilla which neither she nor her husband liked."

"A failure, was it?" Finch asked, deliberately boorish.

"As a matter of fact it was a damned fine piece of work." Templar lay still, staring up into the leaves above him. "Why don't you leave the subject alone?" he shouted in a sudden fury, as if Finch and he had been conducting a long argument on the subject.

"Certainly," said Finch mildly. "What made you come to Hammerford?"

Templar smiled wryly. "That isn't leaving the subject alone. It's just another aspect of it. I saw a photograph of Camilla Ommanney in some magazine or other. I was mad to paint a portrait of her. I happened to see this house advertised to let furnished for the summer. So I took it — on the chance."

Finch nodded. "I can see that wasn't a good choice of mine. This time though I really will change the subject. Tell me, what made Sir Kenneth so angry that he said that either the Major or he must leave the house?"

Templar shook his head. "I've been trying to remember that myself," he murmured into the leaves above him. And he groped for a second bottle of beer.

Finch left him to his beer and his faulty memory. He walked back towards the village. He looked at his watch. It was ten minutes to three. He had learned from Wisbeach that the girl, Mary King, whom he had missed seeing at the Hall, usually came by way of the fields to the village at about that time. He lengthened his stride. He did not want to miss her.

A few people were about now. The grocer had come from his shop and, with a customer, was considering the piles of fruit and vegetables outside the door. A fat woman was crossing the Green towards him carrying a white china jug in her hand. Two small girls were chasing a pale mauve butterfly.

When Finch appeared silence fell like

a blow. Faces were averted. The grocer and his customer went hurriedly inside. The fat woman turned away, waddling grotesquely, sawing the air with her jug. A young woman ran out from one of the cottages and called the children in.

Finch walked on. He turned down a lane that ran beside the Georgian house. A little way along it there was a stile and a path running across a field.

He strolled across the field. Paused to light a cigarette. Beyond, another field unfurled itself, softly green and edged with vivid color where the woods began again. Behind him he fancied that the village would be returning to life again. The grocer and his customer coming out to consider the fruit and vegetables. The fat woman waddling, with her white china jug, across the Green. The two children taking up their pursuit of the mauve butterfly.

It was very peaceful and quiet. The silence was broken by the small sounds of the countryside. The rustle of leaves. Sheep eating the grass. The faraway sound of a farm dog barking.

A tall girl was crossing the further field. She was a blonde and carried herself well, as befitted Carter's aide. She looked alarmed when she saw Finch, obviously guessing his identity.

He raised his great black hat with an air. "Will this path bring me out at the Hall?"

The girl smiled, relieved perhaps at the harmless nature of the question. "Oh, yes. It's not more than a few minutes' walk."

"I don't think I saw you this morning."

"No, sir. I had the table to lay." She smiled at him, flattered but uneasy.

"A pity. I'd been hearing some nice things about you."

"About me? Go on!"

"It's a fact. From Police Constable Wisbeach."

"What did he say?"

"He was comparing you to someone else we both know."

Mary looked lost. Then her smile broadened. "That Dora's a talker," she said. "It always did annoy Mr. Wisbeach."

"We were fortunate enough to get a good account of the quarrel between the Major and his relations from her," said Finch.

Mary King sniffed in a ladylike way. "Dora doesn't know everything," she said, unable to resist the chance to score off her friend.

"She's a sharp little thing." Finch laughed in a knowing way. He snapped open his cigarette case. Offered her one. "Stay and have a smoke with me. I'll take time off my job if you will. It's not often I get the country and a pretty girl thrown in."

Mary laughed coquettishly. "I don't like the country. When I'm married I'm going to live in Market Stalbridge."

Finch turned to look at her, leaning his broad back against the stile. "So you're getting married? He's a lucky fellow. Does he live in the village?"

"Oh no. He lives in Market Stalbridge." Mary spoke as if this alone gave him an exalted position. "His father keeps the bicycle shop in the High Street. Fred — that's my boy's name — has a motor bike." She added with a quick sly glance that Finch affected not to notice, "He came out last night and took me to a dance."

"Why not? It's only grannies that are interested in funerals."

"That's what my boy says." Mary tipped the ash from her cigarette with an elegantly extended little finger. She was being seduced from caution by what one thought of as the sophistication of her position. Lulled into a feeling of security by Finch's softly drawling voice. His air of lazy good nature.

"No one but Dora knew that I was going — not even Mum or Dad. I went up early to my room and then slipped out without anyone seeing me. After Mr. Carter had gone to bed Dora came down and unlocked one of the side doors for me." Mary giggled youthfully. "Mr. Carter wouldn't half be wild if he knew."

"But I expect you girls are careful to choose a door that isn't overlooked."

"That's right. It's on the north side. There's bushes growing right up to the door and no one sleeps on that side. (Except the Major, Finch thought.) Besides from there you can get all the way to the drive gates without being seen from the house."

"That," said Finch, "must be a great help."

"Oh, it is. Me and Dora always go that way if we didn't ought to be out."

"And last night you saw someone else out. Was that what you were going to tell me?"

Mary King's answer took him completely by surprise.

"It wasn't last night, sir. And it wasn't anyone out. It was the morning when old Mrs. Ommanney died that I was going to tell you about. It was then that I saw Mrs. Hugo slip into the old lady's bedroom."

Finch was startled. He felt a surge of excitement. Was this to be the confirmation of the Chief Constable's hidden fears? Of the thought that had lain subconsciously in his mind when he had written, 'Old Mrs. Ommanney is dead?'

He said quietly enough, "I didn't know that her daughter-in-law had been with her that morning. And yet I suppose it was natural enough." His careless way of seeming not to be very interested was a trap into which Mary fell.

She shook her head. "No this wasn't. I'd been up sweeping the passage. We had to get it done by a quarter to eight. I was along in the housemaid's cupboard putting away the mop and carpet sweeper when I found that I'd left a duster behind me. I went back for it, thinking I'd time it just so that Nurse MacDonald, the night nurse, would've gone downstairs. Ever so

166

sarcastic she is, 'Well, Mary, and what have you left behind this time?' she'd say. 'One of these days it'll be your head if you don't take care.'

"I waited until I heard her cross the hall on her way to her breakfast. Then I nipped back and along the passage. I'd just reached the corner when I saw her — Mrs. Hugo — disappearing into the old lady's bedroom.'Course I didn't want her to see me. She might have complained to Mr. Carter. So I popped into a little sort of room they call a powder room. After a minute or so the mistress came out again. Slipped out, if you take my meaning, and stood leaning against the door with ever such a queer expression on her face. Then she looked all around her and nipped off down the stairs. And," Mary added triumphantly, "it was just like everyone says. Two hours later old Mrs. Ommanney was dead."

Finch looked surprised. "What does everyone say?"

"That Mrs. Hugo brings bad luck. People she doesn't like die off sudden-like!"

"But old Mrs. Ommanney had been dying for months."

"Yes — and she wasn't any worse before

Mrs. Hugo visited her than at any other time," Mary retorted with a toss of her head. "I know because I heard the night nurse say so."

Left alone, Finch remained where he was, smoking and thinking. He was disturbed. He wondered how much of Mary King's story was true and how much could be attributed to the girl's obvious dislike of her young mistress.

He became aware that Lionel Glover was hovering among the larch trees that fringed the field. He was watching Finch and his face was angry.

He advanced suddenly. "What has that girl been telling you?" And then, as though despairing of an answer, "It's no good listening to what other women say of Camilla — Mrs. Ommanney. They all hate her."

"Why should they do that?"

"Because they're jealous of her. Even women like my aunt who don't want to attract men. Not," he added with an air of meticulous attention to detail, "that she is my aunt. I just call her that because I was so small when my parents died."

"And you understand Mrs. Ommanney?"

"Of course I do. You see, she doesn't have to pretend with me. She can be herself instead of sort of on the defensive all the time. She really likes simple things. People like Aunt Hilda talk an awful lot of rot about Hugo being her master and keeping her down here. Actually it isn't like that at all. She likes being here. And she'd like to have children, too." He added hurriedly, "I'm sure it isn't her fault that there aren't any."

He blushed with a vividness that startled and impressed the detective.

"I haven't yet had the pleasure of talking to your aunt," Finch murmured.

Lionel looked at him darkly. "You will," he declared gloomily. "She likes speaking her mind."

"Then at least, you know where you are," Finch suggested.

"But it's never where you want to be," cried Lionel in an exasperated voice. "She — she takes all the enjoyment out of things. I don't mind being a solicitor. In fact I think I'm frightfully lucky to have Hugo to buy me a partnership but Aunt Hilda goes on about being properly grateful until in the end one just isn't."

"I can imagine that," Finch murmured.

"Yes — well, that's how I came to fail my Intermediate. Though I didn't know I was going to fail. In fact I thought I'd passed." Lionel's expression was at once haughty and despairing. "And everyone made such a fuss." He looked in a goaded way at Finch. "That's why Sir Kenneth calls me the juvenile delinquent. He thinks it's funny."

Finch would have spoken. He saw, though, that the young man had not finished.

"They all say I spend too much time with Camilla," Lionel muttered, scowling horribly. He went on, speaking hurriedly, "That's why she didn't tell you that we'd been in the Italian House yesterday afternoon. In case Hugo was angry with me, I mean. We went all over it and furnished it in imagination as we thought Sir Kenneth ought to have it done. You know — with elephants' feet made into ash trays and stuffed heads of animals sneering from the walls, and a teak-wood throne on a dais."

"There was a footprint under the fig tree."

Lionel grinned engagingly. "We thought

170

there might be. That's why I told you we'd been there." His sudden laugh startled the sheep. He seemed quite happy now and carefree. "Camilla's awfully sporting," he told Finch.

"Did you turn on the fountain?"

"Yes. We ate some the figs. They were sort of woody so I thought I'd give the tree a watering to help things along. It was jolly difficult I can tell you, getting the thing to squirt the right way."

Finch thought of the shoes he had found in Camilla's bedroom. "It must have been," he said. "Did you leave the fountain on when you left?"

"Not likely. Sir Kenneth would have been furious if he'd known we'd been in his house."

"When were you there?"

"After tea. Camilla wanted to get away from the Hall."

"And how did you get in?"

"I borrowed one of the keys." Lionel grinned widely. "It was jolly lucky I nipped up and put it back before dinner, wasn't it?"

10

MRS. MARKHAM was trimming her hedge when Finch passed. "So you're a detective," she commented. "I never should have guessed it. You don't look like it."

"I don't feel like it," Finch answered sadly. "The locals won't tell me anything."

Mrs. Markham looked at him kindly. She radiated an air of common sense, reasonableness and strength of purpose. She liked people whom she could help. "You find that in small isolated communities," she explained. "They do, on occasions, tend to think as one corporate mind. It can be very exasperating." She added, in what was obviously an extension of the same line of thought, "Shocking thing about the Major."

"Yes — though no one seems very upset. Not even his daughter."

"That's because she scarcely knew him. Camilla Ommanney was put into a convent school in Switzerland and left there, year in and year out. She'd probably be there now if May Ommanney hadn't had such a feeling for family. Not that she'd ever envisaged the girl marrying her own son."

"But surely that possibility must have been taken into account?"

Mrs. Markham smiled. "My dear man, you surely don't suppose that either of the boys were at home at the time?" The clippers were snipping now so that the conversation was carried on as if through a light artillery barrage. "Hugo was with his regiment in Malaya. Arthur was in Ceylon inspecting his mother's tea plantations. That's where a good deal of her money comes from. I can remember to this day May's consternation when Arthur walked in. He'd got tired of Ceylon, so he said, and flown home. But I've often wondered whether the Major didn't write to him and arouse his curiosity. Camilla had half the country at her feet and men can't resist a hint of competition. I must admit, though, they made a handsome couple." She sighed reminiscently.

"Arthur Ommanney was extravagantly endowed with looks and charm."

She pulled off a leather gardening glove

and wiped her face with a red bandana handkerchief. "That's better," she remarked, taking a step back and tilting her head consideringly. "We're great rivals, my next-door neighbour and myself. Miss Buss though has the advantage of keeping her hand in on the topiary gardens at the Hall."

Finch noticed then that the cottage had a monstrous growth of clipped yew trained over it like a pirate's beard. Both gardens were full of topiary trees cut into fantastic shapes.

Mrs. Markham looked sharply and appraisingly at him. "You'd better come in and have a cup of tea. I'm going to."

"Thank you. It's very kind of you to suggest it."

"Nonsense! I want to hear about the murder. Lionel reads so many detective books I feel quite at home with the subject."

The Georgian house had all the charm of its period. A charm that Mrs. Markham's worn, solid and rather tasteless furniture had not been able to destroy.

She settled Finch in one of the comfortably sagging armchairs. She refused his offer of

174

help but left the sitting-room door open behind her so that she could continue the conversation.

She came back carrying a tray. "Can you clear those books off the table?"

"Yes, of course."

The tea cups were large. There was a dough cake. Mrs. Markham poured out two cups of tea and cut several substantial slices of cake. She settled back in her chair with a sigh of satisfaction.

She caught Finch's eye. "The best part of manual labour is when you leave off."

There were three cups on the tray. Mrs. Markham saw Finch looking at them. "In case Lionel comes in," she explained. and then, "Tell me about the Major."

"There isn't much to tell as yet," Finch answered. "The Major, as you probably know, left the village by the last bus." He described the Major's return and his own finding of the body. He padded it out.

In the end he had told her no more than the bare outline.

Mrs. Markham listened intently. "But how very remarkable," she said. "And have you any idea who was responsible?"

"Only in the most general terms. It seems

likely, for instance, that the murderer and the practical joker are one and the same person."

Mrs. Markham stared. "But the practical jokes — as you call them — are so trivial."

"Would you call the destruction of the wreaths in the churchyard trivial — in intent that is?"

"Small-minded." Mrs. Markham was not one to yield a point. "Malicious but small-minded. Murder seems to me to be in quite another category."

"I understood that you reported the practical joke that began the series."

"Not I. It was one of the village women who had come to borrow something. I had left the front door open and she was standing there while I was upstairs. One can hardly," she added drily, "be heard going from room to room calling 'Is anyone there?' without giving some explanation. So I told her about the lights and later on, when other people were doing so, she told Wisbeach."

"Mr. Glover, I believe, was over at the Rectory working for his exam. That seems a little puzzling. I understood that he was training to be a solicitor not a parson."

"It was Hugo Ommanney's idea. He said that if Lionel couldn't be trusted to work alone he'd better take his books to the Rectory, where he could work under supervision. Not that one can depend on the Rector. He's always going into the church to pray and forgetting to come out again."

Finch wondered for a moment whether Lionel could be the Joker. He remembered the mangled wreath frame from which the flowers had been torn and dismissed the idea. The damage inflicted on it had been far beyond the strength of that young man.

Mrs. Markham glanced through the window. "Here comes Miss Buss. Now, don't go. I won't be a minute."

Finch heard the two women greet each other in the hall. "I matched your wool, dear," said Miss Buss. "Fraynes only had two ounces left. I hope it's enough."

"I shall add one ounce to each sleeve," Mrs. Markham answered. "And if it gives out before reaching my wrists I shall have to console myself with the thought that if it's chilly it is, at least, fashionable."

They came into the sitting room together.

Mrs. Markham introduced Finch.

"This is Inspector Finch — Miss Buss. We have been talking about the Major's murder."

Miss Buss gave Finch her hand. "The poor Major! So charming and so distinguished-looking." She spoke with such fervor that Finch seemed to hear Dr. Piper's voice sounding in his ear in satiric echo.

"Stay to tea, Muriel. You're just in time," said Mrs. Markham. "You can have Lionel's cup. He's evidently having his at the Hall — and don't say how nice that is for him."

"If I don't it's only to avoid an argument," said Muriel Buss with spirit. "And you know that Lionel has always been like a younger son at the Hall."

Both women had the light of battle in their eyes.

"We've been arguing this point for over two years," said Mrs. Markham. "I say that those who could not approve of Camilla's second marriage should not have countenanced it by going to the ceremony."

"And I say that there are occasions when a woman has a right to the support of her own sex," declared Miss Buss. She turned to Finch. "It was the saddest sight. The church empty. No one watching for the bridal couple outside. Hugo looking so arrogant that he was positively wooden. And Camilla pale and white like a ghost."

Mrs. Markham made a derisive sound. "Camilla got what she wanted. In fact, I imagine that when she said 'I will' it was the one time we could believe that she was speaking the truth." She broke off, biting her lips. "Forgive me! I shouldn't have said that. It wasn't kind, or even perhaps truthful. The fact is that it gets on my nerves to see Lionel always hanging about in that quarter. Neglecting his work, taking no interest in his old hobbies. And it can only lead to unhappiness."

"But, Hilda, bird-watching is still bird-watching even if Camilla does go with Lionel. And he *was* in his workshop yesterday for I saw him."

"And tidied up after him, I expect."

Miss Buss, who had done just that, maintained a strategic silence.

Finch had an appointment to meet the Chief Constable. Before leaving for Market

Stalbridge he rang up the firm of Skindle and Drew from the call box on the Green. He gave his name and waited.

Presently a voice said, "Good afternoon. Mr. Drew speaking." The voice was high and thin. It might have been coming from very far away.

Finch explained what he wanted.

"The will? I see. Better come to my house. The Mound. Anyone will direct you." The click loud and robust in comparison.

As Finch drove into the police station at Market Stalbridge the Jubilee clock showed the time to be twenty minutes past five.

A police constable came hurrying. "Superintendent Laker is expecting you, sir," he said. He preceded Finch down the dreary, antiseptic-smelling passage.

Laker came to meet him. "How did you get on with Templar?" he asked when they were alone.

Finch told him. He added in conclusion, "I might have done better if Hugo Ommanney hadn't been before me."

"And I might have done better at the Italian House," Laker retorted, "if Sir Kenneth hadn't brought his wife with

180

him. It was no place for a lady. Her being there quite put me off."

"You said they went everywhere together," Finch reminded him.

Laker snorted. "But not there — where a man had been slaughtered with about as much refinement as if he'd been a pig. But there she was, 'in the interests of justice,' walking into the room and looking around as briskly as an auctioneer on sale day. 'The day bed and mirror were here already,' she said, cool as you please. 'The chair must have been brought from the hall.' As for Sir Kenneth, he didn't seem to have any interest to spare from that damned fountain. Seemed to think I'd set it going. 'Are you sure it was on already?' he asked me, smiling up from a place about on a level with my top waistcoat button. And then he rushed off to see if anything else had been tampered with."

"And Lady Sybil?"

"She went with him." Laker's answer was short. He picked up a paper from his desk. "Dr. Piper hurried on with the autopsy. Now he says that the Major was murdered between half past twelve and one o'clock. He asks me to tell you he found the fig."

"Oh, splendid!"

"He says the Major died from the effects of the wound in his throat. He had no other injuries."

"How about fingerprints?"

"We're dealing with those now. The two men I sent up to the Hall had to wait until half past two before the Ommanneys had finished their meal. That's put us back a bit." He banged shut a couple of open drawers in his desk. "Half past five. The Chief Constable will be ready for us."

Colonel Stonor heard their footsteps approaching. Laker and that C.I.D. fellow! He threw a swift glance over his table top. Neat piles of paper covered the worst of the cigarette burns. A London telephone directory stood squarely over the place where he had carved his initials. The desk, he considered, looked neat, businesslike, even impressive.

He raised his voice. "Come in! Come in! Come in!" He rose to his feet. "Mr. Finch? Delighted to see you. And you're willing to take on the case?" A faint note of anxiety came into the Colonel's voice, as if, even at this late hour, the C.I.D. man might wish to withdraw. "You are? Splendid!"

He almost pushed Finch into a chair. He pressed a drink on him and a cigarette. He told Laker to help himself. Then he sat back with a sigh of relief.

"When Laker told me that you'd been at the funeral I thought it must have been you," he continued in an involved sort of way. "Afterwards I wasn't so sure. It was the hat put me off. But I can see now it's a sort of disguise. Makes the village think you're a sort of bullfighter, what?"

Finch had a large collection of hats. Most of them had been, at one time or another, the object of adverse criticism. He was still pained, though, and surprised when it happened. "You don't like it?" he asked now, incredulously.

"My dear fellow, I like it enormously. Puts me in mind of that poster of somebody's port. Spanish chap!" The Colonel had by now almost managed to forget the object of Finch's visit. He caught Laker's eyes and stiffened visibly. "But to work!" He shifted a pile of papers with a businesslike air. This, however, disclosed a long row of cigarette burns and he replaced the

183

pile hurriedly. He glanced slyly at Finch but the C.I.D. man looked bland and withdrawn.

"Better tell you what I've done first," said Colonel Stonor. "To begin with I got the Major's key ring off to London on the 2:15 P.M. train. Then I rang up Sir Eustace and told him you wanted Sergeant Gilroy. One sergeant, for the use of — eh?"

Finch murmured, "Thank you, sir," since it seemed to be called for.

"I asked that this sergeant should be given the keys and sent to search the Major's flat. Then he was to collect all papers and photographs — " Colonel Stonor hesitated, than corrected himself, though without much conviction. "All relevant papers and photographs and bring them down here. He was to make inquiries as to whether anyone had seen the Major this week. He was to visit the Major's bank and see the manager. If there were no bank statements in the flat he was to ask for them for the past twelve months. After that he was to take the next train here."

"Thank you, sir," said Finch again. "Has anything been found out about the Major's journey on Wednesday?"

"Yes, yes. I forgot that. He caught the 10:15 A.M. to Charing Cross. Took a single ticket. A habit of his, I understand, but not much use to us."

Finch gave an account of his activities after parting from the Superintendent. He reported on his interviews with Templar, Mary King, Lionel and Mrs. Markham.

The Chief Constable was upset when he heard that Camilla Ommanney was supposed to have visited her mother-in-law secretly on the morning of her death.

"Nothing in that," he declared firmly. "Old lady had been ill a long time."

"But you did write in your letter to the Yard, 'Old Mrs. Ommanney is dead.'"

"The letter was to my cousin — not to the Yard. A bit of gossip. I'd forgotten that Eustace didn't know Mrs. Ommanney. Come to that" — the Chief Constable brightened — "Eustace may have known her."

"He said not."

"He'd forgotten," said the Chief Constable brazenly. "Anyway," he added hurriedly, "lets get on to the Major. We know *he* was murdered."

"And we know quite a bit about his

movements," said Finch, abandoning but not forgetting the subject of old Mrs. Ommanney and her daughter-in-law. Laker stared at his huge hands with an air both gloomy and disapproving.

"We know that the Major was interested in the Joker," said Finch. "We know that he was making inquiries in the village. Standing drinks in the pub. We know that he went up to London and that, when he came down again, he timed his arrival so that, short of brawling in church, the family had to accept him.

"We know that he and his daughter walked up and down by the lake. And here we have conflicting evidence. Camilla Ommanney says that she and her father were quarrelling. Dora, whose version I prefer since it was uncolored by the knowledge of the Major's murder, says that they walked up and down deep in conversation. So deep that sometimes they forgot to move at all — "

"But that sounds as if they were discussing a subject of equal interest to both of them," Laker interjected.

Finch agreed. "And it is possible," he pointed out, "that Camilla knew the reason for the Major's journey to London. That she was angry, not at his return but because of what that return implied."

"And it was her footprint under the fig tree," said Laker, shaking his head. "Leastways her shoe fitted what there was of it."

Colonel Stonor contented himself with remarking gloomily, and to no one in particular, that he must have been mad to have ever taken on the job of Chief Constable.

"We now get back to something the Major said at the dinner table. We don't know what it was. The butler won't say. Martin Templar won't say. And certainly the family isn't going to. But we do know that Hugo Ommanney finally gave the Major eight minutes to pack and leave the house. He was prepared to throw him out at the end of that time but the Major was ready in seven and a half minutes all told."

"That was queer in itself, wasn't it?" the Colonel said. "I mean it doesn't sound like him."

"The reason, I fancy, was that if he missed the bus Hugo might have run him into Market Stalbridge and put him on the train. And it isn't as easy to get off a train — or to find one's way back eight miles at night. We know from Sir Kenneth that the keys to the Italian House were all together before dinner and that the Major had no chance of going upstairs until he went up to pack. Dora says that he did not come out of his room during the seven and a half minutes it took him to do so. That no one else came up to the first floor and that the Major left neither letter nor message. That being the case we are pretty safe in concluding that when he left the Hall the key of the Italian House was not on him."

The Colonel stared. "Then when did he get it?"

"On his return to the Hall."

"But Carter had locked up the house and the Major hadn't a key."

"A door on the north side was open. One of the maids had gone to a dance and her friend had slipped down and unlocked the door so that she could get in. They made a habit of doing this and since the door was under the Major's window it's more than likely that he knew of it. In which case he would certainly have tried the door that night and found it open."

"But who gave him the key?"

"He might have helped himself but it's more likely that it came from the same person who gave him the roll of bills. And that person might well be the murderer since whoever killed the Major had to know of his intention to sleep in the Italian House. And rather an important point arises here. The Major left Hammerford at 10:10 P.M. He stopped the bus not later than 10:13 P.M. But he did not reach the Hall until just before eleven o'clock."

"You mean he may have called on someone?" Colonel Stonor looked dismayed. "It's a small place. He might have seen almost anyone in the village in forty-five minutes."

"If we knew where he went," said Laker, "we might know the identity of the Joker?"

"Martin Templar suggested that the Rector might be the culprit," said Finch.

Colonel Stonor wagged his head emphatically in agreement. "Something in that. Philip Ommanney's a borderline case in my opinion. You saw him one night, Laker. Walking up and down the churchyard wringing his hands. Remember?"

"Now you mention it, sir, so I did," said Laker. "There're some troops stationed over at Charbury Heath," he told Finch. "One of them had made an attack on an old man who kept a tobacconist's shop and robbed the till. And I'd been over to arrange with their C.O. for an identity parade. It was nearly one o'clock when I came through Hammerford on my way back. And there he was, carrying on for all the world like a character in an old-fashioned ghost story."

"There is one other suggestion as to the Joker's identity. And this comes from the Rector. He suggests that it might be John Marquis."

Colonel Stonor shook his head just as emphatically as he had wagged it before. "Couldn't be Marquis," he said decidedly. "The villagers would never have kept quiet for a comparative stranger."

Finch looked at him quickly. "A stranger? I thought that he had lived there for some time."

"No, no. He was Londoner. Partner with

an uncle in an old established firm of chartered accountants. It was only when it became obvious that he was going to recover his health and not his memory that it was decided that he should come down here to live. Chiefly because of this business of taking to Hugo and not caring a tinker's cuss for his uncle. I remember the whole thing quite well. I was brought into it in my official capacity. Had to be sure they weren't bringing a raving lunatic into the district — and I *was* sure at the time. There was a family council up in the old lady's bedroom. Must have been about nine months ago. (Marquis came out of hospital in February and Swallow Cottage had to be done up for him.) Mrs. Ommanney agreed that he should come to the village to live only on condition that she wasn't expected to meet him."

"Resented that a certain amount of blame for his condition was being laid at her dead son's door, I expect," said Finch. "How did Camilla take the idea?"

"She sided with the old lady and was very much against it. But Hugo overruled her. Said it was their duty to have him. He's always been a man who made his own decisions and expected other people to fall in with them."

"So the family council was really something of a formality," commented Finch. He added, "You know that Camilla is afraid of John Marquis?"

The Colonel looked startled. "I didn't. 'Pon my word I knew no such thing."

A silence fell on the room. An uncomfortable silence, heavy with images half perceived, with ideas as yet too intangible to grasp.

"But I suppose the family did know John Marquis before the accident?" Finch persisted.

"Never met him. Don't think they'd even heard of him. Arthur Ommanney and Camilla lived in London. Had their own set. Smart young people whose one aim in life was to amuse themselves. It was sheer bad luck that Arthur happened to meet Marquis in Bournemouth and take him for a run in the new car." Which was, Finch reflected, rather a different version of the accident than that given to him by the Superintendent.

"What about the woman who looks after him?"

"Mrs. Hookway? She's a very decent, hard-working soul. Looks after him as if he were her own son. Cleans for him, cooks, shops, mends — does everything. Glad of something extra to occupy her time perhaps. She and her husband came from away and that tends to cut them off from the life of the village. He's a shepherd. Their cottage is on the slope above Marquis's cottage and that helps her to keep an eye on his comings and goings."

"And what happened to the male nurse who came down with him originally?"

"Marquis took a dislike to him. The nurse, Cornell his name was, considered it was his duty to follow his patient wherever he went. And, right from the start, Marquis would walk miles. Almost as if he were trying to catch up with himself." Colonel Stonor shifted uneasily. "Dunno though! Probably that's all imagination, and" — he smiled rather bleakly — "imagination's not my strong point, as you'll probably notice. Anyway there they were, Marquis and Cornell, trailing about through rain and sun. Not much fun for Cornell, and when Marquis seized a great chunk of wood and chased him with it he threw in his hand."

Finch stared at the Colonel in some dismay. "So Marquis is capable of violence?"

The Colonel looked uncomfortable. "He only chased the man," he pointed out. "He didn't actually hit him."

There was a knock on the door. A uniformed police sergeant came into the room. "A report on the fingerprints found in the Italian House, sir," he said.

Colonel Stonor took the paper. He read it through. He frowned, cleared his throat uncomfortably. "That roll of bills," he said. "They had Camilla Ommanney's fingerprints on them. She must have given them to the Major."

The Mound was a white Victorian house standing on about half an acre of ground. Here, Mr. Drew, sole surviving member of the firm of Skindle and Drew, had lived alone since the death of his wife many years ago.

He was a tall thin man, so fined down and faded with age that he was like a pencil drawing. His manners were old-fashioned and courtly. He had, Finch noticed, a habit of touching the bowl of roses on his desk as if to affirm his faith that beauty, after all, was the only enduring good.

He made a few conventional remarks about the Major and the manner of his death. His face was in shadow. His voice still sounded as if it came from very far away.

"Major Guy Ommanney told his daughter that he came down expecting that his sister-in-law had remembered him in her will."

Mr. Drew smiled slightly. "I don't think we need take that very seriously. I don't doubt but that the Major saw in Mrs. Ommanney's death a chance to regain his old status at Hammerford Hall and he took it."

"I imagined that it was something like that," said Finch. "And the will itself?"

"It was drawn up about a month ago. The original will, drawn up after Mr. Arthur's tragic demise, left the bulk of her fortune to Mrs. Ommanney's only surviving son, Mr. Hugo, absolutely. This later will leaves it in trust for Mr. Hugo and his heirs. If he has no son the money passes to the next of kin with the estate."

"Why was the change made?"

"Mrs Ommanney believed, rightly or wrongly, that it was her daughter-in-law's fault that there were no children."

"Who knew of the change?"

Mr. Drew said rather stiffly, "Until the will was read after the funeral I was most careful to mention it to no one."

"I see. No children, no money. I take it that Mrs. Ommanney was not actually expecting her son to die?"

"My dear Inspector! You must try and put yourself in Mrs. Ommanney's place — a loving and devoted mother who had had her faith in the stability of the future shattered by the totally unexpected death of one of her sons."

It was an impressive speech. And his voice as he made it sounded like the wind blowing through the halls of time.

"Is Camilla Ommanney entirely dependent on her husband? Were there no marriage settlements?"

"None. The Major was hardly in a position to insist and Mr. Andrew's estate had not then been settled."

"And on her second marriage?"

"Precisely the same state of affairs

prevailed. Though, to be frank, the Ommanneys have always held that the family finances should be left entirely to the husband. The late Mrs. Ommanney was the exception, but then she was a remarkable woman." The voice removed itself by several hundred miles. "A most remarkable woman," it sighed.

"I see. So in the event of Hugo Ommanney's death, the property and the money would pass to the Rector of Hammerford, the Reverend Philip Ommanney."

"That is so."

"But he himself is unmarried. Could Mrs. Hugo inherit through being the Major's daughter?"

"No. The estate is entailed on the male heirs. It could pass through the female line to a male heir but that is all."

"So Mrs. Hugo had no interest in old Mrs. Ommanney's death?"

"None at all." Mr. Drew smiled. "Not even on the grounds that she was an encumbrance. Mrs. Ommanney was a most self-reliant lady. She kept to her room. She had regular visiting hours and saw no one in between."

Finch looked across the roses at him.

"That is interesting — since on the morning of Mrs. Ommanney's death Mrs. Hugo paid a visit to her mother-in-law's bedroom during the absence of her nurses."

Mr. Drew had been smiling and stretching out a skeleton hand to the roses. His smile did not change but for an infinitesimal moment his hand was still, hanging over the flowers. "My dear Inspector, every rule has its exceptions. There was no doubt a perfectly ordinary reason for Mrs. Hugo's visit."

"I have no doubt that Mrs. Hugo could think of a dozen," said Finch drily.

"The utter contempt for truth shown by the ladies," said Dr. Drew, laughing in a ghost-like manner, "has always seemed to me to be one of the strangest of natural phenomena."

At ten minutes to seven a police car from Market Stalbridge put Charles Gilroy down outside the Ommanney Arms. He was a pleasantly ugly young man, tall, lively and talkative. He had with him a small suitcase and a very large bulging one, held together by a strap.

Wyman showed him upstairs. "Second door on the left," he said in a surly voice.

"The Inspector's next door."

"Thanks!" Gilroy put down the suitcases. Before he had time to knock on Finch's door it opened. "Charles! My dear fellow." Finch's eye fell on the bulging suitcase. "What on earth's that? A trousseau?"

Gilroy picked up the large suitcase and dumped it into Finch's room. "That," he said coldly, "contains the papers and photographs from No. 5 Desmond Place."

He bent down and tugged at the straps. The suitcase fell open, disclosing row upon row of smiling and opulent-looking middle-aged women.

"I said all *relevant* papers and photographs."

"I was told *all*."

Finch shook a commiserating head. "Never mind, Charles. We can take them back in the car."

But Gilroy refused to be consoled. "A nice fool I shall look," he grumbled, "if I have to inquire into the love life of that lot."

Supper was served in a small room which, in spite of the fire, still smelt rather damp. The cooking, though, was as good as ever. Gilroy thawed visibly. "I expect you know Desmond Place," he

199

remarked, and was a little dashed to find that his supposition was correct.

Finch nodded. "No. 5 — a greengrocer," he murmured.

"That's right, sir. Major Ommanney had a flat over the shop. Nice-sized rooms. Well furnished, too. A big sitting room, two bedrooms, kitchen and bathroom. And photographs!" Gilroy could laugh about them now. "The Major must have had a sense of humor — or perhaps of gratitude. Because those old trouts had done him proud. He had every imaginable gadget for comfort, from an electric blanket to a fur-lined overcoat. He had dozens of cigarette cases put away, platinum or gold and all expensive."

"The equivalent of diamonds to a woman," Finch murmured.

"There were good modern paintings on the walls. A lovely pair of Purdy's guns. Field glasses and opera glasses. Inspector Drew turned up while I was there. He nearly laughed himself sick when he saw it all."

"Yes, he's always been interested in the Major," Finch answered. He added, "Were you able to trace his movements in London on the Wednesday or Thursday?"

"Only while coming and going from his flat, sir. The greengrocer, a chap called Percy Smith, saw him arrive at about a quarter to twelve on the Wednesday morning. He said that he was in very good spirits but that was nothing new, the Major being a cheerful and affable gent. He arrived in a taxi with his suitcase. After half an hour or so in the flat he left again on foot, and without the suitcase. The greengrocer didn't see him again until the next morning, although he and his assistant were around and about until six o'clock, when they shut the shop and went home.

"I couldn't find anyone who did see him come back but, of course, I hadn't much time. Simpson was with me and I left him to carry on with the inquiries. The greengrocer saw the Major leave his flat early next morning. Early for him, that is. Said he couldn't be sure of the time but thought it was about a quarter past nine. The Major was carrying his suitcase when he left."

"What did this chap think of him?"

"He was frightfully cut up to hear that he had been murdered. Kept saying 'the poor old basket.' And that it was a shame. He seemed to think that the Major's presence lent tone to Desmond Place."

Finch gave a solitary chuckle. "The Major spent his whole life doing just that." He added, "He was a distinguished-looking old boy. We ought to be able to trace his movements even if we have nothing but his looks to go on."

Gilroy put his spoon and fork down on his empty plate. It had been worth coming into the country, he decided if only to taste Mrs. Wyman's pastry. "We have something more than that, sir," he said. "There were two entries for Wednesday, September 16. The first was 'Single fare $1.65 — which must have been the fare from Market Stalbridge to London."

"And the second entry?"

"It said 'Return fare 30c.'"

Finch nodded. "So the Major took another journey by rail or bus. Out of London, but not far out."

He suggested a couple of places that could be visited for that sum. Gilroy, who had looked them up, gave half a dozen more.

Mrs. Wyman came in and cleared the

cloth. "If you want anything more," she told them, "coffee or sandwiches, just come along to our room. Any time before half past ten."

When she had left the room Finch sent Gilroy to fetch the suitcase. "We have to go through it some time," he said. "We may as well get it over."

Gilroy was soon back. He put the suitcase on the table. He took the photographs out one at a time and laid them out like Patience cards. Finch looked at them in fascinated astonishment. At the end he was left with a feeling of respect for the Major's prowess; for if many of the faces were amiable and foolish, others were shrewd. Shrewd enough to be wary of handsome elderly strangers, yet the Major had been as successful with these as with the more gullible.

He spent some time on the diaries and bank statements. From them he received the surprising impression that the Major had led a life as ordered as that of a bank clerk.

He had paid as many visits as the Victorian bachelor of good family. Taken as many motor tours as a courier. He had played cards with a nice sense of the laws of probability. His winnings of dollars on one visit would be balanced by the loss of cents the next. Occasionally, where presumably play was high, he had made a killing. After which his host's name had been struck off his visiting list, though at whose instigation there was no way of telling.

The Major's bank balance had been comfortable. His investments shrewd and profitable, as was not really surprising since most of his hosts were knowledgeable men in the art of money making.

Arthur Ommanney, during the years he had been married to Camilla, had been prodigal of gifts of money. Hugo, on the other hand, had made no presents to his father-in-law other than a cheque for seventy-five dollars on the two Christmases on which he had been Camilla's husband.

There was no record of Camilla herself having made any presents of money other than the forty dollars which she had mentioned. This was entered in the Major's small neat handwriting, "Camilla $40." The sum was hardly less interesting to Finch than the enigmatic "Return fare 30c."

Presently Finch pushed the bank statement over to his sergeant. "Go through those, Charles. See if you can spot anything that looks remotely like a motive for murder."

He turned to the magazines Drew had sent him. These were four. He arranged them chronologically. He turned the pages.

They were mostly of lovelies. At races, at balls, at christenings — and weddings.

Arthur and Camilla had a double page for theirs. Arthur and Camilla on one page. Wedding guests in twos and threes on the other. Hammerford Hall hanging above the bridal couple in a circlet of ribbon and a true lovers' knot.

Camilla, in a cloud of old family lace, was cutting the cake. Arthur Ommanney had his hand over hers, helping her. He was taller than his brother Hugo, but not as broad shouldered. He was not only one of the handsomest men Finch had seen but one of the most engaging looking. Finch wondered whether he was influenced by what he had been told about him in deciding that there was a strain of weakness in the pictured face.

The Major was there with the bridegroom's

mother, old Mrs. Ommanney. Finch was surprised to see that she really did look old until he remembered that Laker had told him that she been in her late thirties when she married Andrew Ommanney.

She was a short plump woman with an air of natural dignity and command. whatever she had thought about the match in private, she was smiling happily in the photograph. And indeed it would have been difficult not to have smiled, so radiant did the bridal couple appear, so pleased with themselves, with each other, with the whole business of getting married.

Finch turned to another magazine. A year had passed since the wedding. Mrs. Arthur Ommanney in black velvet and pearls, "seeing the New Year in at the Dorchester." She had been taken screaming with laughter. She looked lovely, raffish, and more than a little drunk. Her partner was a hard-faced, unscrupulous-looking man in his forties.

Eighteen months later Mrs. Arthur Ommanney, in chiffon and diamonds, was "entertaining some friends at the Moon-and-You, Mayfair's newest and brightest night club." She appeared to be dancing a solo. Her hair had fallen forward over her face. She was holding her skirts up in both hands and her lovely legs were visible to well above the knees. The photograph had a background of smart young people, clapping, presumably in time with the music.

In the fourth and last photograph she was coming down a long twisting Regency staircase. She was alone and stared straight out of the photograph as if the cameraman had taken her by surprise. She wore a strapless evening frock of some light material that seemed to float about her.

She looked, Finch thought, breath-takingly lovely, a vision of sheer enchantment. Only — that hadn't been the first impression that had come into his mind. There had been another, one that he had lost before he could pin it down.

He read the caption underneath.

'The rare and lovely Mrs. Ommanney . . .' So this was the photograph that Superintendent Laker had remembered. It had been taken some three months before Arthur Ommanney's death.

Rare and lovely!

What went on behind those brilliant eyes

and smooth ivory forehead? he wondered. That quarrel between the brothers had been violent and widely known he did not doubt. But what of Camilla's reactions? Had she been as indifferent to the outcome as she had appeared? It did not seem possible.

What had she made of her life in the great silent house with the stubborn old woman clinging to life and the reins of government upstairs and Hugo lording it below? And Hugo himself? Did he, tormented by the thought that she had been his brother's wife, insist that every phase of her life should be the opposite to that which she had led formerly? Did Hugo, perhaps, like his uncle, the Reverend Philip Ommanney, believe in mortifying the flesh? Or was it simply that he liked to be master and disciplined his wife as callously as a small boy might pull the wings off a fly?

Or perhaps Lionel *was* right. Perhaps Camilla liked a quiet life. Perhaps she even liked children. Finch's train of thought was diverted as he recalled the young man's vivid blush. He grinned to himself.

He looked across at his sergeant. "Find

anything interesting?"

"No, sir." Gilroy looked incredulous, even a little bewildered. "Apart from a slight straying from the path in the matter of cards, the Major might have been a bishop."

Finch nodded. "A colonial bishop on holiday — looking up all the people he used to know." He glanced at his wrist watch. "Just half past nine. I'll hop into the saloon bar and get a couple of pints while you pack up this lot."

Templar and Marquis were in the bar perched on high stools. Marquis was engaged in his usual lackluster occupation of staring at his reflection in the long mirror.

Templar had been talking about Cornish oysters. He greeted Finch's appearance with enthusiasm. "For the last ten minutes I've been conducting what amounted to a monologue on the virtues of oysters and I can't get a spark of enthusiasm from our friend Wyman here."

The landlord leaned heavily against the bar. "Personally," he said, "I hate the nasty, flabby things."

"Oh, blasphemy!" Finch murmured, shocked.

Wyman took Finch's order and turned away to fill two tankards. He put the money for it in the till and went back into the Public Bar.

"How's sleuthing?" asked Templar.

"Lousy," said Finch. "You can quote me widely on that."

He looked around the comfortable room. There was something wrong with the place. Wyman had gone but the air was still with antagonism,

He glanced at Templar. He had a double gin in his hand and looked as if, for the moment, he had forgotten the chip on his shoulder. Finch's glance traveled past him. His eyes met those of John Marquis idly in the long mirror and passed on.

It took a second or two to register. Then it felt as if a breath of cold air had blown in to the bar straight from an ice floe.

Marquis had been looking at him with a hard, appraising stare.

Finch took the beer. He went back to his own room. He closed the door very carefully behind him. "Charles," he said, "that fellow Marquis is a fraud."

"In what way?"

"His memory has come back."

"I'll be damned," said Gilroy softly. And then, "But if that's so why hasn't he let anyone know?"

Finch was staring into his tankard like a crystal gazer. It seemed to give him inspiration. "Maybe he doesn't want anyone to know," he said in his soft drawl.

11

FINCH turned his car in under the arch which led to the Market Stalbridge police station before nine o'clock next morning. He had his sergeant with him. To Wisbeach had been left the rather hopeless task of discovering where Major Ommanney had spent the fifty minutes that lay between the time he had left the bus and his appearance at the gates of the Hall.

Laker was expecting them.

He looked harassed. He had always held that there was too much paper work in the life of a Superintendent of Police. This morning, though, he had welcomed it as a symbol of normality. Now, seeing the newcomers, it failed to sustain him.

He looked at Finch. He looked at Finch's sergeant, who was seated and wearing an air of polite attention. He looked at the great black hat lying between them and found its sable extravagance not without significance.

"You saw Dr. Cranley?" Finch asked. This was the doctor who attended Marquis. The Superintendent lived in the same village as the doctor. He had agreed to try to catch him before he set out on his rounds. Now in answer to Finch's question he nodded. He stared morosely at the pencil which he held between his fingers and rolled it slowly backwards and forwards.

"Don't tell me if it's horrid," Finch murmured plaintively.

Laker's face relaxed into a faint smile. "It's not too good," he admitted. "Of course, he's a bit of a windbag and has too much bedside manner to suit me. He told me that very little was known about the human brain. In appearance, he said, it was like a gigantic shelled walnut. In practice it was as mysterious as the Gobi Desert, the functions of only a very small area being known. Then I asked him if he had noticed any change in John Marquis and he said no, though he admitted that he hadn't seen him for the last three weeks as he had been out each time the doctor called."

"That may be significant in itself."

Laker sighed heavily. "So I thought. When I pressed him to say whether it were possible for John Marquis to have regained his memory and, if so, to conceal the fact, he said that he hardly felt competent to answer and suggested that I approach Sir Robert Keeling, the brain specialist, who treated Marquis in London."

"But Dr. Cranley did give you an answer of sorts?"

"Yes." Laker fell silent. He picked up the pencil again and looked vaguely at its sharpened point. "Dr. Cranley," he told it, "said that speaking for himself, he would expect Marquis's memory to return only in part. In a confused and shadowy way perhaps."

"Yes?"

"He said that the shock, if only of a partial recovery, might well be enough to dislodge a man's reason. He added" — and Laker looked directly at Finch for the first time — "that he had always understood that the homicidal lunatic was an adept at concealment."

The two men looked at each other in consternation. Finch was the first to break the silence.

"I don't like that," he said softly. "No, I don't like that a bit."

"Well, there it is! Nothing we can do about it!" Laker pulled one of the table drawers open violently. "The report from the laboratory on the Major's clothes came in this morning. There's nothing to help there. Dr. Piper has made his report on the bloodstains on the Major's overcoat. They were from the same blood group as the Major's. There were no unidentifiable fingerprints in the Italian House, and nothing we haven't already seen in McClansland White's photographs."

As he spoke Laker had been pulling papers from the drawer and slapping them down on the table top. Now he added a large pile of photographs.

Finch took them up, examining each one. He seemed to find one of them particularly interesting. He took out a magnifying glass and studied the print through that. Then he passed both over to Laker.

"Look at this photograph of the mirror," he said. "Look how the camera shows up something we missed. A kink in the wire the mirror hangs by and a brighter length

215

of about six inches."

Laker looked. There was no doubt about it. The wire had been lengthened by some six inches. "It's a queer thing," he said, "but I remember now. I noticed Lady Sybil looking at it once or twice as if something about it surprised her."

"We'll ring her up and ask her — 'in the interests of justice!'"

Laker drew the telephone towards him. "It was Sir Kenneth said that."

"I thought it was Lady Sybil."

"Does it make any difference which of 'em said it?"

Finch shook his head. "I suppose not," he murmured. He had a feeling, though, that it did.

Lady Sybil came to the telephone. "The mirror? I'm interested that you should ask about that. I have an accurate eye for detail and it struck me that it was hanging lower on the wall than I should have expected. I thought at the time that perhaps the Major had altered it. But as it seemed quite pointless I didn't mention it."

"And that's just about what it seems to me," Laker grunted, after he had thanked

Lady Sybil and replaced the receiver. "Pointless."

But Finch was looking at a picture that had risen before his mental view. The picture of a comfortable room in the Ommanney Arms and of a man who stared and stared again at his own handsome image in the long mirror hanging on the wall. "I think it tells us the identity of the Major's visitor," he said slowly. And something of his own inner excitement communicated itself to his hearers. "The mirror hung just where anyone sitting on the one and only chair could look into it. And there's only one person who had fallen into the habit of staring at his reflection — so much so that it has become automatic — and that's John Marquis."

"John Marquis." Laker's eyes narrowed. "But how would the Major have got him to the Italian House?"

"That, I fancy, was arranged during that missing fifty minutes. The Major must have arranged either to send a message to Marquis, or, which is more probable, sent someone to go personally and fetch him. D'you remember Hugo Ommanney said that Marquis was open to suggestion?

217

John Marquis, with his memory gone, did as he was told. John Marquis, with it back again, may have thought it politic to do the same."

"And they were together for at least twenty minutes," said Laker slowly. He was thinking of the three cigarettes the Major had smoked. "If only we knew what they talked about."

"They may have had one interest in common," Finch suggested quietly.

"What was that?"

"Camilla."

"What?"

Finch settled lower in his chair. "You know," he said in his soft voice. "I've always been very interested in that last motor ride of Arthur's. So inconsiderate. So uncalled for — unless, of course, Camilla was John Marquis's mistress and her husband had found it out."

Laker said nothing for a moment. Just stared at Finch while his face turned slowly a dark red. Then he remarked bitterly, "Like mother, like daughter." He was conscious once more of the waste and futility of Arthur Ommanney's death.

Finch's eyes narrowed at this. Someone

else had made very much the same sort of remark. Then he remembered. Inspector Drew! He seemed to hear an echo of his voice. "Just Mother's girl over again. I never could keep track of the number of men she married."

"Suppose Camilla meant to marry Marquis — "

Laker gave an incredulous snort. "Leave Mr. Arthur?"

"But it would explain her indifference to the brothers' quarrel, wouldn't it?" said Finch. "They could do what they liked because she was walking out on them anyway. It would explain Camilla's reluctance to have Marquis down here. Her fear of him. It would explain the Major's visit to London to further his inquiries. His earnest conversation with his daughter by the lake. It might even offer a second theory as to why the Major boxed her ears."

"And why was it?" Laker growled.

"I suggest — sheer exasperation. Camilla's love affair with Marquis had broken up the first marriage. It looked like breaking up her second. And if there was one thing about his daughter of which the Major approved, it was her marriage to one or other of the Ommanney brothers."

On his way back to Hammerford, Finch stopped his car near the gate where he had first seen John Marquis. A rather disquieting idea had come to him. "Just want to see something," he murmured. He opened the gate into the field and passed through. He stationed himself where Marquis had been standing when he had first seen him.

He saw, as he had suspected, that there was a gap in the trees. Through it he had a clear view of the front door of Hammerford Hall. A long narrowing stretch of turf, a glimpse of the lake and, behind it, the clotted darkness of the hanging wood, all dwarfed by distance to the size and significance of a picture postcard.

"Charles! You'll find a pair of field glasses in the pocket of the car nearest to you," he called. "Just bring them here."

Gilroy hurried across with them. Finch focussed them on the distant view.

At once the whole scene came to life. The massive door appeared so near that he could count the studs. The granite chips in the drive sparkled. Some rooks flapped their way into the woods and a black swan swam on the lake.

Finch handed the glasses to his sergeant.

Charles gave a whistle of dismay. "Bet Camilla wouldn't be as keen on walking by the lake if she knew Marquis was watching her," he muttered.

They walked back to the car. "Did he have glasses when you saw him here?" Gilroy asked.

Finch shook his head. "No, but I remember noticing that he had one hand behind his back."

They climbed into the car and dropped rather soberly into the valley. To both of them there seemed something rather ominous in this secret surveillance. It was like the hovering of a hawk before it strikes.

On the outskirts of the village Finch slowed down. "We ought to be able to reach Swallow Cottage, as it's called on the map, by taking a turning somewhere about here."

They saw it a few seconds later. A narrow tunnel-like lane running through a wood, with high hedges on either side.

The land emerged suddenly into rough

open country. The trees here had been felled during the war and not replanted.

A cob cottage with whitewashed walls, old tiled roof and the woodwork painted black stood on gently rising ground. It faced south. A rowan tree, its berries already turning, shot up, straight and graceful, close to the front door.

It had no garden but stood amid clumps of yellowing bracken, blackberry briars and gorse. A track ran past it to Hammerford Hall. In front was an open view of fields and a stream and a fringe of tall trees in the distance.

Another cottage stood higher up and over to the right.

"Mrs. Hookway's," Finch murmured, pointing. He slid from behind the steering wheel. Stood for a moment staring at the cottage. It was well kept and comfortable looking, with something of the appearance of a white broody hen, and its five windows seemed to stare back at him.

"X marks the spot," Gilroy muttered beside him.

They opened the gate that led into the clearing and walked up to the cottage.

Finch knocked. There was no answer.

The front door stood open. Inside they could see a wall with some Hogarth prints on it. A hair-cord carpet in a neutral shade lay on the floor. Some pieces of brass were polished brilliantly and reflected in a distorted way an open door and the room beyond. It was impossible to recognize any particular object. One of them, though, had moved and now was motionless.

"Anyone at home?" Finch called. And a clock ticking away, filled in the vacant pause.

"We may as well have a look around since we're here," said Finch.

At once the reflection moved, expanded. Camilla Ommanney stepped into the passage. She was wearing the drain-pipe slacks. Her hair was still tied by the narrow black ribbon. Her hands were thrust deeply into the large patch pockets of a duffle coat. Its rough surface and turned-back hood made a frame for her fragile beauty.

"Good morning," said Finch. "Is Marquis in?"

"No, I'm sorry. He's out somewhere."

"Pity. Still, perhaps I could have a few words with you instead. It'll save me a journey to the Hall."

"Of course." Camilla smiled carefully. "What did you want to know?"

"Why you gave the Major the key of the Italian House, for one thing."

"It was because he said that he was going to sleep in one of the spare rooms at the Hall."

"Tell me about it." Finch wondered whether Camilla's answer showed a factual mind — or a cautious one.

"It was just after eleven o'clock — I don't know the exact time — when someone knocked on my bedroom door. I said 'come in' and there was the Major. I was afraid that Hugo would come up and be angry so I gave him some money and one of the keys to the Italian House. Then he went away."

Just like that! "What reason did he give for coming back?"

"He said that he was going next day to stay with some friends in the neighbourhood. And that he had no intention of journeying all the way to London and back again."

"What friends?"

Camilla's eyes flickered. "The Applebys at Prickett Point," she said with an air of mild triumph.

"Why didn't he put up at the Ommanney Arms?"

Camilla looked at him in a way that seemed to convict him of stupidity. "He'd have had to have paid there," she said gently. "The Major never paid for anything if he could help it."

"Thank you! That's all quite clear." Finch looked past her into the cottage. "Are you expecting Mr. Marquis?"

"Johnny? Oh no!" Again a careful smile was fixed to her lips. "I came down to see that Mrs. Hookway was looking after the place properly. I often do that."

"You and your husband take a great interest in Mr. Marquis, I understand."

"Yes, we do." Camilla wrinkled her lovely forehead. "It's so odd that he likes Hugo so much."

It was, Finch thought, the only wholly sincere remark that she had made. "He didn't know him before the accident?"

"No, they'd never met."

"But you knew him well?"

"Oh no! He was Arthur's friend." She looked at him solemnly.

"Where did you first meet him?"

"I don't remember. At some party or

225

other. We were always going to parties."

"Did Mr. Marquis come to your house?"

"Oh no!" Camilla hesitated. "Arthur met him outside."

"At parties?"

"Yes."

Finch nodded. "You must forgive me asking all these questions. But I have a special reason for being interested."

"In Johnny?" Camilla's voice was high and thin.

"Yes. It appears that his memory is coming back."

Camilla Ommanney stepped back against the wall. Finch's words wrought havoc with her delicate beauty. Her face seemed all bone. Her eyes grew haggard. It was not so much, Finch thought, that the words came as a surprise. It was more as if they had confirmed some fear that had been already in her mind.

"Martin said that too. But it must be wrong," she whispered. "It can't come back. Not *now*".

"Don't you think that it would be a good thing?"

Her eyes, narrow, brilliant, slid past him. The tip of her tongue came out and moistened her lips. "It would be cruel. To remember — all you'd lost. To realize that you — you couldn't go back." She was picking her words as carefully as a tightrope walker her steps. "To — to your business — and your friends."

"But why should Mr. Marquis make only a partial recovery? His physical health is good. Why shouldn't he get his memory back entirely?"

That Camilla heard him was shown by her answering. She was conscious though of his words only as if they had come from her own mind. "That would be too dreadful," she murmured. She walked past the two men as if they had not been there. Went hurrying with her elegant, catlike walk along the track which led back to the Hall.

"I'll be damned!" said Gilroy for the second time,

"Not one of our best liars," Finch murmured. He stepped into the narrow passage. Stood looking through the inner doorway into the room beyond, Gilroy at his shoulder.

It was a good-sized room and had been made from two small ones. It was very comfortable and well kept. It might have been the country retreat of any man of taste and moderate wealth. To the two detectives its very normality gave it a touch of the abnormal.

There were a great number of books in open shelves. There were some fine pieces of modern sculpture. A handsome walnut desk stood near a window with a graceful chair of the same wood in front of it. A small table drawn up to the fire was laid for luncheon. Flowers were thrust stiffly into vases that had been chosen with taste and discrimination.

Finch looked at the books. There were a few first editions. Some had been chosen for their bindings. The majority, though, were modern. Books of forestry, on British birds. On London, its history, architecture and guilds. A few modern poets and classics. A long row of books on angling.

Finch pulled out one of the drawers on the desk. It was completely and utterly empty. For some reason this took him by surprise. So much so that, for a moment, his mind reconstructed the image of the things that were missing. A box of note paper, a book of stamps, envelopes, a ball of string, some tradesmen's books, a handful of loose drawing pins . . .

But there was nothing and the house appeared what in truth it was. A setting for a way of living that was no longer carried on. Books no one read. Sculpture that no one appreciated. A desk that was never used. A house to which came no news from the outside world. Where the letter box rattled only to the passing wind.

Gilroy had been wondering about it. He picked up a small ivory box. He looked at it, turning it over in his hand, trying to assess its value. Baffled, he put it down again. Stooped to read the titles of some books.

Watching him, it came to Finch suddenly how difficult it would be for a normal man to live this empty life without giving himself away. Never to disturb this orderly vacuum. Never to pick up a book. Never ask an intelligent question. To show no interest in what went on around you.

Mrs. Hookway will know, he thought. Even if it's something quite small she'll have noticed. "Better have a look around before we're interrupted," he told Gilroy. "We'll start on the books. Marquis may have hidden something in them. A newspaper cutting, a scrap of paper on which he'd written — though where he'd get it from in the first place I don't know."

They took the books out one at a time. Ruffling through the pages. Shaking them out.

There were bookplates in most of them with the name John Marquis in heavy ornamental lettering. Some of them bore inscriptions, showing that they had been presents. Finch made a note of the givers' names thinking that they might come in useful.

He pulled out a fat book entitled *Salmon Rivers of Britian*. Holding it by its spine, he stretched open its covers. A snapshot fell out of it.

Gilroy stooped and picked it up. He handed it, without a word, to his superior.

It was a photograph of Camilla Ommanney.

She was wearing a tweed skirt and a short fur coat. A handkerchief was knotted around her neck. She was looking towards the camera and laughing. For background there was a sash window and part of a square-built creeper-covered house.

Finch turned the print over. The back

was plain. "She might at least have put whether she was lunching or sleeping," he complained. "All we can say is that the photograph wasn't taken in the summer or the winter. Her clothes are too thick for the one. And there's a tree in leaf in one corner to disprove the other."

"D'you think this was what Camilla was looking for?" Gilroy asked.

"She had seven months to search — if she'd wanted to. No, I think she was doing the same as we are. Looking for proof that Marquis has recovered his memory. After all, if she'd been his mistress she'd be the first to notice any change in him."

"What's she afraid of, I wonder?"

"That rather depends what sort of man Marquis was before his accident — and on how much he has against her."

Gilroy glanced suddenly from the window. "There's a woman coming in from the road. Must be Mrs. Hookway."

Finch joined his sergeant at the window.

Mrs. Hookway was a pleasant-looking woman of about thirty-eight years of age. Her face was freckled. Her eyes were a clear blue. She wore her hair in a net. She had on a neat navy blue coat and a pudding-basin hat. She carried a bulging American cloth shopping bag.

Finch went to meet her. He introduced himself. "We hoped to have a few words with Mr. Marquis but he's not in."

"No, sir. He passed my cottage about eight o'clock this morning. And there's no telling when he'll be back. He might walk in this very minute or he might not be back for a couple of days." Mrs. Hookway rested her bag on a chair. "I've been in to Market Stalbridge doing some shopping for him."

Finch raised an eyebrow. "He goes off alone? Haven't you any way of keeping in touch with him?"

"I don't need none. Mr. Marquis knows the countryside for miles around. I reckon there isn't anyone who knows it better unless it's Mr. Lionel with his bird-watching and his photographs. No, Mr. Marquis has never come to no harm yet. If he did I'd know soon enough. Mr. Hugo had the telephone put into my cottage for just such an emergency. Anyone can ring me up. Or I can ring them."

"His room looks so comfortable I wonder he can tear himself away."

Mrs. Hookway sighed. "What would he do here, poor lamb? He used to have a gramophone. A wonderful machine. Play a whole opera without stopping, it would. But it only made his head ache. Mr. Hugo had it stored again."

She showed Finch over the cottage. The one big bedroom, so comfortably furnished. A small bedroom. A modern bathroom warmed by a large radiator. A kitchen and pantry opposite the single sitting room.

In the kitchen were cool flags and a lot of fine china behind glass doors. There was an electric pump and a boiler for the hot water. There was an expensive coffee percolator and a wire basket for drying salads.

"I do all I can to keep things as he used to have them," said Mrs. Hookway. "Of course the cooking's not so grand but I use all his table silver and glass."

"And Mr. Marquis seems content?"

"Oh yes, sir," Mrs. Hookway spoke with emphasis but Finch noticed that a shadow had come into her eyes.

"Does he recognize anyone?"

"He knows Mr. Hugo." There was a slight note of uneasiness in her voice.

"He has always known Mr. Hugo. I

meant apart from Mr. Hugo?"

"Apart from Mr. Hugo, me and the doctor there's no one." Mrs. Hookway spoke emphatically. Finch could see, though, that the question was not to her liking.

"Doesn't Mrs. Hugo come here sometimes?"

"Never, sir. It's always Mr. Hugo. He comes in to see if there's anything wants doing. The doctor comes once a week. If Mr. Marquis is out he walks on up to my place and asks me how he's keeping and if I've noticed any change." She seemed to regret the last words as soon as they were out of her mouth.

"And have you?"

"Have I what?" She was pleating the corner of her apron nervously as she spoke.

"Have you noticed any change in him?" Not giving her time to utter the denial he saw forming on her lips, Finch went on, "Since I came to the village it has twice been suggested to me that Mr. Marquis *has* changed, that perhaps his memory has come back?"

"I tell you I've noticed no difference." Mrs. Hookway's voice had risen. She avoided Finch's eye.

Finch knew the value of silence. He walked over to the window. Stood looking out for a long moment. He turned. "If Marquis had regained his memory wouldn't you have expected him to tell you? To come rushing up to your cottage, excited, happy? But he didn't do that, did he, Mrs. Hookway? He preferred to keep the news secret. To tell no one. To leave it to you to find out for yourself — "

Mrs. Hookway threw her apron over her head. She was crying with an abandonment that was surely foreign to her nature. "It was the fish!" she said through her tears — or at least those were the words Finch thought he heard.

"The fish?" he echoed. And Gilroy, who stood now in the kitchen doorway, raised his eyebrow in surprise.

Mrs. Hookway dashed the apron from her eyes. "It was lying on the kitchen table," she cried, "wrapped in newspaper. Mr. Marquis was bending over it. *Reading the news on it.* I know he was."

This was bathos. Neither man, though, felt like smiling. Indeed to Finch it seemed as if a chilling shadow had fallen on the bright kitchen, darkening the day.

"When did this happen?" he asked. And some quality in his voice conveyed a sense of urgency to the woman,

"It was yesterday, sir." Mrs. Hookway wiped her eyes in her apron. "I saw Mr. Marquis come in about four o'clock. And I said to myself, 'He wasn't in for the midday meal. I'll just pop down and cook him a bit of fish for his tea.' "

"Yes?"

"My cottage lies behind his, over to the right." Mrs. Hookway had conquered her emotion. Indeed she seemed more at her ease now than at any time during the interview. "So I can't be seen from these windows. The front door was open and so was this one." She nodded towards it. "Mr. Marquis was in here. He was leaning forward with both hands on the kitchen table. Resting on them, as you might say. And his head was bent over the parcel of fish."

"He hadn't unwrapped it?"

"Hadn't touched it, sir. That's why he was leaning over so far. The fish was right in the centre, where the boy who brought it had thrown it down."

"You're certain that he was reading?"

"Yes, sir." Mrs. Hookway showed signs of returning agitation. "It wasn't only his position. He looked different. Not his face. That couldn't change. The rest of him though looked — well, more all of a piece, as you might say."

"Did you speak to him?"

"No, sir. I was too taken aback like. I went outside and came in again, making a bit of a noise. Mr. Marquis was over by the sink drawing himself a glass of water."

"You didn't make any comment to him about what you had seen?"

"No, sir."

"And afterwards — did he seem any different?"

"He did and he didn't, if you take my meaning. It was him looking and speaking the same and me knowing that it was only playacting that did it."

"It must have been a great shock to you," said Finch.

"It was, sir. I can't hardly believe it even now."

"And you haven't told Mr. Ommanney?"

"No, sir." She looked at him with honest bewilderment. "I don't know how it was, sir, but I couldn't bring myself to do it, and that's a fact."

"Have you seen anything of a knife with two cutting edges, tapering to a very fine point?" Finch was repeating Dr. Piper's description of the knife with which the Major's throat had been cut.

Mrs. Hookway looked disturbed. "There've been no sharp knives in the cottage, sir," she assured Finch earnestly. "We were careful in the first place in case Mr. Marquis was careless with such things and we've just gone on in the same way."

"D'you think you can tell if Mr. Marquis was wearing anything different when he left? Or whether there is anything missing from the cottage? Anything at all — no matter how insignificant?"

Mrs. Hookway was quite sure that she could. She bustled away with Gilroy in attendance. He was soon back to say that Marquis had been dressed as usual. This did not surprise Finch. He had expected nothing else.

Ten minutes late Gilroy was back again. A bottle containing eighteen sleeping tablets had gone from where Mrs. Hookway had kept it behind some tins of grapefruit in the store cupboard.

"From what Mrs. Hookway says they seem to have been phenobarbitone tablets," Gilroy ended.

"Was she in the habit of giving Marquis sleeping draughts?"

"No, sir. Dr. Cranley left twenty-four with her when Marquis first arrived. This is the same bottle."

"When did she see the bottle last?"

"It was there at a quarter to ten last night. Marquis didn't come in for his supper until then and she put a couple of tablets in the tomato soup he had. 'Just to be on the safe side,' as she said."

Finch stared at his sergeant in dismay. Various uses to which Marquis might put eighteen phenobarbitone tablets fled through his mind in a series of fantastic pictures.

"That isn't the only thing missing, sir," said Gilroy. "Mrs. Hookway says that a gallon size tin of black high gloss paint has gone from the scullery."

Finch stared. He was beginning to feel ill-used. "You're sure she said high gloss?" he asked with the utmost politeness.

"Yes, sir."

"I see." Finch was silent a moment. Then he said pensively, "So Marquis is off to the woods with eighteen sleeping tablets and a gallon of high gloss black paint. Rather odd, isn't it?"

"That's not quite correct, sir. The tin only had a little paint in it. Left over from doing the outside doors and window frames."

Finch nodded. "Why didn't you say so at first, Charles? Marquis has gone off with eighteen sleeping tablets and a nearly empty gallon size tin of high gloss black paint. That's quite understandable. The sort of thing I might do myself."

"Quite so, sir," Gilroy agreed with suspicious meekness.

12

FINCH and Gilroy came out of Swallow Cottage. A wandering breath of air caught the front door. It closed behind them with echoing finality.

From somewhere in the woods a pheasant got up with a loud clacking cry of alarm.

Finch glanced at his sergeant. Had Marquis disturbed the bird? They waited. Nothing more happened. The silence gathered again about them. The empty countryside dozed in the sunshine. The mystery of Johnny Marquis with his leather-patched coat and pork-pie hat, his sleeping tablets and his pot of paint remained unresolved.

Finch stopped the car in front of the telephone booth. He called up Hammerford Hall.

Carter answered the telephone. Mr. and Mrs. Ommanney, he said, were out. He was expecting them back to tea. No, he did not know where they had gone. He understood, though, that they were taking advantage of the mild weather to take a run in the car.

Finch thanked him. He left a message to say that he would be obliged if Mr. Ommanney would call up Wisbeach as soon as he got back as he, Finch, was anxious to speak to him. Then he asked if Mr. Marquis had been seen at all that day. Carter said that, as far as he knew, Mr. Marquis had not been to the Hall. And that, no doubt, he was taking one of the walking tours to which he was addicted.

Finch thanked Carter. He replaced the receiver. The butler, he felt, had exhibited an optimism that was likely to be rudely shaken.

He called up the Market Stalbridge police station. He told Laker the result of his visit to Swallow Cottage and asked that a man should be sent around to keep watch on the cottage.

Finch's last call was to the Applebys. He looked them up in the telephone directory. Appleby, G., The Lodge, Prickett Point.

"Is Mr. Appleby in?"

"This is Mrs. Appleby speaking." It was a pleasant voice, though not a young one. "I'm afraid my husband is out still. Can I give him a message?"

Finch introduced himself. "I understand

that you were expecting Major Guy Ommanney to stay — "

A gasp traveled down the line. It was succeeded by a silence, the duration of which was almost as surprising.

"What did you say?" a voice asked cautiously.

Finch repeated his words.

"Oh, dear me, no! There must be some mistake. We weren't expecting a visitor." Mrs. Appleby gave a tinkle of laughter as brittle as glass. "Indeed since we moved into the Lodge we don't entertain at all."

The voice ceased. There followed the faintest of clicks.

"Mrs. Appleby?"

Only the little humming note of the instrument answered him. Quietly and discreetly Mrs. Appleby had hung up on him.

Finch went back to his car. "Don't know what's the matter with the women in these parts," he complained. "I didn't see Appleby, G., but his wife seemed just as upset on hearing the Major's name as Camilla was at that of John Marquis. I suppose we shall have to go over after lunch and see what it's all about."

This, however, proved unnecessary. The two detectives had just finished lunch when Mrs. Wyman opened the door. "Mr. Appleby to see you, sir," she said.

A stout, red-faced man with rather stupid blue eyes and a furious manner pushed past her into the room.

"Who's been trying to involve me in the murder at the Italian House?" he shouted. He looked from Finch to Gilroy and finally settled for Finch. He came nearer. "Whoever it was you can tell them that I only got home yesterday evening — whatever the local rag may have said to the contrary. Yes and you tell them that when I fall out with someone it's final. Tell them George Appleby isn't the man to forgive and forget." He added with a sneer, "He wouldn't even sleep under the same roof as the Major — unlike some people he could name."

"That's very interesting to me," said Finch in his small voice, "though perhaps not to my informant."

George Appleby smiled unpleasantly. He lowered his voice slightly, for which Finch was thankful. "You'll be a damned fool if you believe that. He's hated the Major's guts for thirty years. I was staggered when I heard that he was back at the Hall. I said to myself 'Now, what the devil's the meaning of this?'"

"And what was it?" Finch asked politely.

George Appleby smiled. It wasn't a nice smile. "Don't tell me you don't twig? Why, it sticks out a mile."

Finch sighed. "I haven't the faintest idea what you're talking about."

Appleby looked incredulous. "D'you mean you haven't heard the story?"

"Can't say until I know which story."

Appleby's temper seemed to be subsiding. He smiled. He had an expressive face. It looked now as if he thought that he were being clever. "Look here! I'll make a bargain with you. I'll tell you the story if you'll tell me who it was who said Guy Ommanney was going to stay with us."

Finch considered. "It's a deal."

"Right!" Appleby took the chair which he had refused earlier. He sat straddling the seat. His arms rested along the back. "Must be over thirty years ago now when it happened. We were both in our early thirties. And we both had pretty wives still in their twenties. As a matter of fact

Kenneth's wife was only eighteen at the time — "

Sir Kenneth! Though in a way Finch had foreseen what was coming, it still came to him as a shock.

"He had gone over to Ireland to hunt. He was a game little fellow in those days chock-full of fun — and ambitious as the devil. When he came back he was engaged to be married to Lady Sybil Voase. She was a pretty creature, though you wouldn't think it to look at her now. Rather a shy little thing. Guileless — made you think of apple blossoms and lambs in the Spring. Had expectations, too."

George Appleby broke off to inquire if Finch had ever heard of any wealthy Irish peers. "Well, I hadn't. But Lady Sybil's family were the exception. And there were only the two children, a boy and this girl. Kenneth was sitting pretty. They were married in Ireland and went to Paris for their honeymoon. All proper and correct. After the honeymoon they came back to Hammerford — and Guy was there. He was a fascinating devil in those days. Had the reputation of being irresistible to women."

Appleby's face was settling into ugly lines as its owner's eyes focussed on the past. "Within three weeks of the happy couple's return Guy and Lady Sybil had run off together. And ten days later he left her flat. Posted a letter to her husband to say where she was and walked out on her. There was a rumor that Kenneth had been looking for them with a gun. Perhaps that was why Guy nipped off to America. Anyway, Kenneth was at the beginning of his career and, as I said, he was ambitious. A scandal at that time would have finished him. So things were patched up and he forgave her. Shortly afterwards he got an appointment abroad somewhere and they left the country. Didn't come back to England for about ten years. Didn't come down here until after Guy got mixed up in that card scandal. I suppose Kenneth felt that squared things a bit."

"You mentioned your wife in the same connection, I think."

"Oh, that! Guy had made a pass at her earlier on. Fortunately" — Mr. Appleby spoke with simple pride — "I was always a jealous chap. I made such a hell of a row when I first noticed which way the

wind was blowing that Guy sheered off."
Appleby laughed shortly. "He went to Paris
that time. Guy, I mean. Funny, I suppose,
in a way."

Finch looked at him curiously. "That's
all there was to it? And yet you have never
forgotten it?"

Appleby rubbed the side of his nose. He
looked almost shy. "Fact is," he said at
last, "I've never been quite sure my wife
wouldn't have gone off with Guy if he'd
given her a chance."

"I think you said that you had an alibi
for the night of the Major's murder?"

"Eh? Yes, of course. My wife and I slept
the night at Southampton and motored
home yesterday. Just back from the States,
see? Stayed at the Dolphin in High Street.
They know me there. You ask 'em." He
smiled with simple triumph. "Well, that's
all. Your turn now. Who told you than Guy
Ommanney was going to stay with us?"

"His daughter — Mrs. Hugo Ommanney."

Appleby stared. His face fell comically.
"That little thing! She wouldn't even have
heard any of what I've been telling you."
He looked soberly at Finch. "You're pretty
smart, aren't you?"

"What me?" Finch shook his head. "I only want things to be nice and ordinary," he said. "I get worried when they're not."

Gilroy saw Appleby off. A crestfallen Appleby, since he would not have told Finch the story of Sir Kenneth's misfortune had he not felt certain that Sir Kenneth had first told Finch of his.

Finch sat silent, thinking over what he had just heard.

That their visitor was wrong on one point he was certain. Kenneth Ommanney had not forgiven his wife. But then Appleby G., was a simple soul. There were in existence refinements of cruelty that were undreamed of in his philosophy.

Gilroy came back. "We had that handed to us on plate," said he cheerfully.

Finch was pensive. "That must have been quite a dinner party. No wonder the butler was upset."

"I haven't seen Lady Sybil yet."

"I suppose she does have her informal moments." Finch sounded doubtful. He added, "She certainly had a strong motive for murder. Since whatever excuses she might have made in the past for the Major, her feelings must have changed to hatred to hear him bring up the story of their abortive romance so causally at the dinner table. A motive for Sir Kenneth, too. His inflated ego might well have felt that only the Major's death could avenge the injury done to it."

"And once inside the Hall, the Major may have visited other people beside Camilla. Or been seen hanging around and followed to the Italian House by one of the inmates."

But Finch was thinking of something else. "I wonder if Camilla appeared at the inquest on her husband? And if so, what impression she made." He rose to his feet. "Charles, I'm going across to the police station and have a talk with the Ringwood police. You stay here, and if that chap arrives from Market Stalbridge, send him up to the Hookways'."

Wisbeach was at home but was just going out. He was disappointed at not having been asked to do more. He had by now rather the look of a terrier asking with diminishing hope to be taken for a walk. He showed Finch into the room which he used as an office. It was clean and bare and a telephone stood on a desk with a pile of directories beside it.

Finch's call to Ringwood came through. He asked to speak to someone who could give him the details of a fatal motoring accident that had taken place two and a half years before. "A Mr. Arthur Ommanney was killed. His passenger was badly burned."

"Inspector Dawlish was in charge of that, sir. If you'll hold on I'll see if he's in the station," said the sergeant who had answered the telephone.

A moment later a brisk voice said, "Mr. Finch? Dawlish here. We've been wondering whether we'd be hearing from you."

"Why was that?"

"Just a general feeling that there was a great deal more behind that motor accident than came out at the inquest. And that it was just possible that the murder of Major Ommanney might have been tied up in some way with the death of Arthur Ommanney."

"That's very interesting. What was wrong about the motor smash?" This sounded promising. Finch blessed the impulse that had led him to get in touch with the Ringwood police.

"For one thing there was a mysterious woman mixed up in it," said Dawlish. "She checked out of the Isaak Walton where she and Marquis were staying as man and wife on the morning of the accident."

Finch was conscious of a sudden feeling of excitement. "Can you lay your hands on a description of her?"

"I can give it to you. I turned up all the details we had out of curiosity yesterday, so I'm well briefed."

"Splendid!"

"Here it is then. Age about twenty to twenty-five, not more and might be less. Height about five feet two inches. Slim build. Eyes greenish. Hair — this is a good touch — a faded tortoise shell. She's three-and-a-half — "

"That's the one!"

"You recognize her?"

"At the time of the accident she was Arthur Ommanney's wife."

Inspector Dawlish gave an expressive whistle. "Boy, oh boy! Then she and Marquis must have known that her husband was on the way down. No wonder she moved out."

"Was the Isaak Walton a rather square

252

house with sash windows and covered in Virginia creeper?"

"How did you know?"

"I found a snapshot of Camilla Ommanney in a book called *Salmon Rivers of Britian*, belonging to John Marquis. The Isaak Walton — and the name makes it perfect — was in the background."

"Damn!" said Dawlish. "That book was listed as being among his effects left at the pub. And I remember seeing it there. I never thought of looking inside it though. And talking of photographs, the chambermaid at the pub said she thought the she'd seen one of the supposed Mrs. Marquis in some society magazine. She promised to let me know if she saw another but she never did."

"Never did let you know, I expect," said Finch dryly. "The beautiful Mrs. Ommanney was always being photographed. But the family are rich and there was rather a tragic sequel to the accident connected with it, quite apart from the actual accident. Arthur Ommanney's mother became bedridden as the result of the shock. Arthur, it seems, was the light of her eyes. So that those who didn't fall for bribery were probably got at by sentiment."

"Don't know that I blame them. The pub's a quiet little place, too. Expensive and select. And not much patronized by the locals. So only a few people would have been involved."

"Who identified the body?"

"Hugo Ommanney, the brother. I took him to the mortuary myself. Never saw anyone nearer the point of collapse than he was when he came out."

A picture of Hugo Ommanney floated before Finch's mental vision. The bullet head, the bold gaze, the arrogance of the frog face. "I find that a bit hard to imagine," he murmured. He was doing his best but with little success.

"You ought to have seen the body," Dawlish spoke feelingly. "It wasn't human any more. Hugo Ommanney could only identify it by the teeth."

"I was told that Arthur died of a broken neck. I had imagined that, in some way, he had been thrown clear of the car." Finch spoke slowly. A strange and rather terrifying idea had come to him.

"As far as actual burning was concerned Arthur Ommanney had the worst of it. He was making no protest and so, presumably, was dead. Marquis, on the other hand, was screaming for help and fighting to get the door of the car open. Naturally we concentrated on getting him out first."

"We? You were there then?"

"Yes. I happened to motor past a few seconds after the crash. Only just missed seeing it."

"Could you tell the relative positions of the two men?"

"No. The car had turned right over and was resting on its hood. The driver had slipped clear of the steering wheel. He and Marquis were in a sort of huddle just inside the jammed door."

"I see. D'you happen to know what Hugo Ommanney recognized about his brother's teeth?"

"Two back teeth on the left-hand side filled with gold. And a gap between where a tooth had been drawn."

"Did Hugo tell you this before or after he'd looked at 'em?"

"Now you mention it, it was after," Dawlish spoke slowly. He was beginning to see where the C.I.D. man's questions were leading.

"Did anyone look at Marquis's teeth?"

"Not as far as I know."

"Then you have only Hugo Ommanney's word for it as to which man was which?"

The Hampshire man was silent for a moment. Then he said, "Had he any particular reason for wanting his brother out of the way?"

"He married his widow and came in for the estate."

"But, of course, the second man wasn't expected to live."

"Only the dead are beyond recovery."

Again there was a pause. "Looks as if you'll have to try and trace this chap Marquis."

Finch laughed mirthlessly. "No difficulty about that. He's been living in the village for the last seven months. He was brought down here from the hospital with his memory gone. It's only just been discovered that he's got it back without telling anyone the glad news."

"But could his brother afford to have him down there?"

"Could he afford to have him anywhere

else? With a watch dog set to report any change in him. And a telephone so that it can be done in the shortest possible time."

"Then Hugo Ommanney knows that his brother (if it is his brother) remembers who he is?"

"The watch dog failed in its duty for purely sentimental reasons. For all that" — and now Finch was speaking slowly — "Hugo may have discovered it for himself."

"How's that?"

"A few weeks ago the man known as John Marquis was found shut up in a burning barn with the door jammed. A nice lonely barn, too."

Again Dawlish whistled. "What happens now?"

"I wish I knew." Finch's voice was sad. "Marquis — or Arthur — set out from his cottage this morning. He's done the same thing before. But this time I have a nasty feeling that he's not coming back."

For a time the two men discussed what could be done. Dawlish was a sensible and quick-witted police officer. When he suggested visiting the hospital in which Marquis had been a patient for nearly two years, Finch jumped at the offer.

This hospital had been started in Hampshire during the war to deal with badly burned service men. It had acquired a reputation for plastic surgery that was almost world-wide.

"I'll find out if Marquis has ever done or said anything to suggest that he is Arthur Ommanney," said Dawlish. "And, at least, I should be able to find out about his teeth."

Finch next put through a call to the Market Stalbridge police station. Laker was out, he was told. He would be connected to Colonel Stonor.

There should be, Finch reflected as he waited, some instructions in the police manual as to the breaking of unwelcome news to sensitive police constables.

"Good afternoon, sir," he said in his soft voice. Adding cautiously, "I've found out why the people of Hammerford are behaving so oddly."

"Oh?" The single word oozed with mistrust. "Why is it?"

"They think that Hugo Ommanney identified the wrong man. And that John Marquis is, in reality, Arthur Ommanney."

Colonel Stonor drew a deep breath. "This is intolerable. First you want to dig up old Mrs. Ommanney. Now it's her son — "

Finch was charmed. "That," he said happily, "is a splendid idea."

Colonel Stonor made a noise like a wounded elephant. Finch did not hear him though. He had replaced the receiver prepatory to ringing up New Scotland Yard.

He asked to speak to Sir Eustace Anson. He explained what had happened. "As things stand at present, sir, we've no way of telling whether Marquis is Marquis or whether the village is right and he is Arthur Ommanney."

"Whoever he is," said Sir Eustace, "it makes no difference to his potentiality for mischief."

"That's quite correct, sir," said Finch. "It means that as things are now, in the event of a showdown, Hugo is at a great disadvantage. His position is analogous to that of a lonely outpost where the inhabitants are, at best, neutral — but are more likely to be hostile."

"I don't think on present evidence that

there is a chance of the Home Office giving you permission to exhume Arthur Ommanney's coffin. Indeed I don't see why it should."

"It's a question of speed, sir. Of convincing the natives. No doubt we shall be able to settle this question of identity to our satisfaction but will the villagers believe it? You know what they're like."

"I know what you're like," said Sir Eustace unkindly. But he promised to do what he could.

Gilroy was standing in the sun in front of the inn. He saw Finch coming. He came to meet him. "If ever I become stone deaf," he said cheerfully, "this is where I shall come to live. Lovely scenery, good food, no one pestering you with casual conversation."

"I've found out the reason for that," Finch rejoined. "Let's walk around to see Templar. I can tell you about it on the way."

When they were well away from the village, he said, "You remember I told you that Arthur Ommanney died of a broken neck and must have been thrown clear of the burning car?"

"Yes, sir."

"I was wrong. His body was so badly burned that Hugo could only identify it by the teeth. And Marquis" — Finch accompanied this by a sidelong glance from under the broad brim of the assassin's hat — "Marquis was never identified at all."

"You mean — ?" Gilroy looked startled.

"Exactly. Hugo may well — and for obvious reasons — have identified the dead man as his brother."

"But why should that frighten the locals? What do they expect?"

"Work it out for yourself. They knew those two. And what they knew had decided them, that the safest thing to do is to retire inside their cottages. To answer no questions and to ask none."

"Do you believe it, sir?"

For a moment Finch did not answer. He was seeing again the powerful figure of the man known as John Marquis as it brooded over the dreaming loveliness of Hammerford Hall. Experiencing again his own sensation of uneasiness, almost of fear that had sprung up in him at the sight. He stood again in the Ommanney Arms watching Marquis's stony profile and the

261

sweat breaking out on Wyman's forehead. Saw Camilla, a shivering, frightened soul with all her beauty gone.

"Camilla believes it," he said. "Not," he added, "that we can go by that. A trickster's daughter. What else could she believe?"

Gilroy had forgotten Camilla. "What a ghastly position for her," he said. "She doesn't even know whether she was a widow or not when she married Hugo."

Finch wagged his head. "She was a widow, all right," he said gloomily. "Trouble is to know whether it was grass or sod."

"How are we going to find out — one way or the other?"

"The A.C. thinks it shouldn't be difficult. I wanted to dig up the body and have a look at it."

Gilroy was startled. "What did the A.C. say to that?"

Said Finch sadly, "He was against it." He continued murmuring unhappily. "I can't help thinking what a weapon this could be in some unscrupulous person's hands. Even supposing that John Marquis is John Marquis and not Arthur Ommanney what difference does it make if someone makes him believe that he *is* Arthur Ommanney?

That Camilla is, in reality, his wife and Hammerford Hall the home of which he has been dispossessed?"

"Yes," said Gilroy doubtfully, "but could they?"

"As regards Camilla what could be simpler? In the back of his mind Marquis is probably aware of dim and yet intimate images, such as might linger in the memory of a lover — or a husband."

Gilroy had another thought. "But why should anyone try to influence Marquis against Hugo and his wife?"

"I was thinking," said Finch, "about Sir Kenneth. Suppose he could get Marquis to remove the Rector and Hugo, how he would revel in being Squire of Hammerford Hall. Then he really could make his mark."

There was someone at work in Martin Templar's cottage. Standing at the front door, the two men could hear the clattering of china. A woman was singing a popular tune of the day.

Finch knocked. The singing went on. He waited until the singer hung on a low note then knocked again.

The singing and the rattling of crockery ceased. A middle-aged woman came to the door. Mr. Templar, she said, was in. She showed them into a sitting room overlooking the front garden.

The room might, originally, have been prim and rather austere. Now papers and books were strewn around. Cushions, collected from all over the cottage, were packed into a large armchair. They were flattened as if someone had recently been sprawling there. A used glass lay overturned on a newspaper on the floor. A faint smell of whiskey rose from where a trickle of liquid had soaked into the paper.

Finch bent and righted the glass. He straightened his back — and there was the painting. It hung on the wall before his eyes.

It showed a landlocked sea, bleached grass, swans asleep with their long necks stretched along their backs. Houses on two sides reflected in the water. And, over everything, the clear thin light of a spring day.

The painting was signed M. Templar and dated May 1952.

Gilroy made a warning movement. Finch turned. Templar stood scowling at him from the doorway.

"You here again?"

"Looks like it." Finch saw that the painter was drunk. His walk was steady. His speech clear — for all that he was drunk. Nothing was wrong — and nothing was absolutely normal.

"Nice place, Christchurch," Finch murmured. And Gilroy glanced quickly at the painting. "Always makes me think of salmon."

"Can't say it does me. I'm a painter. Not an angler," Templar growled. "Still, I don't suppose you came to discuss fishing with me."

"I came to see you in connection with something you said to Mrs. Ommanney."

"Mrs. Ommanney?" The painter seized on the only word that caught his attention. "Dear little Camilla!" He went to a table. Poured himself half a glass of whiskey and drank it neat. "So that's how it's done," Finch thought.

"You know" — Templar wagged the empty glass at Finch — "that girl has an absolute passion for the state of matrimony. That's how Hugo got her. But I'm the one who understands her. If you don't believe me look at that portrait I did of her. Best thing I ever did. But he (alluding presumably to Hugo) couldn't take it. Didn't want people to think of her *as that*."

"As what?" Finch's voice was quite colorless.

Templar shook his head. "Never you mind." He added with immense dignity. "If the family don't want you to know, as a gentleman, I can't tell you."

Finch tried again. "What don't the family want me to know?"

It was no good. Templar was searching his conscience. "A gentleman? Well, why not? I was brought up as one. Give us a child for the first seven years of its life, as they say — "

"I understand that you told Mrs. Ommanney that John Marquis had recovered his memory?"

"Eh?" Templar stared. He gave a roar of laughter. "Not a word of truth in it. I made it up."

"Why did you do that?"

"Because I'm a malicious chap." Templar nodded his head solemnly. "Yes. That's me. A damned malicious chap."

Finch was delighted with the result

of their interview with Martin Templar. "That's one person we can wipe off our list of suspects," he told Gilroy as they walked back towards the village. "He didn't mean any harm when he came down here. He just wanted to seduce Camilla. And," Finch added firmly, "compared to murder, seduction is a lighthearted and commendable pastime. Did you recognize the painting?"

"No, sir — I saw the date though."

"Exactly. I'll get it confirmed but there's not much doubt about it. Martin Templar was at Christchurch painting, probably at the same pub, when John Marquis and Camilla were there. Templar was one of those men for whom Camilla had a tremendous fascination. But what was the good? She was rich, secure, happily married. He got on with his painting and hoped he'd work her out of his system. But he didn't and perhaps because of that he kept the painting, which he associated with her.

"Two years later, and here probably he was telling me the truth, he came across a press photograph of her. Mrs. Hugo Ommanney. He made inquiries. Found that she had been Mrs. Arthur Ommanney and Mrs. Hugo Ommanney. But never was Mrs. John Marquis. So that was the sort of woman she was! Full of hope, he scouted around and found this cottage. Came down here, bringing, as a reminder, the painting on which she must have seen him at work. And, for good measure, adding the date May 1952. The year and month of Arthur Ommanney's death; though it seems obvious that Templar must have left the Isaak Walton before the accident and gone where he saw no photographs of the newly made widow. Probably abroad or 'to sea.'"

Said Gilroy thoughtfully after a pause, "I don't think he can have made it. After all, when he came down here Templar didn't know that Hugo was in his wife's confidence."

"On the other hand he's been here since May. A lot can happen in four months. Perhaps he did make it — and it wasn't what he had expected."

Finch fell silent. His mind was full of conjecture.

That a painter often saw more in his sitter than was visible to the layman was a truism. That what he saw was sometimes apprehended only by some intuitive hinterland and was conveyed from there to the brush, by-passing the conscious mind, was an accepted fact.

Finch supposed that something of this sort had happened to Martin Templar. But what had he discovered? Had the façade of lighthearted promiscuousness revealed on closer inspection rooms that were dark, echoing and slightly sinister?

"In fact," Finch murmured aloud, "did he

Change in a trice
the lilies and langors of virtue
For the roses and raptures of vice?

Gilroy looked startled.

Finch wondered what had made him quote Swinburne, a poet he did not much admire. Then he remembered that it was Templar who had first associated Camilla and Swinburne in his mind.

Laurel is green for a season
And love is sweet for a day.

269

Templar had not recited the next two lines but they must have been in his mind.

But love grows bitter with treason,
And laurel outlives not May.

Finch could see now what the painter had meant.

13

FINCH and Gilroy motored up to the Hall. They turned in between the great wrought iron gates, where the two strange beasts stared down and the interlacing trees made green twilight of the drive.

At the end was a gleam of water like stretched blue silk. Beyond this and over a bridge was a wide gravel sweep and the long lovely façade of the great house.

Carter opened the front door to them. He showed them into a room which overlooked the formal gardens on the south side.

The room was some thirty feet long. Surprisingly enough it was shabby and comfortable. It was full of rich dark colors. The color of calf-bound books, of faded rugs, to a great jar of autumn leaves. And, over all, the flickering mellow light of a wood fire. A door on the far side led into another room.

"This must be the small library," Finch

remarked politely.

Gilroy nodded. "The large library must be quite a room."

They waited. Through the windows they could see the topiary gardens. Dwarf trees, clipped yew hedges, strange beasts and birds and, in the center, a set of chessmen playing out their game on squares planted in two alternate varieties of grass. Beyond these were lawns and ornamental shrubs and trees that grew thicker and thicker until they merged into the great woods of Hammerford.

Finch looked out of a window. He whistled a sad little tune. "I have a feeling that we're going to hate all this cover before we're through."

"You'd have a job to find anyone in that lot," Gilroy agreed, staring fascinated at the chessmen.

The door opened. Hugo Ommanney came in, Lionel Glover at his heels.

"Good evening, gentlemen," he said. "What can I do for you?" He motioned them to sit down. He walked over to the fireplace. Stood there, one foot resting on the steel fender, looking at them coolly and quizzically. He seemed to personify, in an attractive and virile manner, a whole age of cultured leisure.

"I came to Hammerford in the first place because of the strange behavior of its rural inhabitants," Finch explained in his gently drawling voice. "They shut themselves in their cottages. They were evasive. They avoided Wisbeach. They refused to answer questions. Now I find that the reason for all this lies in their conviction that John Marquis is, in reality, your brother, Arthur Ommanney."

Hugo nodded. "I see that we are in the same boat, Inspector. I too, have just learned the same thing — from my cousin here. Though what grounds the villagers have for their extraordinary assumption. I cannot imagine. Lionel seems unable to help me there."

The young man squirmed unhappily under the bold, slightly contemptuous ferocity of his cousin's glance.

"You and your brother were, I understand, great practical jokers?"

Hugo raised an eyebrow. "We were — when we were young men."

"There has been a practical joker at work in the village."

"My brother's efforts were easily recognizable. It was Voltaire who said, 'If God did not exist it would be necessary to invent Him!' We went further. We decided that since God obviously had no sense of humor it was necessary to endow Him with one." A gleam of faint retrospective amusement flitted across the frog face. "It led to some most remarkable results. As the Deity's deputy Arthur had a most inventive mind."

"The person at work in the village shows no invention at all."

"Which the village, no doubt, put down to the injury sustained to his brain in the accident," said Hugo with the greatest possible courtesy.

"No doubt," Finch agreed. He continued, "Does the phrase 'Hello there, Bill Bowman. Same as usual' convey anything to you?"

Hugo's face changed color. "Arthur used to say that."

"John Marquis says it now."

"Someone must have put him up to it."

"It is possible," Finch conceded. "The villagers believe, though, that John Marquis — as we must continue to call him — has recovered his memory. Have you noticed anything to support the suggestion?"

"It never occurred to me for a moment. Sir Robert Keeling, the brain specialist, said that such a thing was virtually impossible."

This sounded a dangerous admission. Finch, though, thinking it over, could see the wisdom, on Hugo Ommanney's part, of carrying on the conversation on the assumption that Arthur's death was not in doubt.

Said Lionel "You don't think that because Johnny lost his memory in a fire getting shut up in that burning barn may have brought it back?"

Hugo looked at him. "You read too many detective stories," he said with tolerant amusement.

"I don't see why it shouldn't be true," Lionel urged. "Anyway we could ask Sir Robert. He was frightfully interested in Johnny's case."

"It'd be a good idea to have him down to look at Johnny anyway."

"You'd have to arrange first for Mr. Marquis to be at home, wouldn't you?" There was something in Finch's voice that made Hugo glance at him sharply.

He walked over to the telephone extension

and dialed a number. "Is Mr. Marquis in?" There was a murmur of words from the other end. A pause followed, during which, Finch thought, Mrs. Hookway must be looking from her window to see if there was a light in Swallow Cottage.

Her voice sounded again. "I see. Thank you." Hugo put back the receiver. He stood for a moment staring down at the machine. Then he said quietly, "Johnny hasn't come home yet."

There followed an odd little silence. As they had talked the darkening sky outside had been taking the light from the room. Now Lionel stirred uneasily. And the shadows, filling the far corners, added their own uncertainties to the scene.

"But Johnny's often away for days on end," Lionel cried. "And anyway he's no more dangerous than — than Carter." He looked at Finch, adding a belated, "Is he?"

"Safer, perhaps, to assume he is. That's why," Finch added placidly. "I've brought you Wisbeach."

Lionel looked startled. Hugo thought of his wife. "Lionel, you'd better see Camilla is safe."

"Right."

"Not a word about Johnny though."

"Of course not."

When the door had closed behind Lionel, Finch said, "Your wife is afraid of John Marquis."

"Many people have an instinctive aversion to the abnormal."

"We traced Mrs. Ommanney to the Isaak Walton at Christchurch."

Here Hugo was vulnerable. His face colored. The color receded leaving him unnaturally white. "Camilla," he said stiffly, "was unhappy with my brother. She had written to ask him for a divorce. No doubt it would have been better if she had told him straight away that she was going to Johnny instead of letting him believe that she was with friends."

"Better, perhaps, if she had stayed at the Isaak Walton to see him."

Hugo shrugged. "It would only have precipitated the row that both she and Marquis had hoped to avoid."

"When did Mrs. Ommanney learn of the accident?"

"That same afternoon. The news that there had been a motoring fatality was chalked up on a news agent's board. Knowing my brother's temper, she had been nervous all day. She bought a copy of the local evening paper and learned that, of the men, one was dead the other reported to be dying."

"Must have been a terrible shock to her," said Finch sincerely. "How was she able to identify the car as her husband's?"

"The front number plate had become detached. The police had it reproduced in the local press in the hope that someone would come forward and identify it. Fortunately Camilla called me up before going to the police. I was able to persuade her to leave the district at once and lie low with some cousins of ours, Bob Ommanney and his wife, who live in Surrey. I told her what I believed to be true. That if the newspapers got hold of the fact that she had left my brother for Marquis the scandal would kill my mother."

"Then you had news of the accident in advance of the police message?"

Hugo smiled thinly. "Beat them by an hour and a half. Camilla telephoned about five o'clock. I didn't dare to speak to Bob on the telephone here. I motored into Market

Stalbridge and called him up from a booth. Even then I was afraid that the operator might be listening in. I introduced myself to Bob by the name I used to be known by when we were both kids. It was all very cloak and dagger."

For a moment Hugo's face looked grey and tired, the skin stretched tight over the bone, so that Finch saw him for the moment as he must have looked that May afternoon. Stripped of his magnificent assurance, torn by the horror of what had happened to his brother and by his love for that brother's wife.

"It's always been rather disconcerting when life has to be accepted on the level of melodrama," said Finch.

"You were going to tell me something about Johnny," said Hugo.

Finch nodded. "It was this. There seems little doubt but that a change has come over John Marquis's mental state during the last few days. I can't say that he has recovered his memory because Dr. Cranley thinks that that is unlikely. What he thinks may have happened — and we must rely on his opinion until we have that of a brain specialist — is that Marquis will have recalled his past only in a very fragmentary and confused manner. Enough perhaps to connect your wife — or yourself — with some unpleasant experience in his past life. He may feel that he owes you a grudge. He may perhaps feel a hatred for you wife." Of the second, and to him far more dangerous idea that there might be someone behind Marquis, he made no mention. "There is nothing really tangible to go upon. And yet the very fact that Marquis has not told anyone of the return of his memory seems ominous."

Hugo nodded. He stared down into the fire so the top of his bullet head and the crisp, lively looking hair was presented to the detective's view. "It seems then," he remarked meditatively, "as if from now on I had better go about armed."

"If you were to kill Mr. Marquis I am afraid that we should look on it as murder," said Finch politely.

Hugo's glance, cool, critical and yet tolerant, swept the two men. "I'll tell you something for your own good. About six weeks ago an elm tree came down in the park. I sent down a portable crane to lift the sawn timber on to a truck. When I went down to see how things were progressing there were two agencies at work, the crane and Johnny Marquis. It was a most impressive sight. No, no! If either of you come up against Johnny take my advice. Either shoot or run like hell."

Hugo saw the two detectives to their car.

"If you or Wisbeach should see anything of Mr. Marquis let me know," said Finch as he slid his inordinately long legs into the space behind the steering wheel.

"We most certainly will," Hugo answered in his pleasant impersonal voice.

Gilroy, about to get into the car, paused. He thought that he had heard a rustling in the shrubs, but very faint.

"The wind," said Hugo, noticing his glance. But his eyes studied the shrubs thoughfully. "It was the wind," he said again. "Good night."

They left him standing before his front door. He was staring once more at the dark clump of bushes on the far side of the gravel sweep. Wisbeach had joined him.

"D'you think it's safe to leave him?" Gilroy asked uneasily.

"I don't think I've ever seen anyone

more capable of looking after himself."

"From the description I thought he must be a bit of a sissy."

"Charles! No one who had met Hugo would describe him in those terms."

"I dunno! Small mouth, curly hair, touch of the exquisite. It might add up to that."

Finch stopped the car outside Wisbeach's cottage. He walked up the path and knocked. Mrs. Wisbeach opened the door. "There's been a message for you from the Ringwood police," she told Finch. "I wrote it down. I was waiting to see you pass before running over with it."

"It's a shame to give you so much trouble," Finch answered. He and Gilroy followed her into the house. "Would you like me to send a man out from Market Stalbridge?"

"Not unless you'd rather, sir. With my husband out I've nothing much to do."

The message from Inspector Dawlish had been written on a sheet of paper and now lay neatly folded by the telephone. Finch was about to pick it up when the telephone rang. Scotland Yard was on the line in the person of one Detective Sergeant

282

Pollick. So far, he reported, they had not been able to unearth anything that could be said to establish the identity of the man known as John Marquis. They had traced his manservant. The only dentist he had known his employer to patronize had been blown up in and with his house, by a flying bomb towards the end of the war. The manservant had said that Marquis had several back teeth filled with gold. He could not remember their number or their precise position. He said that Mr. Marquis must have patronized another dentist since he went regularly but he did not know anything more than that.

They would, no doubt, said Sergeant Pollick, soon unearth the right man.

The police had had one success. They had found out where Major Ommanney had gone on the Wednesday. He had paid a visit to Arthur Ommanney's ex-valet, who was in service in Dulwich (return fare 30c).

This man had admitted reading of the Major's death in the newspapers. He had not come forward for the usual reasons. He had not wanted to get mixed up with the police.

The Major had suggested to him that perhaps Arthur Ommanney was still alive. He had discussed with him whether Arthur had had any habits or mannerisms strong enough to have survived the loss of his memory.

"And had he?" Finch wondered why he himself had not thought of this line of inquiry.

"He used to sing in his bath." The sergeant sounded apologetical.

"Splendid! Show me the man who doesn't."

"He had a passion for French mustard."

"We must try him with some — and some salt on his tail. Was that all this cretinous manservant could suggest?"

"Yes, sir. That's the lot."

"And Sir Robert Keeling, the brain specialist?"

"Taking a holiday in Norway."

"How about John Marquis's uncle?"

"We went around to see him but he was out. Wasn't at his office in the city, either. We're trying again later. There's the War Office, too, sir. They've promised to try and unearth something tomorrow."

Finch replaced the receiver. "Unearth! Unearth!" he muttered fretfully. "Why can't they let me unearth that fellow in the churchyard?" He picked up the sheet of paper on which Mrs. Wisbeach had written the message from the Ringwood police.

Inspector Dawlish had spent the entire afternoon at the hospital where Marquis had been a patient for so long. He had interviewed the doctors and the staff. Not one of them had noticed anything to suggest that Marquis had been wrongly identified. As for his teeth, they had all been extracted. This had been necessary as some new bone had had to be grafted in his jaw. They had not kept any records or casts of the mouth as it had been.

Finch passed the paper to his sergeant. "So that's the answer! Nothing! Nothing at all! Marquis might be the King of Siam for all these fellows know."

"Sure to take a bit of time," Gilroy murmured soothingly.

"Time!" It was a word that now had a sinister notation to Finch. "What time have we to spare — with Johnny Marquis loose in the woods and night coming on?"

He called the Stalbridge police. No, they had no news of the missing man. They had been making inquiries all the afternoon. There were few farms still unvisited. Barns and outbuildings were being searched but so far without success.

Laker came to the telephone. He had been around to see the leading dentist in Market Stalbridge. This man, a Mr. Snow, had been Arthur Ommanney's dentist up to the time when he had gone to live in London. He could vouch for the fact that Arthur had had one gold-filled tooth on the left-hand side and a gap next to it. He could not say anything about the second tooth except that he had not filled it. He would be able to recognize his work, though he hoped that it would not be necessary.

The two police officers talked for a while, comparing notes as to the appearance of John Marquis and Arthur Ommanney. Superficially they had been very much alike.

Finch left his car outside the inn. He had an uneasy feeling that he might want it in a hurry.

He went into the saloon and found it empty but for Wyman. He brought up the subject of John Marquis. He bullied, argued and cajoled the landlord. He emerged from the interview looking shaken.

"Hammerford's obsession isn't as absurd as it sounds," he told his sergeant. "From what Wyman says it appears likely that it *was* John Marquis who died in the accident and Arthur who survived."

He repeated what Wyman had told him.

Gilroy was startled. "I suppose Hugo might have made a genuine mistake," he said doubtfully.

"I'm afraid," said Finch pensively, "that even so his brother would still take a poor view of his carelessness."

They had supper. After it Mrs. Wisbeach ran over to say that Scotland Yard were on the line and would like to speak to Finch.

It was Sergeant Pollick. He had had an interview with John Marquis's uncle. There had been, old Mr. Marquis told him, no means of identifying his nephew. He had described him as 'a body wrapped entirely in bandages.' A creature more than half dead who groaned even under the drugs that had been given him. He had seen his nephew before he left hospital to go down to Hammerford. He had not been able to recognize him. He had not seen him since, Sir Robert Keeling having advised against it.

"He said that his nephew, though much in demand, being a wealthy bachelor and his uncle's heir, was not a society man," Pollick added. "He was a great walker and reader. Went salmon fishing in the spring and early summer and hunted in the winter. He was by nature a reserved, quiet sort of man."

"Liable to go off the deep end?" Finch inquired.

But Sergeant Pollick had not thought to ask. "Sorry about that, sir," he said. Adding consolingly. "You'll be able to ask him yourself, sir. The old gentleman's motoring down first thing tomorrow morning. So he'll be in at the death, as you might say."

Sergeant Pollick was not a tactful man.

Finch and his sergeant walked back to the inn. It was dark now. The leaves rustled overhead in a breath of wind and a chill seemed to have come with the evening.

A shadow moved under the dark trees in the churchyard. In full moonlight it resolved itself into the tall figure of the

Reverend Philip Ommanney. He was buttoned elegantly to the chin in his black cassock. He was progressing towards the church in his own eccentric manner.

The two detectives stopped to watch.

He swooped towards the iron railing that enclosed the old stone vault. Circled a young tree like a morris dancer, his hand touching the spiked fence that protected it from straying cattle or destructive children.

He took a bound on to an unbroken flag and three little shuffling steps on one that was much cracked. He vanished into the black cavern of the porch. A moment later the light was switched on inside the church On, off, on, off. A pause, On, off —

"What is it?" Gilroy asked, staring. "A code?"

"No. The Rector has a thing about lights." Finch was counting the flashes as they came in multiples of four. Sixteen, twenty — The light burnt steadily.

Gilroy shook his head. "For heaven's sake," he muttered.

Finch went upstairs with the intention of writing his report. Instead he crossed over to look from the window. A faint light came from the church and from a lopsided window in a cottage that otherwise was invisible. Apart from this there were only the darkness of the great woods of Hammerford and a rustle of leaves that was like the surf breaking on some quiet shore.

His unique mind projected itself into the quiet churchyard to linger inquisitively before the marble cross which bore the words 'Arthur Bliss Ommanney.' It went through moon-haunted lanes, peered in at the windows of Swallow Cottage. It reconstructed from emptiness and the shadows cast by inanimate objects the figure of a man that leaned across the table, reading with avid eyes the news of a world that had been lost to him for more than two years.

Went on, up the rough track, haunted now by the small scurrying figure of Camilla Ommanney, to stand at last in front of the great silent house. A voice whispered now in his ears. 'About three o'clock . . . Finds a way in . . . No burglar more persistent or more successful.'

Gilroy came up the stairs with his brisk light tread. He knocked and opened the door.

Finch spoke from the window. "Turn on the light, Charles. No! Hang on a minute."

The Rector had emerged suddenly from the west door. He came striding down the path towards the lych gate and went up the road in a great hurry.

"Looks as if he's making for the Hall," Gilroy muttered.

"But what happened in the church to send him off like that?"

Gilroy gave a sudden muffled snort of laughter. "The black paint, sir," he explained. "I was wondering whether Arthur Ommanney used it to write rude words on the church wall."

Finch stared. "You might be right!" he said slowly. "Yes, you may very well be right."

He led the way out of the inn and across the Green to the church.

A single cluster of lights burned high up under the roof of the church. Beneath it lay a pool of light and the shadows streaming away. The silence was intense. Pale tablets hung unrelated in space. Effigies of men and women long dead glimmered wanly in the gloom. And the cold rose up as if from the opening of old graves.

Finch told Gilroy to find the electric light switches and put them all on. His eyes passed swiftly along walls, searching the pews, the shadows, the carved pulpit.

Nothing. No sign of disorder. He walked slowly up the south aisle.

On all sides, on tombs or marble tablets, were recorded the lives of dead-and-gone Ommanneys. The elder sons had been landowners and occasionally statesmen. The younger had been for the most part sailors and soldiers. They had been dashing and efficient since those who had survived to return to Hammerford had, almost without exception, attained high rank. They had been tough, too, for they had lived to a ripe old age even in times when life for the majority had been short, vivid and violent.

Of those who had not returned their tablets recalled old skirmishes and battles forgotten except in the dusty pages of history.

He came on four weeping cherubs, supporting a placque. *Sacred to the memory of Georgina, only child and heiress . . . And wife of Ralf Ommanney. She survived his death for over forty years* . . .

In a side chapel was a great stone with an inscription deeply incised.

Behind this tablet walled in until all eternity
lie members of the Ommanney family

That was all. And the date. *12th November, 1852.* The day Ralf Ommanney had died.

The family, Finch reflected, had been taking no chances.

And then he saw it. Newly painted and glistening. In words roughly printed some five inches high.

IT IS APPOINTED UNTO MEN ONCE TO DIE,
BUT AFTER THIS THE JUDGMENT.

"Charles!"

"Yes, sir." Gilroy came hurrying.

The two men stared at the inscription for a moment in an uneasy silence.

"That accounts for the paint," Gilroy muttered.

"Not rude but ominous," Finch murmured. "What is it, d'you think? A declaration of war?"

"He must have been here," said Gilroy. "Here in the church while we were going about outside."

For answer Finch touched the crudely painted letters. He drew his finger away, wet with paint.

"A good place, really," he murmured. "The Rector was bound to find the message in a matter of hours."

"He might have come in and disturbed the chap at work."

"Not if this were done during the afternoon. It's Saturday. The Rector probably composes his sermon for tomorrow on Saturday afternoon. Arthur — if it is Arthur — would have known."

"But there were other safer ways for him to have threatened his family."

"Yes, more dramatic, too."

Finch had a vivid imagination. Now it supplied him with half a dozen methods to indicate to someone, already on the lookout for signs and portents, that Arthur Ommanney had returned from the grave.

A telephone call in a remembered voice. Some symbol or act peculiar to Arthur. From all accounts he could find his way in and out of the Hall easily enough.

His favorite chair pulled out. The door of his old bedroom opened and the bedclothes rumpled as if he had slept there. His hat on the hall table as if he had just returned and cast it down.

Then why had he chosen this method? Finch's mind busied itself with the inscription. "It is appointed unto men once to die." Arthur had done that. "But after this the judgment." But judgment against whom? Against Hugo? Camilla? Or against the whole family?

And suddenly an icy finger seemed to touch some hidden nerve in his spine. A chilling presentiment crawled through his brain.

He had a mental picture of the Hall drive, dark, silent and gently curving. Empty but for those two. The thin elegant figure of the Reverend Philip Ommanney and the shadow of the man who had come back from the dead.

Finch looked at Gilroy and saw his own fear spread like a contagion to his sergeant.

"The car," said Finch urgently. "We may catch him up."

They turned and raced for the door.

Silence now was gone. Their footsteps clattered, the sound echoing against the walls.

Outside the darkness was complete. The car's powerful head lamps lit up the impassive boles of trees, their vast arching branches and the drive itself, unwinding before them, length upon length of emptiness.

A man stepped suddenly into their path. A tall man, so that for a moment both Finch and Gilroy felt their hearts leap with excitement. The man turned and stared, screwing up his face in the glare of the head lamps.

Finch saw then that it was the man whom he had seen on his arrival at the Ommanney Arms. The man who had advised him to book a room at the Bull in Market Stalbridge.

Finch drew up beside him. "Who are you?"

"Keeper, sir. Spurling's the name." The man was surly. He touched his cap politely enough.

"Seen anything of the Rector?"

"He passed me about five minutes ago."

Finch was startled. "Passed you? Which way was he going?"

"Towards the Hall."

"Then you — ? I see. You passed him and then turned back. Why?"

Spurling answered him sullenly. "I did think that I heard a cry." His eyes were evasive. "There's so many sounds in a wood though. Owls or a small beast caught in a trap. I couldn't rightly tell."

The trees were spaced in such a way that it was useless to try to take the car across the turf. Finch did, however, turn it so that the head lamps blazed into the woods. They lit up the quiet trees, the roughly cut grass, an occasional ornamental shrub. Of the Rector or the man known as John Marquis there was no sign.

The two detectives struck across the grass diagonally. Gilroy was some five paces from Finch.

"You don't think that the Rector did reach the Hall after all?" Gilroy asked under his breath.

Finch shook his head. "Look at Spurling. He heard that cry all right."

The gamekeeper was standing still, watching them with a dark sullen look on his face.

Gilroy gave a sudden exclamation. He

stopped dead in his tracks. "Look there, sir." He pointed to where a sluggish stream made a wide miry path for itself. In the soft mud were the prints of a man's shoes.

"He was running." said Finch uneasily.

"From someone?"

"The devil himself wouldn't have made him do that." Finch turned, following the course of the stream. "Only the one pair of prints. Why should he have run? It was dark, too. Did someone show a light or cry for help perhaps?"

They stood still and listened. The silence was profound.

"Give him a call, Charles. Make it a good loud one."

Gilroy obeyed, shouting the Rector's name.

The tall listening trees gave it back to him in muted echo. There was no other answer.

Finch came to a lump of bracken. It was broken and crushed. When he shone his torch on to it he saw that in one place it was dappled with blood!

The two men began to cast about them, the keeper glowering darkly from a distance.

That the Rector had been attacked and

wounded seemed obvious. It explained, too, the cry that Spurling had heard. But if the Rector had been capable of crying out why had he not called for help?

But then the Reverend Philip Ommanney was not concerned with things of the body but only with those of spirit. That his own body should be in danger seemed perhaps but a small thing compared to the peril in which stood the immortal soul of his assailant.

Gilroy gave a sudden cry. In a clearing sprinkled with bleached branches like a ships' graveyard he had come on a pool of blood and an unlighted torch which told their own tale.

The Rector had fallen. Fallen and not risen again. The trail now was plain enough. Crushed and broken bracken. A path brushed clear of leaves by the skirts of his cassock. Blood —

The two men followed the ominous spattering.

On every side here the yews raised their great bushy head, blue black and faintly smelling. They sprawled upon the ground, were twisted in every shape and size.

They parted and the pale beauty of the

Italian House rose up before the two men. Its windows glimmered in the white stare of the moon as if every room were occupied and every light blazing.

Halfway across the clearing something dark and still was lying. It was the Rector. One arm stretched out in front, a leg was extended behind. His narrow head lay, face downwards, as if death had actually met the crawling man in a head on collision.

Finch fancied that Philip Ommanney died as he knelt beside him. "He's gone," he murmured.

"Damn and blast!" said Gilroy fervently.

Spurling, standing in the open between the yews, gave something that was between a curse and a groan.

The actual cause of death had been a single fierce blow that had crushed in the front of the unfortunate Rector's skull. The trail of blood, though, had come from a deep knife wound in the chest. This would, in any case, Finch thought, have proved fatal.

Standing there he recalled Templar's saying that nothing came easy to the Reverend. And certainly the manner of his death had not been so. Finch had a picture of the dying man driven by his indomitable will almost to his murderer's feet. He had raised himself up — for what? To cry repent? and so had met that last brutal blow.

Finch was aware of a sick feeling of regret and of a cold anger against this callous murderer.

He felt in his pocket. He had detached the key of the Italian House from the Major's key ring before sending the main bunch up to London. Now he gave it to Gilroy, "Ring up the Hall. Tell Wisbeach what has happened. Ask him to check on who's in the house but not to let anyone know what has happened. Tell him to be doubly on his guard."

Half an hour later Finch and Gilroy arrived at the Hall. They had gone out by the iron gate set in the yews at the back. The path emerged from the woods near the edge of the artificial lake.

Finch touched Gilroy's arm. "Look!" he said, pointing.

A haze lay over the water like a shroud. Even as the two men watched it moved forward, ghostly and nebulous, on to the grass and up towards the house.

"That," said Finch sadly, "is just about all this case needed."

Wisbeach saw them coming. He opened the front door.

"How've you been here?" Finch asked.

"All quiet, sir, so far. Mr. Hugo heard you ring up. He asked me if it were anything important. I told him that you had rung to know how things were going. He didn't say anything further. He looked though a bit old-fashioned, as you might say."

"Where were they all when I rang up?"

"It's a bit difficult to say, sir. Mr. Hugo came in through the front door just as I was taking your message. Sir Kenneth came in about ten minutes after that. He volunteered the statement that he'd been walking in the topiary garden, enjoying a cigar."

"You sound a bit skeptical?"

"Well, sir, he'd got something heavy in the pocket of his dinner jacket. I managed to brush against it and it felt to me like a revolver."

"And was Mr. Hugo armed?"

"Yes, sir. Had a 20-bore shotgun."

"And the ladies?"

"Both in the drawing room, sir. They went upstairs a few minutes ago and are still up there."

Hugo came hurrying down the stairs. "What's the news, Inspector?"

"Bad, I'm afraid. The Rector was murdered not half an hour ago while on his way here."

"Uncle Philip? I thought he'd live for ever." It was, Finch thought, an odd sort of remark. "Here! I must have a drink after that."

Sir Kenneth appeared suddenly in the doorway that led from the inner room. Like Hugo he was wearing a dinner jacket. He was smiling, too. "Anything wrong, Hugo?" He nodded a greeting to the two detectives.

"Uncle Philip has been murdered."

"Really? Philip dead? Why that leaves only you and me to represent the main branch of the family."

As Finch refused the drink Hugo offered him he reflected that Sir Kenneth's reaction to his news was even queerer than that of his nephew. He was positively pleased.

"How did it happen?" Hugo asked, glass in hand.

Finch told him.

"That damned place! I'll have it pulled down."

Sir Kenneth's smile became fixed. "You forget, my dear boy, that I intend to live there."

"I still mean to pull it down."

"But I wish to live there."

"Lady Sybil may prefer to live elsewhere."

"I have been put to considerable expense."

"Please send all the accounts to me."

"How nice," said Sir Kenneth with a smile of the utmost ferocity, "to be so rich."

The discussion was being carried on around the unmentionable fact of Lady Sybil's naughty behavior in the distant past. And of Sir Kenneth's belief that, considering the origin of the Italian House, it would, in the interests of justice, be a fitting place of residence for the light woman who was his wife.

The phantom conversation went on. Finch suddenly became weary of it. "You don't have to consider me," he said in his small voice. "I know the history both of the death of Ralph Ommanney and of Lady Sybil's connection with the Major."

The dispute ceased. The two men turned and stared. Sir Kenneth's face became a startling shade of red. His smile grew diabolical.

"How did you find out?" Hugo asked curiously.

"I have been down here since Thursday," Finch offered.

"I consider, Hugo," said Sir Kenneth icily, "that our conversation had better be deferred until some other time." He walked with an odd, stiff-backed walk from the room.

Hugo looked at Finch. His glance was friendly and appraising. He repeated his question. "Tell me, how did you find out?"

"About Lady Sybil? Your wife had to account for the Major's determination not to leave the district. She explained it by saying that he was due at the Applebys' on the following day. Mr. Appleby was annoyed."

Hugo laughed. It was not, though, a particularly amused sound. "Bless her! I suppose it was seeing Appleby's name in the local paper. She could scarcely have made a worse choice," he said. He drained his glass. "What do we do now?"

Said Finch simply, "We must, I think, look to our defenses."

Hugo grimaced to himself. "That's not easy." He went on to enlarge upon the peculiarities and disadvantages of the house. It had no less than eleven recognized entrances and exits. The window latches on the ground floor level were not of any particular complexity and the mist, which was even then rising from the lake, was not going to make things any easier.

"Superintendent Laker could bring up half a dozen men."

"A score could patrol the house and not be noticed. And Johnny has always shown a remarkable flair for getting into the house. He — "

From somewhere upstairs came a wild screaming cry. The sound tore through the house, leaving a startled silence behind it.

"Camilla!" Hugo shouted.

He plunged for the door, Finch and Gilroy following after him.

Carter, his face drained of blood, was in

306

a listening attitude at the foot of the stairs. "The long gallery, I fancy, sir," he gasped. He closed in at the rear. Lady Sybil came from her bedroom.

The scream had not been repeated.

Hugo threw back a door on the first floor. It opened on a long shadowy room Just inside the door lay the body of young Mrs. Ommanney.

"Camilla!" Hugo dropped on his knees. He bent over her. "Fainted," he said a moment later. "Thank God she's only fainted. I'll take her along to her room."

He lifted her up and carried her from the room. Lady Sybil hurried after him.

In some perplexity Finch and Gilroy stared down the long length of the room. Near them a table lamp stood on a small table. A cheerful fire blazed on the hearth. Two chairs were drawn up before it. A book lay open beneath the lamp, a silver paper knife lying on it as if to mark the place. It was a copy of the *Kon-Tiki Expedition*.

Beyond this small oasis of brightness the room stretched away into the shadows for some sixty feet, a vista of dark diminishing furniture and portraits staring dimly from the walls.

"But what made her faint?" Gilroy muttered.

Finch shook his head, frowning. "She was sitting there reading — "

Carter interrupted. "It wasn't her," he said. His face was ghastly.

Finch turned and looked at him. "Who was it?"

The butler's answer brought with it a disturbing suggestion of the abnormal. "It wasn't anybody, as you might say. That far chair was always used by my late mistress, old Mrs. Ommanney. Until she took to her bed this was her favorite place for sitting."

"And the other chair?"

Carter gave a groan. "That used to be Mr. Arthur's. He was reading that book aloud to the mistress that last time he was here."

14

MISS BUSS had been reading. The book though, no longer held her attention. She found her eyes straying towards the entrance to the dark passage which led to the kitchen.

Something had happened to disturb her. She realized that. But what had it been? She sat still, listening.

To the ticking of the clock on the mantelpiece. To the sound of her own heart beating. There was nothing else. The silence was profound. Miss Buss returned resolutely to her book.

She became conscious that she was sitting rigid, curiously receptive to sight and sound in a house that was utterly and completely silent. The fire blazed up suddenly and a dozen furtive shadows moved in the little sitting room. A board cracked in the kitchen.

Miss Buss turned her head sharply in the direction of the sound. She knew that board. It was loose and made a noise if anyone stepped on it. It lay just inside the kitchen door.

Miss Buss was not a nervous woman. That she did not at once walk into the kitchen or call out 'Who's there?' was due to the strangeness of life in Hammerford these last few days. And to the extraordinary immobility of whoever was in the kitchen.

But perhaps no one was there. Miss Buss leaned forward listening. After a moment she fancied that she could hear the sound of breathing.

Out of the corner of her eye she saw something move. She turned her head. A tiny scream tore from her throat.

A man was looking in at her through the uncurtained window. An unknown man, his head wreathed and made indistinct by mist.

The head vanished suddenly. Listening, Miss Buss heard footsteps going round the cottage. In the kitchen the board cracked again. The back door opened. There was a wild scurry of feet in the garden. A crash and then the sound of someone swearing.

Miss Buss ran through the house and out at the back.

The front door of the adjoining house flew open. Mrs. Markham hurried out. "Muriel! What's happening? Are you all right?"

A very young policeman came up the garden path. "I can't find a way out," he said in an aggrieved tone of voice. "I thought I'd got him, but it was only a bush. By the time I'd picked myself up he'd got away. I could hear him on the other side of the hedge making off — and that was all."

"There *is* a weak place in the hedge," said Miss Buss apologetically. "You push and there you are. On the far side."

Mrs. Markham came out of the garden and into that of her friend. "Muriel, what is going on?"

The policeman answered for her. "I saw a man slip around the corner of this house," he said. "I walked up the path. I couldn't hear anything amiss. I looked at the window — "

"You frightened me horribly," said Miss Buss.

Said the constable with relish, "From what I could see, ma'am, you were frightened before that."

"Oh, I was." Miss Buss nodded her head. "You see, I heard someone in the kitchen. I couldn't see anyone though. It was all dark — "

"I can't make head or tail of it," Mrs. Markham declared. "Someone breaking into *your* cottage."

The constable shook his head. "He never broke in. Just opened the door and stepped inside. He knew the house all right. Just as he knew the garden. Not that I mightn't have caught him if it hadn't been for that bush." He turned to look where it rose up, a dark column almost at his shoulder. He saw that there were others, looming up in the mist for all the world like human beings.

Miss Buss hoped that the policeman had not damaged the topiary trees. She felt though that it would seem ungrateful to inquire.

Mrs. Markham looked uneasily about her. "You'd better come back with me, Muriel," she said, "while the constable looks around."

"That's right, ma'am. I'll have a look around and then I shall have to report this." He sighed. Superintendent Laker,

312

he felt, would not be pleased.

Miss Buss, looking back, saw him standing in the path. Already he was scarcely distinguishable from the topiary trees growing up about him in the mist.

Sitting in front of the fire, the two women discussed what had happened. Mrs. Markham was convinced that the intruder had been a thief — though what he could have hoped for from Muriel's cottage she could not imagine. "That young policeman," she said in her authoritative way, "probably made that up about the man knowing the house and garden to explain how it was he got away."

"Perhaps you're right," said Miss Buss placidly. She looked up a moment later and caught her friend looking at her in an oddly speculative way.

"You don't think," said Hilda Markham impressively, "that the man in the kitchen meant to murder you?"

The idea, put into words, seemed so ridiculous that both women burst out laughing.

A bell in the church tower began to toll. The melancholy, eerie sound rang out over the village. Echoing in the high trees.

Finding its way through locked doors and into closed rooms. Setting their occupants crouching nearer to the fire.

Mrs. Markham put down her knitting to listen. "Lionel said that he saw a lot of policemen pass in cars," she said.

"When you think of it," said Miss Buss, "it was odd to find a strange policeman in one's garden."

"But at such an odd time." Mrs. Markham was thinking still of the bell. She looked toward the telephone. "Shall I — ? No, better not, perhaps. Lionel is sure to know when he comes back."

"He is out?"

"Yes, he was working upstairs. The policemen, though, were too much for him. He finds murder even more distracting than Camilla."

The front door flew open. Lionel burst in. "It's the Rector now," he blurted out. "He's been murdered."

"Lionel! You can't — !" Mrs. Markham's voice died away. She was badly shaken.

Miss Buss stared. She shook her head in an incredulous way.

"Can't mean it? It's the police who say so — and old Nixon. Not me. He's in the

church there — all alone. Tolling away."
Lionel shivered suddenly. His eyes were
widely dilated. He had not liked the Rector
but he had known him all his life. Murders
in real life were not like murders one read
of in books.

If only that damned bell would stop. He
tried to close his mind to the sound. To
forget the way the mist had touched his
face like cold trailing fingers. And the
church! Dark where he had expected a
blaze of light, if only to dispel shadows
and ghosts and — murderers.

And the sound of old Nixon's voice
raised to a screaming pitch above the
crash of sound that in itself was like
a blow. "It's for the Rector," he cried.
"The Rector! It's only right. He's dead.
Murdered!" And the bell overhead had
crashed out, drowning them both in a
flood of reverberating sound.

The two women listened intently while
he told them what he had learned. "I didn't
know the bobby at the park gates," he
ended, "but I got quite a bit out of him.
I daresay I could have got him to let me
go in if I'd tried."

"What we want," said Mrs. Markham,

"is a drink. Lionel, be a dear and put on the kettle."

When he had left the room the two women exchanged glances.

"I'm afraid Lionel thought us trivial."

"The young are so intolerant."

"And tea! We ought to be drinking something more dramatic."

"Vodka, my dear. Or absinthe. Nothing less."

Miss Buss's mind went off at a tangent. "It's most odd but I seem to have mislaid the wire frame I use for making a wreath. Not the best one, Hilda. May Ommanney had that. This is one we mended at one side."

"It's sure to turn up," said Mrs. Markham. "You're always so tidy. It can't be far."

"And white flowers. I don't think I shall have enough — "

Lionel had not told anyone of the conversation at the Hall between Hugo, himself and the C.I.D. men. He had liked the sense of power that the knowledge had given him. Now, though, the weight of it was almost an actual pain.

He came in with the tea tray. He put it down on the table, looking at the two women with a sidelong glance. "As a matter of fact," he said in an offhand manner, "John Marquis has got his memory back. At least, if he *is* John Marquis. The police think that Hugo identified the wrong man and that he's really Arthur. Inspector Finch came up to the Hall to see Hugo about it this afternoon."

If he had hoped to cause a sensation he had succeeded. Miss Buss and Mrs. Markham sat frozen, staring. They looked, Lionel thought, quite stupid. He thought it, though in quite a kindly way.

"Lionel, what an extraordinary boy you are!" Mrs. Markham cried. "Why didn't you tell us earlier?"

"As a matter of fact," said Lionel casually, "I guessed it long ago. About Johnny being Arthur, I mean."

Miss Buss sat up very straight. "But it isn't true," she said severely. "Hugo would never do a thing like that."

"I quite agree with you, Muriel. Now if it had been Sir Kenneth who had had the chance. He has always resented the fact that he was a younger son."

"Yes indeed, dear! I've always thought that that was the most dreadful part of that story about him shooting those natives. That one could believe it so easily."

A knock sounded on the front door.

"It's the policeman," said Miss Buss.

Lionel looked at her in surprise. "What policeman?"

"The one who chased a burglar out of my cottage."

Lionel, going to answer the door, turned a moment, grinning. "Really, Aunt Muriel, what a strange woman you are! Why didn't you tell me earlier?" he mocked.

Miss Buss waved a hand to him. "Too demoralized," she said, though it was not true.

Seen in the light, the police constable proved to be a thin wiry young man with a thread of dark moustache. "I've been over your cottage, ma'am," he told Miss Buss. "I couldn't see that he'd taken anything." He reflected that he couldn't see that there had been anything to take. As a matter of form, though, he asked Miss Buss if she had any valuables in the house.

"None at all, Constable. There wasn't a thing to attract a burglar."

The policeman looked at her sharply. The very senselessness of the affair was in itself disquieting. "Better spend the night with friends," he suggested.

"Yes, of course. You must sleep here." Mrs. Markham turned to the policeman. "You don't think perhaps that it was a tramp passing through the village?"

The policeman shook his head. "This was no tramp. He knew that garden like I know my own. He was off in the mist and dark like — like greased lightning, as the saying is."

The telephone rang suddenly and stridently, startling them all.

"Best see who it is," said the constable in a boding voice.

"Of course! What can I be thinking about?" Hilda Markham was shaken out of her usual calm. She took up the receiver. "Hugo! Yes, hold on. She's here." She extended the receiver full length to Miss Buss. "For you Muriel."

The subsequent conversation exhibited all those characteristics so maddening to those who listen to telephone conversations.

"Hugo! I am sorry . . . Yes, most disturbing . . . Has the doctor been? . . . The poor Rector." (That at least was understandable.) "Of course I will . . . That

319

is kind of you . . . Good-by then for now."

Miss Buss replaced the receiver. She turned to meet the battery of three pairs of eyes. "That was Hugo," she said unnecessarily. "He says that Camilla has gone quite to pieces and would I go and spend the night at the Hall."

"Were you thinking of walking, ma'am?"

"Oh no!" She had never liked the drive. "Mr. Ommanney is sending a car for me."

"I'll go with you," said Lionel, delighted. "And bring my gun — in case we're attacked on the way."

"You'll be wanting to get some things from the cottage then." The constable was pursuing his own line with the tenacity of a pedigree bloodhound. "I'll come in and wait while you collect them."

Miss Buss shook her head. "Quite unnecessary," she said firmly.

Miss Buss and Lionel arrived without incident at the Hall. Miss Buss had on a black woollen frock with long sleeves and a most unsuitably scooped out neck. Over this she wore a black homespun cloak. A black and gold silk square was tied over her hair.

320

The chauffeur carried in her night bag. He put it on a chair and went back to his car.

Lionel had his gun with him and was in the wildest spirits.

A few minutes later the Chief Constable arrived. Carter brought in drinks and coffee. Hugo acted the part of host with cool urbanity. Lady Sybil and Camilla stayed upstairs and only Finch was haunted by the thought of the malignant ex-Colonial Governor sitting solitary somewhere thinking out unpleasantness for those who had crossed him.

Colonel Stonor buttonholed Hugo and took him off for a chat. Finch, his long length draped over the back of a high chair, listened while Miss Buss gave him an account of her experience earlier that evening in her cottage.

Lionel, sprawled comfortably in a big leather armchair, was amused and skeptical. Miss Buss herself made light of it. Finch, like the constable, was worried by the seeming purposelessness of the affair.

In the drawing room an embarrassed Chief Constable was trying to get at the truth of the rumors current in the village. He was getting no help from his sardonic host.

"This is bad business," he declared. "A very bad business indeed." And then, after clearing his throat, "About this rumor, Hugo, my boy! If you do think you made a mistake in identifying your brother now's the time to say so. Murder, y'know! Facts are bound to come out."

"I can't see that it makes the slightest difference to you," said Hugo hardily, "whether Johnny is Arthur or not. I can't even see why you should think that he'll come up here tonight."

The Chief Constable looked gloomy. "Fellow's got nothing to wait for," he pointed out. "Can't spend the rest of his life in the woods." He sighed heavily. "Well, no more to be said, I suppose. But it's a bad business. A damned bad business."

Miss Buss and Lionel had gone up to Camilla. Miss Buss came down again. "Mrs. Ommanney wants her embroidery," she told Finch as she bustled past him into the small library.

As she seemed to be there some time, Finch went to see what she was doing.

She had parted the curtains a little at one window and was looking out on the topiary gardens.

There the mist had, in a measure, given ground to the moonlight. The clipped and fantastic yews were swathed but not entirely hidden in mist. They *did* bear a resemblance to human beings, she thought. The kings and queens were giants, of course. But the knights and the bishops —

Miss Buss gave an exclamation of dismay.

"Anything wrong?" Finch asked.

Miss Buss turned, letting the curtain fall into place. She saw the tall detective filling up the doorway. "That wretched man Masters, the head gardener, you know. He's cut down the white bishop after all." She added tragically, "The original white bishop — or so we've always believed."

"Why should he do that?"

"Why indeed? True a dead branch had left an unsightly gap in the Bishop's mitre but he was perfectly healthy. By next spring new growth would have taken the place of the dead wood and could in time have been trimmed perfectly satisfactorily, Oh, it was too bad of him!" Miss Buss struck her hands sharply together in her annoyance.

"The work of centuries gone," she cried, "just to satisfy Masters' ambition to clip a whole new bishop for himself."

Finch wagged a doleful head. "Too bad," he murmured in his soft drawl.

Miss Buss bit her lip. Then laughed. "I'm a ridiculous old woman," she declared. "Now, where is that embroidery frame?"

"How is Mrs. Ommanney?" Finch asked, joining in the search.

"In rather a peculiar frame of mind," Miss Buss rejoined "I suppose it's to be expected under the circumstances."

The missing embroidery frame was found by Gilroy on the floor behind a big chair in which Camilla had been sitting earlier that evening. Miss Buss took it and hurried away.

The two detectives heard Colonel Stonor condoling with her over what he called "the fellow in the kitchen." He spoke heartily and as if he regarded the whole thing as a joke in rather bad taste.

He came into the small library, followed by Hugo. As he did so the smile vanished from his face as if a hand had wiped it off. "That's a queer story of Miss Buss'," he said uneasily.

Finch nodded. "The queer thing is that it happened."

Colonel Stonor glanced askance at him. "A burglar, *d'you think?*"

"Not a chance. Miss Buss had been in next door to supper. Plenty of time for a burglary while she was away."

"But murder! She seems so harmless."

Finch shook his head. "Difficult problem," he murmured. "Still, it did happen."

Colonel Stonor walked over to the fire. "Better decide on a plan of action, eh?"

Finch nodded. "Charles had better see that we're not overheard."

"Histrionics!" Hugo smiled angrily.

"Someone in the house gets around far too easily for my peace of mind," said Finch.

Hugo's face stiffened. "The chairs in the long gallery."

"Your wife saw nothing beyond the chairs and the book?"

"She says that she saw Arthur standing by the door at the far end of the gallery."

"Good God!" said the Colonel. He looked startled.

"Not clearly then," said Finch. "There was only the one table lamp alight."

"How could it have been clear?" asked Hugo. "Arthur has lain quiet enough in the churchyard for two years. Why should he disturb himself now?"

"A trick," Finch mused.

"What else?" Hugo's tone was haughty. His face, though, was grey under its tan.

It was a mad business. Discussing the resurrection of a man long dead in this room where everything breathed of security and the orderly passing of days. But the memory of the powerful figure and faultless profile of the man known as John Marquis kept coming to Finch, so that he could see him all around outlined menacingly against the yellow fire-lit walls. John Marquis or Arthur Ommanney! It mattered little which one was dead.

"We'd better get up more men," said Colonel Stonor uneasily. "We could collect a couple of dozen, though it may take a little time."

"If we do that," said Finch, "we'll drive him back into the woods."

"What's the alternative?"

"To put a guard over the upstairs bedrooms. To achieve his object, which is, I imagine, to kill Mr. Ommanney"

(Hugo bowed ironically), "and possibly his wife, Marquis will be forced to venture upstairs. When he does, we should be able to nab him."

"A bit risky, isn't it?" said the Colonel.

"Anything we do is risky," said Finch. "The whole situation bristles with risk. Chiefly because Marquis seems to have his own way of getting in and out."

"I am quite willing to be a decoy," said Hugo with finality, "but not upstairs. And not confined to any one part of the house. I shall move about freely and if I should meet Johnny I reserve the right, much as I have liked him in the past, to blow him as full of holes as a colander."

"Legally I believe you'd be within your rights," admitted the Colonel dolefully.

Finch put in a plea for what he called 'no wanton spilling of blood' but Hugo Ommanney only smiled fiercely.

"I can't help feeling that it'd be fairer on your wife if you stayed upstairs," said Colonel Stonor.

"If Johnny should fire first my wife will have a son to carry on the name." Hugo spoke stiffly. Both his listeners, though, felt the undercurrent of emotion in his voice. "I mention this because I understand from Mr. Drew that there has been a certain amount of misapprehension about the visit she paid to my mother's bedroom to give her the news on the morning of her death."

Colonel Stonor would have congratulated him, but Finch spoke first. "Who knows of this?" There was an urgency in his voice that made both men glance at him in surprise.

"Only myself. Camilla told me about half an hour ago."

"Good." Finch hesitated. "No, Miss Buss knows." He recalled that lady's parting remark. "And if she has noticed, so may others."

"Does it matter?" Hugo asked.

"It matters so much that if the knowledge gets out your wife may be in the most terrible danger."

"Yes, yes. Can't expect — the murderer to care about the idea," said the Colonel.

Hugo was walking to and fro. Now he stopped and said politely, "By all means, Colonel, allude to him as Arthur if you find it easier."

Colonel Stonor colored. He opened his

mouth to make some hasty remark, then closed it again, the words unsaid.

"I apologize," said Hugo stonily.

"Any idea how Marquis gets in?" Finch asked.

"None — except that I met him several times in the old part of the house. He appeared quite suddenly, too."

"Have you a plan of the ground floor?"

"Yes. There're a whole lot of plans in the tallboy here." Hugo crossed the floor. "The one we want — yes, here it is." He brought it back and spread it out on the center table.

"Good." Finch crossed over to look at it.

"Are we all armed?" Hugo asked. He turned to the Chief Constable. "How about you, sir?"

"I'm quite handy with a pistol, if someone can lend me one."

"I'll get you one from the gunroom." Hugo hesitated. "Perhaps you'd like to come and choose it?"

"No, no. I'll leave it to you." Colonel Stonor spoke rather stiffly. "I fancy I'd be better employed refreshing my mind with a look at this plan of yours."

Hugo went out.

"What's meant by the old part?" Finch asked.

The Colonel pointed. "It's there. The John Ommanney who built the Hall in the reign of the first Elizabeth incorporated the original medieval manor into his plan. The electricity's never been put in. It's dark and rambling. If — " He hesitated over the name. Then substituted another word " — the murderer comes in that way he's playing on an easy wicket."

The library door opened. Hugo came in quite quietly. He closed the door carefully behind him. In spite of this something about him gave an impression of suppressed agitation and alarm.

"At some time during the last two hours," he said, "the gunroom has been broken into. A Colt .45 is missing."

"A heavy revolver then." Finch was thinking of the blow that had killed the Rector.

The Colonel stared at Hugo in dismay. "Now that is awkward," he said. "Damned awkward." He added lamentably, "Arthur was the finest pistol shot I ever saw."

Finch called Gilroy into the small library to study the map. He took him on a northerly circuit of the lower rooms.

Small dining room, the music room, two drawing rooms. As Hugo had said the windows had no particular protection. A pane of glass pushed in to fall silently on the thick carpet. A hand put through the opening. It would be easy enough.

But Johnny Marquis had found a way in through the old part of the house.

Finch opened a door into a small room with paneled walls. Facing him over the mantelpiece was Martin Templar's portrait of Camilla Ommanney, so real, so lifelike that both men stood silent, staring.

She had been painted wearing a yellow gown and a large dipping hat of coarse yellow straw. From under its brim she gazed out with the tragic and bewildered gaze of a lost child.

As Finch looked, the word that had come into his mind when he had first seen her photograph returned. Forlorn, that had been his verdict on the rare and lovely Mrs. Ommanney and as forlorn Martin Templar had seen her. And perhaps because of this he had painted in, as background, a grey and fading landscape of infinite melancholy.

So this was Camilla. This was the secret that Templar had revealed for his own undoing. So that he must remain, expecting nothing, hoping for nothing, half foe, half knight in shining armour.

"The sentimental bastard," Finch murmured.

The humor of the situation struck Gilroy suddenly. He gave a yelp of laughter. "So there's Templar's siren. Think of waiting two years to discover that."

"I can't help feeling," said Finch, "that he must have been annoyed at the time."

They went on.

Down stone passages. Under great stone arches. Through shadows dark as velvet. A door barred their way. It opened on the blackness of the pit, Finch switched on his flashlight. It lit up a bleak stone vault with a grooved roof and squat pillars. An open stone staircase wound upwards in one corner. The windows were small and crooked and an outer door hung askew though it was strong enough for a prison.

The air was cold and damp and smelled

slightly foul. Small dark rooms opened off the main hall.

"If Marquis gets in here," Finch murmured, "he must know of a secret — " He broke off suddenly. Stood tense, listening.

Footsteps had sounded suddenly on the stone steps. They ceased. After a moment they recommenced, light, furtive, retreating now up the stairs. Very faintly there came down to the listeners the creak of a dry hinge — then nothing more.

Finch and Gilroy raced up the stairs. These spiralled upwards to emerge on a wide passage, quiet and empty.

"It might have been one of the family," Gilroy ventured.

"Why run — unless it were Johnny Marquis?"

"Johnny?" Gilroy's thoughts were on that other.

Hugo turned the corner and came towards them. He had a gun tucked comfortably under his arm.

"Did you meet anyone?" Finch asked.

Hugo shook his head. "Should I have done?"

"Someone came up those stairs in front of us."

Gilroy was opening and closing doors, though without much hope. Hugo watched him and eased his gun a little under his arm.

"How do we get back to the main staircase?" Finch asked.

"I was going this way." Hugo opened a door. Its hinge gave a dry squeak as it swung back.

They looked into the long gallery from the opposite end. It was empty. In the distance the fire burned cheerfully. *The two chairs had been pulled out again. Under the lighted table lamp a book lay open.*

Hugo stood staring. The uncanny suggestion of those two chairs seemed to strike him dumb for a moment.

They walked the length of the gallery. They halted and stood staring.

The silver paper knife was back, marking the place in the *Kon-Tiki Expedition*.

The ghosts had read a further twenty-seven pages.

"Nice going," Gilroy murmured. His eyes, though, were uneasy, faintly shocked.

A photograph frame lay on the floor. Hugo bent and picked it up. He glanced at it. "What's that doing there?" he muttered. He set it down on a side table. He looked with an angry face at the two chairs.

Finch stood staring silently at the photograph.

It was of a wedding group. It had been taken outside the West Door of Hammerford Church.

There was the Major, as Templar had described him on another occasion, smiling on a mouthful of teeth like a horse. There was the Reverend Philip Ommanney with his haunted eyes and hollow cheeks. Miss Buss was there smiling with determined cheerfulness. Hugo and Camilla, arm in arm, gave an odd effect of clinging together. Lionel's face could just be seen in the shadowy porch.

"Were those the only guests?" Finch asked.

"They were. The marriage wasn't exactly popular."

"Then the Major and Miss Buss — ?"

"Were the witnesses. The Rector performed the ceremony . . . " Hugo's voice died away as a thought struck him. He glanced sharply at the two detectives. He caught up the photograph, stared at it.

"The Major, the Rector and Miss Buss," he cried, "in that order." He looked across at Finch. There was a strange, almost wild expression on his face. "It seems then," he said, "that the unpopularity of our wedding was not undeserved."

15

TIME seemed to have ceased to exist. Or, at best, to be something marked only on the dim faces of clocks. Hammerford Hall had become a world of its own, a house, fortress and prison all in one. Mist-hung and haunted, given up to a boding silence.

Two police constables walked with echoing tread outside the library windows. Their footsteps rang out monotonously on the still air and the mist pressing against the windows gave curious suggestion of isolation and mystery to the house's many rooms.

Inside, the lights blazed and fires roared up the chimneys. Candles were clustered at strategic points, so that the place could not be given over wholly to darkness should the power fail for any reason.

In her bedroom Camilla, in a pale blue satin rest gown, whiled away the night hours playing cards in company with Lady Sybil and Miss Buss.

The chauffeur dozed in a comfortable chair outside the maidservant's room, a gun across his knees. Carter appeared at regular intervals like a comet, with coffee and sandwiches and to make up the fires.

Two more policemen walked the passages outside Camilla Ommanney's bedroom door and Laker, who had brought them to the house, visited them, as well as the two outside, at regular intervals.

Hugo, after the finding of the photograph, had shut himself up in his bedroom. Lionel indulged in a series of sorties and planned ambushes in the furthest corners of the great house. Sir Kenneth, in a dark blue dressing gown, passed like a malignant cloud, a smile of the utmost ferocity on his face and a pearl-handled pistol in his hand.

No one method was more successful than the other. Johnny Marquis — or Arthur Ommanney — seemed to come and go as he pleased.

Doors opened and closed. Footsteps broke out in rooms that, an investigation, proved empty and dust-sheeted. A vase fell from a niche in the music room and all the doors in a disused wing banged one after another.

One o'clock, two —

An owl hooted quite near the house. The stable cats began a quarrelsome courtship beneath the drawing room windows.

Finch, walking with Gilroy, halted by one of the windows. "What was that?"

"I didn't hear anything."

They stood listening. There was nothing. The silence remained unbroken.

"I thought that I heard a voice outside calling," said Finch slowly. He turned and led the way downstairs.

They went out by the front door. Stepped into the thin faintly luminous mixture of moonlight and mist.

A man was standing at the corner of the house looking towards them. Finch flashed the light of his flashlight on and moved off in an agreed signal. The man did the same. He did not move, since he stood at the limit of his beat, but waited for Finch to join him.

"Anything wrong?" Finch asked.

"I don't know, sir." The man was doubtful. "I thought I heard someone calling down there by the lake."

"Calling what?"

The constable coughed. "It sounded like 'Arthur,'" he said apologetically, for he had heard the rumors, "but I may have got it wrong."

The three of them stood still, listening and peering into the mist. A wall of silence hemmed them in, palpable as the shifting vapor. No sound but that of their own breathing and the mournful drip-drip of moisture from a nearby shrub.

Then suddenly, startling them, came the cry of a human voice. "Mister Arthur! Where are you?"

"That's it," said the policeman uneasily. "That's what I heard."

Finch caught Gilroy's eye. They moved quietly in the direction of the sound. The voice was silent. The constable at the corner of the house receded from view. The lights from the house faded. There was left now only the shifting wall of vapor. It moved with them like a tent. The same white walls, grass underfoot, the bole of a tall tree.

The voice that had fallen silent spoke suddenly almost at Finch's elbow. "Mister Arthur," it said, whispering. And then,

"Mister Arthur, is that you?"

The landlord of the Ommanney Arms stepped suddenly into view.

In the rose and white bedroom Camilla threw her cards down on the table. Lady Sybil and Miss Buss exchanged troubled glances. It had been impossible for them not to be aware of the change the hours of waiting had made in their hostess. The pinched face, the fever-bright distracted eyes, the wandering attention.

Now she pushed the loose hair back from her face with frantic hands. "All my life," she said in a high, reed thin voice, "I've wanted only one thing. To be ordinary. I begged and begged Arthur to settle down, but he wouldn't. He liked being popular. And the more people he knew the more popular he felt. He liked living in a luxury hotel, too, and throwing money about. He and the Major — they both liked it. Throwing money about, I mean. It was Uncle Andrew's money. But they knew Aunt May had plenty more.

"They liked my being notorious, too. I don't suppose either of you know what it's like to be notorious." The wild bright eyes

341

sought those of her guests. "No," she said with finality, "you wouldn't know. But you can take it from me, it's just hell. That's why I decided I couldn't bear it any longer. I'd met Johnny by then. He was quite different from Arthur. He liked books and being quiet. He liked children and I did so want some. He was jealous, too. He'd say. 'Camilla, if ever you let me down I'll kill you.'"

She smiled brightly around her. "That's why it doesn't really matter to me whether Johnny is Arthur or not. But it'll matter to my baby if he's ever born. He'll be notorious like his mother. A bastard, too, poor little thing. Hugo shouldn't have done that. He should have thought of my baby. I told him that. I knew I'd have one if only I could feel safe. Safe in my mind, I meant — "

"Camilla, I'm sure you're wrong about Arthur." Miss Buss spoke earnestly. "Hugo would never have pretended that Arthur was dead. He — "

"Oh yes he would," Camilla interrupted. "He told me so. He said he'd marry me if he had to kill Arthur to do it. And Hugo always tells the truth. Not like Lionel and me. We hardly ever do. But that's because we've never felt secure. People without background of their own can't afford to tell the truth. They pretend. Pretend to be happy. Pretend to be satisfied. Pretend they haven't done things they have . . . " The thin reedy voice ran on.

Miss Buss looked across at Lady Sybil. "A doctor," she breathed at her, nodding her head. She said aloud, "What we want it a cup of tea. I'll tell Carter to bring some up."

Unfortunately Miss Buss had the intellectual type of mind that, quite literally, did not believe in violence. She traveled in railway carriages in company with a lone man without a thought of being raped. She could hear unmoved a solitary walker overtaking her in a quiet lane.

Finch's warning made no more impression on her mind than a gypsy's prognostication of ill fortune.

She ignored the remonstrances of the two policemen. "Mrs. Ommanney needs a doctor," she said firmly. She walked down the stairs and along to the telephone room.

She rang up Dr. Cranley, who said that

he would dress and come out immediately. It was characteristic that she quite forgot to mention that Hammerford Hall was virtually in a state of siege.

She crossed the hall and rang the bell by the fireplace. No one came. She rang it again with a like result. Carter, then, had retired for the night. She knew where the pantry was situated. She decided to make the tea herself.

At this point it did strike Miss Buss, that considering the number of people about, the place seemed singularly deserted.

As she passed the foot of the stairs she caught sight of Sir Kenneth looking down at her from the landing. She waved to him but he only made a singular grimace in answer and vanished. His head had only come just above the balustrade in any case.

She pushed open a baize door. A long bleak passage lay in front of her. For the first time some faint misgiving seized on Miss Buss's mind. She banished it resolutely. She walked down the passage.

It seemed very long and once or twice she could have sworn that she was not alone, though from where or for what purpose she was being spied upon she did not know — or would not accept.

She opened the door into the pantry. The light was on here and for a moment this disconcerted her with its suggestion that the room was already occupied. She remembered though, that the lights had been on everywhere.

She picked up a kettle and took it into the adjoining room. This was known as the flower room. Here there was a sink and a coldwater tap. There were long trestle tables and shelves and built-in cupboards full of vases and bowls and flower holders of various types.

Miss Buss had put out a hand to turn on the tap when she saw it.

The crushed and mangled wire frame that had been found in the churchyard. It had been mended in one place. Miss Buss could not mistake her own handiwork.

This, then, was her missing frame.

In that moment of heightened sensibility Miss Buss's brain worked clearly and with surprising speed. Even so, the conclusion to which it came was reached only just in time.

Footsteps were approaching along the corridor.

Miss Buss turned the tap full on in the hope that the running water would drown the sound of the window opening.

The news of Miss Buss's disappearance caused consternation. Lady Sybil was the first to be worried. Where was Muriel Buss? She whispered the question to one of the men on guard. He passed it on to Wisbeach, who raced downstairs and told Laker.

The Superintendent hurriedly assembled his forces. Colonel Stonor, Lionel, Wisbeach, Carter (the butler had been on the top floor chatting to the chauffeur), himself — Sir Kenneth — was nowhere to be seen.

"Mr. Finch and his sergeant are in the grounds somewhere, sir," Wisbeach said. He had heard the news from one of the men on duty outside.

Laker grunted. A fine time to be away. He and the Chief Constable decided on a plan of campaign. Lionel, though, did not wait. He went hurrying, white-faced, from room to room calling "Aunt Muriel" in a distracted manner.

Sir Kenneth appeared. He had, he admitted, seen Miss Buss leave the hall and go down the passage leading to the kitchen.

"But why didn't you stop her?"

said Colonel Stonor. "You knew it was dangerous."

"I never liked the woman," said Sir Kenneth blandly. He stood there, swinging his pistol around on one finger and exuding malevolence.

Laker stared at him, shocked and incredulous.

The hunt began. The searchers were oppressed by their knowledge of the complexity of the great house. Haunted by Lionel's voice still calling, the sound running in front of them like their own thoughts made audible.

It was Colonel Stonor who heard the tap running. He and Laker went to investigate.

"Must have been struck down as she turned on the water," said the Colonel in a hushed voice. He turned off the tap and the silence was glacial.

The Superintendent felt that their search was over. His heart was heavy as he bent to open the cupboard doors.

Miss Buss was not in any of them.

Both men turned and looked at the window. It was unlatched. "Probably pushed her through it." Colonel Stonor felt that this time they had the solution.

Miss Buss, however, was not lying outside the window.

Laker called the others. The search was transferred to the garden. Here it was more difficult. Trees and shrubs were shrouded in mist. Recurrent yew hedges and dim green alleys made it difficult for those unfamiliar with the garden to be certain that they were not traversing the same ground over and over.

A policeman spoke to the Colonel. "I fancied just now that one of those shrubs moved, sir," he said. His voice was uncertain.

"The chessmen?" Colonel Stonor declared.

They had all walked across the board. Still — He turned, moving between the rival sides. "Eight pawns," he muttered. "Castle, knight, bishop, king, queen, bishop, knight, castle."

He was not an imaginative man but his spine was crawling. They looked, he thought, if not human then near enough to be disconcerting. He turned about, counting the pieces of the other side under his breath.

'Eight pawns, castle, knight, bishop, king, queen, bishop, knight, castle.'

Damn fool that policeman was! Not

exactly his fault though. Colonel Stonor moved off the chessboard.

Miss Buss felt quite faint with relief. This, though, was no time for fainting. She could not even put her head between her knees. 'Now if only I had been one of the lizard-like creatures crawling over a globe,' she told herself, 'I could have fainted quite comfortably and no one been the wiser.'

She was feeling slightly lightheaded. But then, she thought, it *was* disconcerting when one's would-be murderer had passed quite close to one. Might even, she acknowledged to herself, have spotted the deception and be awaiting a more propitious chance to return.

Finch came back to the house.

In the hall the fire was almost out. Carter was snuffing the guttering candlewicks one by one. "We've run out of candles, sir," he said apologetically, turning a grey face.

"What's happened?" Finch asked him. He threw his hat down on a side table, where it lay looking in that bleak place rather like a dead vulture.

"It's Miss Buss, sir," said Carter. His face twitched in a sudden spasm of nerves.

"She's disappeared. Seems as if she must be dead. We've called and called but she doesn't answer."

As if in eerie confirmation of his words there came floating down the stairs the voice of Lionel Glover. "Aunt Muriel!" it called "Aunt Muriel!" And the walls gave back the name. "Aunt Muriel! Aunt Muriel!" they echoed, faintly mocking.

Finch held a consultation in the small library with the Chief Constable and Laker. Then he went upstairs to see Hugo. In each case Gilroy waited outside the door to see that no one overheard the conversation.

Wisbeach was sent to find Lionel.

In the hall Colonel Stonor was speaking. His ruddy face showed signs of strain. His voice rose as he spoke, as if it were not entirely under control.

"I'll ring up for more men," he said. "When they get here we can make a thorough search for poor Miss Buss. In the morning I'll have the troops over from Charbury Heath. They can go through these damned woods and the house until they do find Marquis." He added feelingly, "I wouldn't endure another night like this, no, not if Her Majesty the Queen were to decorate me for it every morning before breakfast."

"But it'll be hours before the extra men get here and we begin looking again," Lionel protested. As no one spoke he turned and went off to continue the search by himself.

Hugo laughed. He seemed to have taken new heart from the discouragement of the others. "Give him time," he cried. "Johnny Marquis never appears until around three o'clock."

Colonel Stonor looked up at him where he stood on the stairs above. "It lacks twelve minutes to the hour," he said bleakly. He turned and walked away in the direction of the telephone room.

A door opened upstairs. There was a confused babble of sound. Camilla appeared at the head of the stairs. She came darting down. The small pale face was haggard. The green eyes were glinting and distracted. "I can't bear being shut up any longer," she said in an exhausted voice. She cowered over the dying embers of the hall fire as if her body were immune to its heat.

Lady Sybil followed her down the stairs more slowly.

351

"The hall is hardly the safest place in the house," said Colonel Stonor, returning.

"From Arthur?" Hugo laughed. "I tell you he's dead. Quite dead now."

And softly and deliberately in the silence that followed footsteps could be heard approaching across the parquet floor of the drawing room. Instinctively they all turned to face the sound. Camilla's face was ghastly.

"Who's there?" Hugo asked sharply.

Laker marched across the hall. He threw open the drawing room door, pressing it right back. "No one," he said. "Nothing but an empty room."

"Arthur was always fond of that room," Camilla said. She shivered suddenly.

"Arthur's dead," said Colonel Stonor uncomfortably.

"Of course." Hugo smiled bitterly. The sad little conversation faded and became part of the silence.

"It's nearly three," said Lady Sybil. She shivered. The room now seemed dominated by the slow ticking of the grandfather clock. The small sound was like an inexorable whisper in the silence. Seven minutes to the hour. Six —

Sir Kenneth stalked in. He looked at the group by the fire with an envenomed stare. "I hear that Camilla is pregnant," he said loudly. "I congratulate you, Hugo."

"Kenneth!" cried his wife in sharp protest.

"Damn you, Uncle Kenneth!" cried Hugo furiously. "D'you want to kill Camilla?"

"My dear boy! What a suggestion." Sir Kenneth smiled savagely.

Lionel came down the stairs. "Why don't you do something?" he cried. "Just waiting — " He made a nervous gesture, nearly dislodging a standard lamp which stood on a table close at hand. His own clumsiness seemed to upset him. He fell silent, peering uncertainly, his face anxious.

The tension was growing. Fear had stretched to every corner of the great bleak room.

The clock struck the hour. It was three o'clock.

Carter burst into the room. He was the image of terror.

"He's coming!" he shrieked. "He's coming!"

"Who's coming?"

"Mr. Marquis. I saw him."

"Which way?" Colonel Stonor demanded.

"There! There!" The butler's fingers stabbed the air in the direction of the passage up which he had just come. It was one that led from that ancient and unlighted portion of the building that Johnny Marquis had made his own.

In the deathly silence that followed on the butler's screaming voice footsteps could be heard approaching.

There was now in the passage an unaccustomed gloom. Details were blurred or lost completely. Only a few surviving candles burned somewhere out of sight in a faint and wandering manner. And past that light and into the gloom beyond the footsteps walked.

A tall figure appeared dimly in the passage. Recognizable chiefly for the leather-patched coat, the pork-pie hat, the broad shoulders —

The lighting failed suddenly. Darkness swooped in the hall. Except for Lionel the far end of the room was empty — and it was from that end that the danger threatened.

Laker stood before the fire, peering down the length of the hall, adding to the shadows and dimming still further the faint light of the dying fire. Colonel Stonor moved to interpose his body between Lady Sybil and possible danger.

Camilla scrambled to her feet with a scream of terror. Hugo hurled himself towards her, carrying her in his rush toward a door on the far side of the fireplace.

The figure of the intruder stood motionless for a moment, as if enjoying the sudden panic. Then Lionel moved. Sprang forward.

"Take care! Camilla!" It was like a battle cry.

A big-caliber revolver barked hideously again and again. It sounded in that confined space like the thunder of ships' guns. A confused and furious fight broke out at the end of the room. The plug of the standard lamp was jerked from its socket. Reinforcements appeared from the library.

The big-caliber gun spoke again. Then fell, slithering away across the polished wood floor to come to rest under a great oak chest. Chairs were scattered. A grandfather clock toppled forward its face and all its works jangling and banging.

A table was overturned.

Dr. Cranley drove up to the Hall. Getting no answer to his ring, he opened the front door. The murderer, seeing the moonlight beyond, made a last bid for freedom. He threw off his assailants and bolted for the opening. He struck at the man who appeared suddenly to bar his passage and his pursuers were on him again. They all fell in one savage heap on the threshold.

There was a click. "Got him!" panted a voice out of the dark. And then "Lights! Can't we have lights?"

They came on as suddenly as they had failed. The seething mass broke up into its component parts. Gilroy with his captive, one of the Market Stalbridge men, Wisbeach — Dr. Cranley staggered groggily to his feet from beneath them all.

The two police officers and Sir Kenneth came hurrying down the hall.

Lionel Glover, gasping and wild-eyed, stared incredulously at the handcuffs on his wrists. "But it was Johnny," he cried. "You've got it all wrong. It was Johnny Marquis."

"Mr. Marquis isn't here," said Finch.

Lionel turned, staring incredulously.

The man in the leather-patched coat was Finch's own sergeant, Charles Gilroy.

Lionel sprang at him. "I'll swing for you, too," he screamed.

When things had quieted down again Colonel Stonor said thankfully, "No casualties? That's good."

Dr. Cranley came in from the grounds, where he had been spitting out two front teeth. His collar had burst from its moorings. There was a rapidly swelling lump on the back of his head. "What about me?" he asked bitterly. "What would you call me?"

Sir Kenneth cackled unfeelingly. "I'd call you damned lucky," said he. "My brothers were the last to get in the way of the juvenile delinquent and they're both dead."

In the safety of the passage Hugo paused to listen. He smiled grimly. From the sounds coming from the room which they had just left it seemed that the furniture was to be the main sufferer.

There was a bar of light shining under the drawing room door for that room was on a different electric circuit. He pushed open the door.

A tall handsome man in his shirt sleeves

rose from one of the deep armchairs. His gaze was friendly, smiling, a little quizzical.

Camilla saw him. For a moment she stood frozen. Then she moved slowly, uncertainly forward. "Johnny!" she whispered incredulously. "Johnny is it you?"

Marquis smiled. "No one else," he said gently.

"Johnny! Johnny!" She fled across the room to him. Throwing her arms about him. Crying, pressing her wet cheek to his shirt. "It *is* you! And I've been so frightened, so terribly frightened."

He held her tight. "Not of me, Camilla. Never of me."

"I was! I was! I thought," she added confusingly, though both men knew what she meant, "that if you *were* Arthur I wouldn't be married to Hugo at all and Baby would be a bastard. And that if you *were* you, you were angry because I'd married Hugo."

"Oh, Camilla!"

She laughed shakily, rubbing the tears from her cheeks with the back of her hand. "That's just what you used to say. 'Oh, Camilla!'"

Above her head the eyes of two men met. It was, for them, an oddly emotional moment.

Hugo smiled. "Hello, Johnny!" he said. He held out his hand.

16

FINCH walked in the topiary garden. The dark clipped hedges towered above him. Peacocks, lizards, dancing bears, mist-hung and fantastic, hemmed him in. He came to the chessboard and walked between the opposing factions. "Bishop's move, Miss Buss," he said in his small voice.

One of the white bishops stirred. Moved from its square against the towering white queen. "Is it all over?"

"Yes. No one was hurt." Finch thought of the once dapper Dr. Cranley. "At least, not fatally," he amended. "Lionel, though, was caught red-handed."

"Lionel!" Miss Buss shivered. She looked at the strange ranks of her late companions. "Isn't that odd? I was so angry with Masters but if he hadn't cut down the white bishop . . . " Her voice trailed away light as the mist that swallowed it up.

"Colonel Stonor tells me that he came out here and called you by name."

"He did. But Lionel was there, in that opening in the hedge, looking in all directions. He would have killed me long before I could have reached the house. He is a first-class shot."

Finch nodded. The Ommanneys, he thought, were far too fond of firearms. "Tell me what happened to you. But first, how about going somewhere warmer?"

"Into the Hall?" Miss Buss shook her head. "Besides, I must get back to break the news to Hilda."

They fell into step, pacing slowly towards the front of the house.

Miss Buss told her story. "And then," she ended, "I saw that wire frame. The Rector brought it up to show Hugo. I knew that it had been found in the churchyard. But, looking at it, I saw that it was one that I had missed from my cottage. I rememberd how I had seen Lionel come out of the workshop on the afternoon of May Ommanney's funeral. And how I had gone in to clear up after him. There had been an old torn pink silk curtain lying on the bench and one or two threads caught in the vice. I wondered at the time what he had been doing. When I saw my wreath frame I knew; for there were a couple of tiny strands of pink silk caught in the wire."

"I see. He had used the curtain to wrap around the wire frame so that it didn't show any marks of having been in the vice," said Finch. He added slowly, "I never thought of a substitute wreath." It had been a clever idea. It had not only given the impression that the wreath had been destroyed by someone of maniacal strength but it had shortened the time that Lionel had had to spend in the churchyard. He had only to scatter the flowers and trample on the other three frames.

"Of course," said Miss Buss, "it wasn't only the wreath. There was the man in my kitchen. So immobile. Lionel had trained himself to stand like that when he was taking his photographs of bird life. And besides he was always bitterly resentful of the fact that Arthur and Hugo were sons of the house and that he was not. That was why May and Andrew always made such a fuss of him. To make up to him for not being their son, I mean."

Finch glanced at her quickly. "So that was what Mrs. Markham was alluding to when she said that only unhappiness could come of his habit of hanging around the Hall. I thought she meant that he was in love with young Mrs. Ommanney."

Miss Buss shook her head. "Lionel loved only himself," she said sadly. "He was so attractive, though, that none of us thought of him as being really bad."

Except Sir Kenneth, Finch reflected. He put Miss Buss into a police car, a small, shaken and yet dignified figure. He waved in farewell and Miss Buss waved back.

The car moved off and the sound died away. There were now only the shifting mist, the tall trees and the great house which Lionel had coveted so bitterly and so long. It rose up behind Finch, ghostly and beautiful in the moonlight and with the lights shining again from its many downstairs windows.

In the hall Gilroy, Wisbeach and two of the Market Stalbridge men were still busy. An air of cheerfulness pervaded the scene.

"Lucky that meat's off the ration," said the Colonel, catching sight of Wisbeach's fast discoloring cheek. "Your wife'll have to put a bit of raw steak on that bruise."

Wisbeach grinned cheerfully. He touched the place lightly with his fingers. "It was worth it, sir." Though he did not realize it, his cheerful pugnacity had done more to arouse the Chief Constable's interest in him than any amount of devotion to duty.

"You fellows certainly had all the excitement," the Colonel remarked.

"We must have looked like hens when a fox is raiding the roost," said Laker sadly. He thought that he had played a poor part.

"Hens?" Colonel Stonor shook his head. "It took a gamecock to act as a fire screen when there was shooting going on. You were the most tempting target I've ever seen. Damme! I nearly potted you myself."

Laker's face was suffused with a deep reluctant color. He had thought little of the risk, only envying the younger men their rough-and-tumble with the murderer.

Finch came in from the garden.

Colonel Stonor went to meet him. "Miss Buss all right?"

Finch nodded. "I took the liberty of sending her home in one of your cars, sir."

"Quite right! Quite right! Know what we found in young Lionel's pocket?"

"Possibly a bottle with about thirteen phenobarbitone tablets in it. And certainly a glove of some sort."

"That's it. An old leather glove. After he dropped the gun he must have managed to get it off and into his pocket."

"Lionel didn't mean there to be any other fingerprints on the gun when he pressed Marquis's fingers around it." Finch added with a faint touch of grimness in his voice. "He may not have been as careful when he tampered with the lights."

Gilroy grinned. "There's a lovely impression of his fingers on the bulb and a rather blurred print on the sixpence we found under the bulb."

Colonel Stonor shook his head. "My education's been neglected," he declared. "I never knew you could fuse electric lights so efficiently." He looked at Finch. "How about getting Marquis's story, eh?" He lowered his voice. "Young Mrs. Ommanney has gone to bed. She went all to pieces when she realized that Lionel was the murderer. The doctor has had to give her an injection to keep her quiet. Seems that Lionel was around under her window that night and that she told him where the Major was sleeping."

Hugo Ommanney and Marquis were sitting in front of the fire in the drawing room in a companionable way. They spoke or were silent as they pleased. Marquis's dependence on Hugo was gone. But the strangely forged bond between them still held.

Finch looked at them with interest. 'David and Jonathan,' he thought. Like most men, he was a sentimentalist at heart.

"How's your wife?" Colonel Stonor asked.

"Gone off to sleep. Aunt Sybil's sitting with her until I go up."

Colonel Stonor drew a deep breath that was almost a groan. "Bad business that. Shock to the nervous system, eh? Still, might have been worse."

The door opened and Sir Kenneth came in. He seemed not at all put out by the coldness of Hugo's reception.

For a few moments, while everyone was being settled and supplied with drinks, the conversation was general. Soon, however, it reverted to the murders.

"You guessed that Lionel was responsible?" the Colonel asked Hugo.

"Not," said Hugo grimly, "until I caught sight of his face as the lights failed. But what on earth induced him to do it?"

"It was your mother changing her will," Finch answered. "However much Lionel Glover coveted this place it was no good to him without the money. But with the money — ! There were four lives between him and the property. Five, if he had but known. He was willing to spare Sir Kenneth. It would look better and besides, he was a sick man."

"But the others," said Hugo, "were — well, middle-aged and they had no sons to inherit. Why not just have killed me?"

"The answer to that," said Finch drily, "can be seen on the tablets in Hammerford church raised to your family. Lionel didn't mean to wait another twenty or thirty years for his inheritance. It was difficult, though, for him to see how to proceed and yet not be suspected. Then Mr. Marquis was rescued from a burning barn and that gave Lionel an idea. He was a great reader of detective fiction. And in a book there's the story of a man who lost his memory in one fire and regained it after being involved in another. This was only fiction but he felt that he could sell the idea quite successfully. He knew from Camilla that Mr. Marquis might be supposed to have a grudge against the family. It was only later that a more daring idea came to him. To make people believe that it was Marquis who had died in the motoring accident and Arthur who had survived. Arthur, if he were alive, really would have cause to start a vendetta. Furthermore he would have the sympathy of the village behind him. We saw the advantage of this to the murderer in Spurling's half-hearted search for the Rector, whom he had heard cry out when Lionel stabbed him."

At this Hugo's expression boded no good to his gamekeeper.

"From these beginnings," Finch continued, "was evolved the idea of murdering all those who had attended Camilla's second wedding. True this would necessitate the murder of Miss Buss. Even so the advantages from Lionel's point of view far outweighed its disadvantages. Her murder would seem so senseless, so outrageous that even the wildest of motives would be considered, and if no one thought of the right one then Lionel was all ready to help with his photograph of the wedding group planted in the long gallery. Here, though, he was unlucky since, when ured us there, Mr. Ommanney was with us. His remark of 'What's that doing here?' betrayed the fact that the photograph did not belong there but had been planted for me to find."

"Was that what you saw in it?" Hugo demanded. "Not that my wedding guests were doomed but that Lionel was the murderer?"

"Exactly! I'd had the idea for some time that if Marquis were indeed the murderer, then he was being prompted to violence by someone else. My mistake was in thinking that the someone else was Sir Kenneth."

"You flatter me," said Sir Kenneth sardonically, though Finch did not think that he had — at least, not in the sense that the ex-Colonial Governor meant.

"I had recognized my mistake, though, when I first saw the two chairs pulled out and the book opened in the long gallery. Sir Kenneth and his wife had been abroad so long that it was highly unlikely that he would have known that his sister-in-law and her son were in the habit of sitting there — and more than unlikely that he would have known that Arthur had been reading the *Kon-Tiki Expedition* aloud when he was last home."

"But why did you fix on Lionel?" Hugo persisted.

"Because right from the start two things struck me as important, the outbreak of trivial practical jokes and the death of Mrs. Ommanney. And yet when I considered them, they seemed to be in reverse order, as one might say. First came the practical jokes and then the death of the woman of fortune. Yet I felt that they must be connected. Now, looking at Lionel lurking so appropriately in the background of that photograph, I realized that he was perfectly placed to have discovered the contents of the old lady's will, which was drawn up a month before her death. Then again, Lionel was tall and broad-shouldered. He could have impersonated Marquis had he wished. He knew Arthur's voice and his mannerisms."

Here Hugo glanced sharply at the detective. But Finch did not elaborate the point, since the explanation would come later from Marquis.

"Lionel was on good enough terms with the villagers to be able to hint that Arthur was still alive. And though it may be true that we are all capable of murder, Lionel was a recognizable type. He was conceited, self-centered, charming, unscrupulous and utterly callous. The annals of crime are littered with names of men of a like disposition.

"I realized then that, with the Major and the Rector dead, only Hugo Ommanney stood between Lionel and his desire to be recognized as the heir to the Hammerford estate. I knew then who it was who had taken the black paint and the phenobarbitone tablets, and to what use the latter were being put. I remembered that Wisbeach had mentioned some concrete pillboxes in the woods. I was wondering how I was to find them when I heard Wyman down by the lake calling on Arthur Ommanney to answer him."

"And you hadn't suspected Lionel before?" Colonel Stonor asked.

"Yes I had. Right in the beginning. When Lionel tried to explain away Sir

Kenneth's name for him — the juvenile delinquent. It's a curious thing about nicknames," Finch added meditatively. "If they are bestowed jokingly and in kindness the recipient will accept them in the spirit in which they are given. But Lionel, by going out of his way to bring up the subject, betrayed the fact that something unsavory lay behind his nickname."

Sir Kenneth nodded. "Old Drew, the solicitor," he explained, blandly disregarding Hugo's movement of protest, "rang up and complained that Lionel had been stopping late at the office and examining letters and documents that had nothing to do with him. I couldn't get the others to take the matter seriously though."

"We were too used to Lionel's inquisitiveness," said Hugo.

"Which extended, I suspect, to Mrs. Ommanney's will," said Finch drily. He was recalling the rather curious and precise choice of words with which Mr. Drew had answered his inquiry as to who knew about the contents of the will. He added, "Of course, as you are all now aware, Lionel's final plan was quite simple. It was to

372

release Marquis, wait for him to appear in the hall in search of Hugo, then under cover of darkness, shoot Hugo and Camilla Ommanney," (Finch avoided stressing this last name in deference to Hugo's feelings. As it was his brows darkened ominously as he recalled Sir Kenneth's treachery.) "using the gun that he had stolen earlier from the gunroom and which he had used already to club the Rector to death. He would then leap on the unsuspecting Marquis, press the gun into his fingers and force him to shoot himself, leaving it to appear that he had been killed unavoidably in the struggle. It was to force Lionel's hand that I asked the Chief Constable to say in his hearing that we were sending for more men and that the soldiers from Charbury Heath would be over next day to search for Miss Buss, actually to release Mr. Marquis. Though," Finch added, "if I had known that Mrs. Ommanney was going to come down into the hall, I should never have dared risk it."

"It worked damned well," Colonel Stonor declared.

"It worked," said Finch, "because of one miscalculation on Lionel's part. He never realized that Mr. Marquis had had his wits restored."

Marquis smiled rather ruefully. "Not surprising really, seeing how little use I made of them." He was silent a moment, collecting his thoughts. Then he said, "My memory came back to me in the night, after Wisbeach got me out of that burning barn. I awoke then at two o'clock and remembered who I was. Or rather I remembered only that. For me it was the night following that motor accident and all that had happened since was forgotten.

"Lying there in my bed, I recalled how incredulous Arthur had been about the idea of Camilla wanting a divorce — and how almost insanely angry when I had convinced him that it was true. I lay there in the dark wondering what had happened to him. I thought of Camilla as waiting for me in the Bournemouth hotel. I thought that I must be in a hospital or nursing home. I was amazed that I felt no pain, but supposed myself to be under the influence of drugs. I groped for a bell, and found the switch of a bedside lamp. I turned on the light. To my amazement I saw the furniture,

374

carpets and curtains of my London flat, but in a totally strange room.

"I called out but no one answered. I got out of bed and opened the door. I looked into the bathroom and saw another man there. I said 'Where the devil am I?'or something like that, and saw the lips of the other man moving. It was fantastic, horrible. I put my hand up to my head, and so did the other man. It was then that I realized that I was staring into a mirror. That what I saw there was my own reflection. I was that man and that was my face.

"I rushed from the room calling — I don't know what. I went downstairs. Opened the front door. There were only fields and trees and emptiness. I was conscious suddenly of a great weariness. I crawled back to bed and fell asleep. Perhaps it was that saved my reason.

"When I awoke it was to hear someone moving about downstairs. Then I heard them coming upstairs. I pretended to be asleep and lay there following their every movement in my mind. A tray placed by the bed, curtains drawn back —

"I opened my eyes in time to catch sight

of a country-looking woman disappearing through the door.

"Presently I dressed — there was no one now in the house but myself — and walked down the road. I came to a sign that said Hammerford and I remembered that Arthur lived there. I went on into the village and, with some vague idea of finding the name of Ommanney (at least that would be familiar) I walked into the churchyard. I came on a tombstone with Arthur's name on it — and it looked as if it had been there some time.

"I wandered into the woods, hopelessly confused, taking a sort of comfort from the great trees everywhere. I had always loved trees. I came to the fringe of the woods and saw a red brick Elizabethan house in front of me, and knew that it must be Hammerford Hall. As I stood staring, two people came out from the front door. One was Camilla — and the other — Hugo — was a man whom I could not remember ever having seen before.

"My first impulse was to call out to Camilla. I was held back by the sudden realization that the sight of her no longer moved me. I felt that if my love for her had gone, then I was a different man indeed. I sank down on the stump of a tree and so remained for some time. When I got up I walked back to the village, instinctively following a path that actually I knew very well. There was a shop in the village, and an elderly man behind the counter. I asked him the date. He didn't seem surprised, and he called me by my name. 'Mr. Marquis.' he said, and told me that it was Saturday, August 4, 1954 — two years and four months after the accident. I realized then what must have happened. The motor accident that had killed Arthur had destroyed my face and my memory. I found my way back to the cottage where, it appeared, I had been living. My mind, after its previous turmoil and confusion, felt almost tranquil, and because of that, I began to recall my second life. To merge one with the other. This process continued for several days during which I avoided as far as possible speaking to anyone."

"And in the end you decided to go on playing the man without a mind?" It was Finch who spoke. Up to then his hearers had sat in silence.

"On the contrary I decided to tell the truth."

"Then what stopped you?"

"A visit from Lionel Glover and a quite erroneous belief that whatever his game was I was more than a match for him. He kept telling me that when I went to the pub I must say 'Hello there, Bill Bowman. Same as usual'. He told me this over and over as if he were teaching something to a talking parrot. It never seemed to occur to him that I was in any way different, and this, after he'd gone, made me congratulate myself on my own cleverness.

"Later that same day I stopped to admire old Tom Delves' garden — he was there with his back to me, digging — when a voice spoke behind me. A voice I didn't know, though it had in it something reminiscent of both Hugo and Lionel. 'Well, Tom', it said, 'what happened to those two camellia cuttings I gave you? Sold them, I suppose?' And old Delves answered 'That I didn't — ' And then he turned; his face was as white as a ghost's. 'Did you say that?' he asked. I didn't answer him. Just turned on my heel and walked hurriedly away. As I did so I saw

Lionel slipping from behind some bushes. This made me the more determined to discover his game and beat him at it.

"This went on for a couple of weeks or so. Lionel, I discovered, had a coat and hat like mine so that I knew that he was impersonating me. I spent a lot of my time in the woods and, if I'd been wiser, I'd have taken fright from the ease with which Lionel would find me there. And all this time it was becoming more and more difficult to keep my secret. I was like a returned prisoner of war. I wanted to stare at everything. To speak to everyone. Again and again I caught myself looking at people. Newspapers or indeed any form of writing had a tremendous attraction for me.

"Then old Mrs. Ommanney died and the Major came down. And that did it. He was such a fine-looking old boy and yet I sensed something bogus about him. I was having a good look at him when I suddenly became aware that he was having an equally good look at me. When I heard next day that he had gone up to London I felt certain that his journey was connected in some way with me. So I wasn't surprised to see him come into the church next day. That evening late, it was after eleven, Eli Skinner walked into my cottage and asked me to go with him. I felt pretty certain that this was the Major's work, I thought that I was being taken to the Hall. I was amazed to find myself instead approaching the Italian House. More amazed still to find the Major camping in one of the rooms.

"When Eli had gone — and he seemed only too anxious to get away — the Major came at once to the point. He asked me if I were Arthur Ommanney and I assured him that I was not. He then told me that the village was convinced that I was Arthur and I told him that that was Lionel's fault. We discussed what that young man was after and decided that if he thought he was going to make trouble for Hugo by persuading people that Arthur was still alive it would be nothing to the trouble that we would make for him. Eventually we agreed that the Major should go around next morning and tell Hugo everything and then that they would both come over to my cottage to see me."

John Marquis glanced briefly at Finch. "You know what happened. I waited and waited and when I eventually went around to the Hall I saw a police car drawn up in front of the house and three — or rather two — obvious police officers talking to the family on the lawn for you" — he spoke directly to Finch — "were not my idea of a policeman. I put on my usual blank expression and joined them. And you can imagine my feelings when I learned that the Major had been murdered during the early hours of the night. It was the first indication I had that something far more deadly than impersonation was in Lionel's mind and that I was to be the scapegoat.

"After that matters went from bad to worse. Poor Mrs. Hookway caught me reading the news on a piece of newspaper that was wrapped around some fish. She very tactfully backed away and came into the cottage again with a great deal of noise. But even if I hadn't seen her moving away from the kitchen doorway I should have known that something was wrong. She kept looking at me in such a woebegone manner and I heard her sobbing to herself in the kitchen. Then at the pub, you" — Marquis looked at Finch — "caught my eye in the mirror. I suppose I should have spoken, but by then I was panicking badly.

"I went to bed and, to my surprise, slept soundly. When I awakened it was with the determination to carry out my original intention of going to see Hugo and tell him everything. I dressed, drank the coffee from the thermos on the kitchen table and set off. I hadn't gone far when I felt the most extraordinary drowsiness coming over me. I felt quite stupid with sleep. Even so I should have reached the Hall had I not been attacked from behind as I was going through a particularly lonely part of the wood. I fell to the ground and, once there, lost all inclination to get up again. I remembered nothing more until I felt someone shaking me and a voice saying in my ear, 'Drink this.'" He caught Finch's faintly amused eye. "Yes, you're quite right. Like the coffee, it was drugged. And the next thing I knew I was being shaken again and someone saying 'Mister Arthur' right in my ear."

Finch chuckled. "You repudiated the idea so violently that poor Wyman was practically convinced of his mistake on the spot."

"I'm sorry I upset him. I was so sick at

my own stupidity. I was still a bit woolly, too, and surprised to find that it was dark outside. But to continue, I heard Wyman say, 'I'm satisfied, sir.' And another voice, yours — " Marquis looked again at Finch, "said, 'Keep a watch then outside and don't let anyone surprise me here or the whole show will be ruined.' By this time I'd made out that I was lying on a bed of bracken in some sort of concrete hut. My head ached and my tongue felt as if I'd been on the tiles for a week."

Finch reflected that this was not surprising since Marquis had been drugged three times in under forty hours. Once by Mrs. Hookway and twice by Lionel Glover. "There was nothing wrong with your wits though," he said aloud. "You took in what I told you and followed instructions to the letter."

"I went to sleep again as soon as you'd gone," Marquis retorted ruefully, "and woke up to find myself being shaken again, this time by Lionel. He got me to my feet and helped me into the open air. He kept saying, 'Hugo wants you.'" Marquis smiled grimly to himself. "I don't think I have ever been so tempted to hit anyone as I was to hit that young man. The effort not to do so added years to my age. I set off for the Hall, conscious at first that Lionel was keeping pace with me and later that I was alone. I got into the house through a window that the Inspector had left open for me — and where the idea originated that I had some secret way in I don't know."

Hugo grinned. He rumpled his crisp curly hair. "I was responsible for that," he said apologetically. "I got the idea after meeting you several times in the old part of the house."

Marquis was surprised. "Wonder what I was doing there?"

"Your past may yet rise up and surprise you," sneered Sir Kenneth. It was, for him, rather a halfhearted attempt. Finch though, thought that he was pleased about something.

Hugo looked angrily at Sir Kenneth. It was obvious that the older man was no longer a welcome guest at the Hall.

Marquis smiled good-humoredly. "My behaviour was innocent enough tonight. I climbed in by the window left unlatched for me and walked along into the old part of the house. As I came into the passage beyond I heard someone cry out and saw Carter running up the passage in front of me. Then Sergeant Gilroy appeared, snatched off my jacket and hat and was off, following in Carter's wake, switching off the lights as he went. And there," Marquis added regretfully, "my share in the affair ended."

The Chief Constable nodded. "It was Mr. Finch's plan. It worked — but it was damned dull for most of us."

"That was inevitable," said Finch. "We had to bait the trap. From Lionel's point of view the setup was ideal. Everyone standing at the far end outlined against the fire. The fire nearly out so that he himself would be in almost complete darkness when the lights had been fused. Marquis coming in quite close to where he was standing. My only fear was that he might think it too good and suspect a trap. That was why I persuaded Carter, on the plea that we were short of men, to watch for Marquis and give the alarm. Carter's obvious and natural alarm was sufficient to throw Lionel a little off balance. He did just what I had hoped that he would do. He pressed down the switch of the electric lamp with his foot where it was plugged into the wall without waiting to make certain that it *was* Marquis coming along the passage."

"It was a great responsibility for your sergeant," said Colonel Stonor, shaking his head. He had never really liked the idea.

"Gilroy's part was almost foolproof. Lionel had to shoot from close beside him to give the impression that it was Mr. Marquis shooting and" — here Finch emphasized the words — "Lionel was totally unsuspicious. For all the attention he gave him his intended victim might have been a dummy from a shop window."

"Lionel kept his head enough to save the last shot for the supposed Mr. Marquis," Colonel Stonor pointed out.

"Yes, Lionel was a quick-witted fellow. He must have reasoned that if Marquis died during the struggle he, Lionel, would not only save himself from the hangman but would appear as something of a hero. And who knew what opportunities for getting rid of Mr. Ommanney and his wife might present themselves in the future?"

"Why did he make that bolt for the

front door then?" Sir Kenneth asked.

"I fancy it was because he began to be afraid that Marquis was going to kill *him*. That was a possibility that had never previously occurred to him. Seeing the front door open, he lost his head and made a bolt for freedom. It was in this way that Dr. Cranley became involved."

Colonel Stonor pulled a long face. "That was unfortunate." As no one else spoke he added, "Damned unfortunate."

"Can't say I grieved over it," said Hugo.

"Nor I," said Kenneth.

"There was," said Finch, "a sort of poetic justice about it, for it was Dr. Cranley's lurid description of Mr. Marquis's possible mental state that had us all running around in circles."

The thought of Dr. Cranley's misadventure seemed to cheer everyone. The conversation became general, though scrappy and rather disjointed.

"D'you think Lionel guessed that it wasn't me with whom he was struggling?" Marquis asked.

"It never crossed his mind." Finch described Lionel Glover's rage and astonishment when he, at last, saw his antagonist.

"It doesn't seem possible that it's Lionel we're talking about," said Hugo in a quick dry voice. "The whole thing seems unreal."

The Chief Constable asked Marquis his plans and was told that he intended to go back to the family business.

"Hugo has suggested that I keep on the cottage here," he ended, "so I shall be down pretty often. I shall like that."

"We might do something about the fishing," said Hugo. "Wyman would like that."

Marquis smiled into the fire. "Poor old Wyman! How I frightened him."

The Chief Constable said that he must be getting home.

He got away with the minimum of embarrassment. As Hugo had said, the whole thing *did* seem unreal. That it would grow successively more and more real and more menacing was, happily, lost to all of them, but the C.I.D. man. He thought of this as he accompanied Colonel Stonor from the room.

Sir Kenneth called after them, "If I'm

wanted to give evidence at the trial I shall have to come over from Ireland."

Colonel Stonor paused. "You're going to Ireland?"

"To my brother-in-law's place. He has asked my wife several times since he was left a widower to go and keep house for him."

Colonel Stonor looked amazed. "And you're going with her?"

Sir Kenneth affected to misunderstand him. "There's plenty of room, I can assure you. My brother-in-law has a very large property. Very large indeed. He lives in quite feudal state. And since he's something of an invalid I shall be able to take a good deal of the management of affairs off his hands."

Hugo tipped his head back, a mannerism that increased his naturally supercilious look. It was one that Finch had come to recognize as a sign of temper. "I had no idea that you thought of leaving us so soon, Uncle Kenneth?"

Sir Kenneth smiled up at him. "My dear boy," he said blandly, "I have been feeling for some time that I need more scope — "

Colonel Stonor pulled the door shut with an indignant bang. The rest of the sentence was lost.

"Perhaps someone in Ireland *will* shoot Sir Kenneth," Gilroy muttered when the Chief Constable had been seen off. He had been searching for the bullet holes made by the big colt. He had found them all but one and now looked on it as a point of honor to find that.

"In these cases there's usually a streak of weakness in the victim that encourages the aggressor." Finch was watching his sergeant. "Lady Sybil should have walked out on her husband when she found that he didn't mean to live with her again."

Gilroy gave up looking for the last bullet. He looked curiously at Finch. "How d'you know he doesn't? Live with her, I mean."

Finch was surprised. "Why, Templar — But, of course, you weren't there. Templar, who'd heard the whole story at the dinner table, alluded to Sir Kenneth as a rogue elephant — and you know what they suffer from."

"Did he tell you why the Major walked out on her?"

"No — I got that out of Carter. And he heard it at the dinner table. It seems that the Major thought that Lady Sybil had had big marriage settlements but actually, as the Ommanneys refused to make any, so did her people. She only had an allowance — and that was cut off when she eloped."

Gilroy returned to his search. "The Ommanneys seem a queer bunch. Take Camilla — she doesn't seem to have been in love with any of the three men she's lived with — "

Finch nodded. "As our friend Swinburne has it:

Ah, beautiful passionate body
That never has ached with a heart."

Gilroy's expression showed that the poet was no friend of his. "I — " He broke off with a cry of pleasure. "Here it is! This must be the shot that was meant to blow my head off." He pointed. "We were struggling there on the floor . . . " His voice faded away. A hideous possibility had seized on him.

It came to Finch, too. He picked up his

assassin's hat. He turned a tragic face to his sergeant. "Charles," he said, "that bastard has blown a hole right through the crown of my hat."

THE END

Other titles in the
Ulverscroft Large Print Series:

TO FIGHT THE WILD
Rod Ansell and Rachel Percy

Lost in uncharted Australian bush, Rod Ansell survived by hunting and trapping wild animals, improvising shelter and using all the bushman's skills he knew.

COROMANDEL
Pat Barr

India in the 1830s is a hot, uncomfortable place, where the East India Company still rules. Amelia and her new husband find themselves caught up in the animosities which seethe between the old order and the new.

THE SMALL PARTY
Lillian Beckwith

A frightening journey to safety begins for Ruth and her small party as their island is caught up in the dangers of armed insurrection.

THE WILDERNESS WALK
Sheila Bishop

Stifling unpleasant memories of a misbegotten romance in Cleave with Lord Francis Aubrey, Lavinia goes on holiday there with her sister. The two women are thrust into a romantic intrigue involving none other than Lord Francis.

THE RELUCTANT GUEST
Rosalind Brett

Ann Calvert went to spend a month on a South African farm with Theo Borland and his sister. They both proved to be different from her first idea of them, and there was Storr Peterson — the most disturbing man she had ever met.

ONE ENCHANTED SUMMER
Anne Tedlock Brooks

A tale of mystery and romance and a girl who found both during one enchanted summer.